Whacha Wanna Do?

CONFESSIONS OF A *MISCHIEVOUS* REFORMED ALTAR BOY

GARY S. EDELEN

 FriesenPress

Suite 300 - 990 Fort St
Victoria, BC, V8V 3K2
Canada

www.friesenpress.com

ISBN
978-1-5255-6934-0 (Hardcover)
978-1-5255-6935-7 (Paperback)
978-1-5255-6936-4 (eBook)

1. FICTION, COMING OF AGE

Distributed to the trade by The Ingram Book Company

ACKNOWLEDGMENTS

To my wife, Faryl, whose constant encouragement and tireless reviews and editing of this work motivated me to complete this endeavor. Faryl, you're the best!

I would also like to recognize my friend Tom Holloway, who constantly prodded me to put my pen to paper. Finally, special thanks to my friend Yonetta Beagle, who refused to accept any excuse for failure by me to publish this work.

Chapter 1
PAROLED FOR THE SUMMER

Come on, I thought as I waited for the bell to signal the end of the school day, the end of the school week, the end of the school month, and the end of the school year! I was sure that when the school bell rang, the heavens would open up, and we would all hear a loud "Hallelujah!" The seventh grade had been the longest school year I had ever survived. As I looked up at the clock on the classroom wall, I thought that it must have been the slowest clock in the entire city of Louisville. Heck, it was probably the slowest clock in the entire state of Kentucky.

All around me, my classmates, for the most part, were watching the clock tick down to that magical time of two thirty in the afternoon. The gates of the prison would soon burst open, freeing us from this nine-month-long ordeal of torturous, mind-numbing nonsense that included force feeding us "new" math, catechism, spelling, history, and any other stupid educational fad that swept into the principal's office. Don't know if it was really her fault for coming up with all of those corny new classes that were dumped into our classrooms, but I guess it's okay to put the blame on her, especially since I didn't like her much in the first place.

In all fairness, I don't think she was all that fond of me either. Well, maybe she should share the blame with our dumb school board for coming up with all of these dumb subjects. I think they must just sit around all day thinking up dumb ways to make students like me miserable for nine months each and every year.

My name is Scott Stiles, and this was a very important day for me. Actually, it was the most important day of the entire school year. I had been waiting for this moment all year long—the last day of school! *Go down clock*, I thought. It seemed like the only good parts of coming to school were the hot lunches, recess, and then getting out at two thirty. I was one of the few kids who actually thought that the hot lunches were pretty good.

Oh, one other nice thing about going to school was that I got to see that pretty little Lori Ann Lake. She was the prettiest girl in my class, or at least that's what I thought. However, I was forced to admire her beauty from across the classroom … *way* across the classroom. It seemed like bad luck always worked against me when it came to the seating assignments. Ever since I first noticed just how pretty Lori Ann was, not once was I ever assigned to a nearby desk. I don't know just how the nuns knew that I wanted to sit by her, but I was sure that they knew. I might as well have been living on another planet as far as Lori Ann was concerned.

Darn nuns! Maybe they received some divine inspiration when they planned the seating assignments and figured that I needed a bad seat as extra penance. Darn nuns! Nope, I think they did it just for pure meanness. Since Saint John Bosco was a Catholic school, we had to attend Mass every school day and also go to Confession at least once a week. Oh, Saint John Bosco was the patron saint of hopeless boys, at least that was what my mother told me, so this had to be the best school for me, or so she said. I wasn't quite sure what she was trying to tell me.

Anyway, it really became tough to come up with a couple of good sins worth reporting to the priest in the confessional. Sister Mary Wackenhammer called it confessing, but I think that when I am forced to admit to some small, insignificant blemish on my otherwise fairly clean spiritual record, "reporting," or "checking in" with the priest in the confessional, would be a more accurate description of the whole darn process. I would call it dumb, but Sister Mary Wackenhammer told us all that if we ever made fun out of anything religious, we would bypass purgatory and go straight to hell, and we "wouldn't" be roasting marshmallows when we got there.

Oh, Sister Mary Wackenhammer was not really her real name. Her real name was Sister Mary Wackenmeister. However, she got that nickname, and I didn't give it to her, because if you were bad in her class, she would make you walk up to her desk and place your hand on her desk. Then she would whack you across the knuckles with her ruler. She told us that this punishment caused her great pain. She acted like she expected me to believe that. Well, I wanted to tell her to put her hand on my desk and let me whack her knuckles with my ruler, and then she would know what great pain really was or really felt like. That was never going to happen, ever!

She would also tell us not to forget to confess our classroom offenses in the confessional. I bet that she had a checklist that she went over with the confessional priest every week just to see if we were reporting our sins accurately. Anyway, I heard on good authority that the priests were not really listening but were reading the newspaper and eating beer nuts while we were in that little confessional spilling out our guts. I think that sometimes they would fall asleep, because I thought that I heard a visiting priest snore in the confessional one time. I remember thinking that I needed to come up with something more creative and interesting for both me and Father Taurman. I mean, anyone would get tired of hearing the same story week after week. Just how much mischief can a good little boy like me get into, anyway?

Back to Father Taurman. He kinda just sat there as I confessed. I often wondered that if I told him I had robbed a bank, would I receive the same penance as the usual five Hail Marys and five Our Fathers? He never smiled. When you never smile, you're either weird, mean, crazy, or in a coma. Maybe he was just sleeping. Well, when he wasn't sleeping, he seemed to enjoy my stories ... I mean my confessions. But most of the time, I think he was sleeping. I would tell him that I'd committed a mortal sin by eating a piece of bologna on Friday. Now for us Catholics, eating meat on Friday will get you a ticket straight to hell. Sister Mary Wackenhammer told our class that if you eat meat on Friday, you will go to hell, and when you get to hell, the devil will cook up a juicy cheeseburger when you're hungry and then eat it right in front of you. To make matters worse, when he would finally give you a cheeseburger, you would find out that it was a fried liver sandwich, and he would make you eat it. There is nothing in this entire world worse than fried liver.

I thought about telling Father Taurman about the rousing poker games played after altar boy training class, but I decided that he might use my confession to bust up our card games. That was a story I didn't make up, because we did play poker, even though Sister Mary Wackenhammer lectured us about the evils of gambling. I didn't have much to gamble with, except for my lunch money or candy or something like that. I had never progressed much beyond rummy, so I kinda stayed out of those high-stakes poker games. I had lost my lunch money one time too many, so I mostly just watched some of the other guys. I did learn some poker words like raise, call, and fold. I folded a lot when I played. It kind of helped me not to lose any more money by raising. Raising always got me into trouble and ended up causing me to lose more money or candy.

Back to confessions. Just to spice things up, I would tell Father Taurman about dropping my pencil on the floor in order to look up Gloria's dress. I did have to sound like a regular boy, didn't I? Guys were always dropping their pencils on the floor in my class in order to take a peek up the girls' dresses, but not sure if anyone was confessing to Father Taurman about that. Probably not, I bet. Us guys weren't particular about just whose dress we looked up. Whatever was available seemed to work out fine.

I was always careful to disguise my voice so that Father Taurman wouldn't recognize me. However, it seemed like every time I finished my confession, Father Taurman would say, "Go in peace, Scott." *Ugh,* exposed and humiliated again. Hope that Father Taurman never gets cross examined by my mom. She would get it all out of him, and I would be grounded until college. She was good at stuff like that. Even I had an awfully hard time dealing with her tough interrogations, and I had gotten a whole lot of practice handling interrogations from the principal at school.

Just a few more ticks of the clock and then paradise! Yup, in a week or two I would be able to attend the altar boy picnic at the swimming lake. I guess that place had a name, but we called it the swimming lake. This was the ultimate payback for all of those weekday and Saturday-morning church Masses that we served at as altar boys. Free hamburgers, hot dogs, potato chips, and soft drinks for everyone! We even got to go canoeing on the lake. Who would get up at six o'clock in the morning and walk to church in the cold to serve Mass for about six people unless there was a payback like the altar boy picnic?

Looking around the classroom, I knew that I would miss some of my classmates whom I wouldn't see during the summertime. Lori Ann Lake—I sure would miss her a lot! I would often gaze at her long brown hair and her beautiful brown eyes and think and sigh, and think and sigh, and think and … *Gee she barely knows that I am in her class. She is just missing out,* I would tell myself, only to be followed up by the thought that I was really the one missing out, because I really didn't have a chance in, in, in heck, I didn't even have a little chance.

Well … darn it anyway. I'll go to hell if I use those bad words that I really want to use, even in my thoughts. At least that is what Sister Mary Wackenhammer told us. Oh well, this summer would be the best summer ever, and I had plenty of friends to pal around with for three whole months. Sister Mary Wackenhammer. Why do all of the nuns have names that begin with Sister Mary—like Sister Mary Holy Rose, Sister Mary Glory Be, Sister Mary Matilda, and Sister Mary Punchy? Not sure where that name came from. However, she did live up to that name, because she was quick to punch you in the arm or the side of the head if you misbehaved in her class. But it really was her real name!

R-R-R-R-I-I-I-I-N-N-N-N-G-G-G-G! The bell finally rang, and we were freed from our academic forced bondage!

"Have a nice sum …" That is all I heard Sister Mary Wackenhammer say as I dashed out the door and headed down the hallway toward the stairway to the front door. I had to make it out before anyone had a chance to grab me for some last-minute spiritual guidance that would be meant to last me all summer long. That kind of spiritual guidance usually came with a yardstick and left me not wanting to sit down for the rest of the afternoon.

I rounded the first flight of stairs, and the front doors came into sight. I was almost there, almost free, almost uncaged! Then it happened!

"Oh Mr. Stiles, would you come over here please?"

It was not a question. It was a command from the school warden, Principal Miss Penny Pennyberry. What a name! Over the past year, we had enjoyed many one-on-one conversations in her office. Well, I think she enjoyed them. Me, not so much, because they were mostly one-sided. Most of the one-on-ones came from her one yardstick being applied to my one botchacoocka as retribution for some trivial, insignificant, and practically innocent offense. With Miss Pennyberry, I was always guilty and never presumed innocent.

I winced as I pondered this last meeting of the ... minds. "Yes, Miss Pennyberry," I replied while noticing that the school secretary had moved toward the front door, assuring me that I had no possible escape. Miss Bunch, our school secretary, was always nice to me, but this was rank and file, and Miss Pennyberry outranked both me and Miss Bunch in this case.

Many times after my special meetings with Miss Pennyberry, Miss Bunch would look down at me through her beautiful blue eyes, smile as she pushed back her long, wavy, blonde hair, and say to me, "Scott, you really should try a little harder to follow the rules in school. Not that I don't like seeing you, but it would be so much better for you." Then she would give me that big, beautiful smile. She would always slip a piece of peppermint candy into my hand as I left her office. Then she would whisk me out with that beautiful smile. She always made me forget about my sore botchacooka.

However, this time she was allied with the enemy, and I understood why. "Mr. Stiles," said Miss Pennyberry. "I expect that over the summer you will learn that when you come to school it is a privilege, and as such you are expected to behave according to the rules of this institution of higher learning."

She stopped me for this? I thought. At least I hadn't been busted for my parting gift of gluing her yardstick to the top of her bookcase. Maybe she hadn't discovered that fact yet. "Oh, you're so right, Miss Pennyberry," I said, "and I have taken steps to make sure that you will never have to use your yardstick on me again. As a matter of fact, I am so convinced that I'll come back a reformed student, I think you can go on and get rid of your yardstick right now, or after we all go home. You know, it really clashes with the lovely decorations in your office. Am I free to go now, Miss Pennyberry?" I asked with as much of an innocent look as I could fashion on my face.

"Yes, you are, Mr. Stiles," Miss Pennyberry replied with narrowed eyes as she nodded to Miss Bunch to stand down from her post at the front door.

As I dashed out the front door, Miss Bunch smiled, winked at me, and said, "I'll miss you this summer, Scott."

She said that she would miss me! Miss Bunch, who must have been a beauty queen before coming to Saint John Bosco, she said that she would miss me. I was so caught up by her words that I didn't see the door post ahead of me as I ran right into it. I saw stars. There was no pain, only rapture. Miss Bunch had noticed me and was going to miss me. Wow, this had to be a message from heaven that this would be a special summer. I felt that I could sprint all of the way home, and I did!

Chapter 2
THE ADVENTURE BEGINS

Monday morning, the first real day of my vacation, was here! Boy, it felt good not to have to go to school! Time to kick back and relax, but I thought that I could relax better after breakfast. "Let's see, what do we have here?" Mom had decided to let us sleep in, me and my brother and sister. But it appeared that she had left a note for us. I bet that it was something to brighten up our day while she was at work.

The ladies who lived on both sides of our house always kind of kept watch over us while Mom was at work. I think they felt sorry for her being a single mom and having to raise three kids by herself and all that. Mrs. Holloway was pretty nice, but I think that she had her hands full just keeping up with her three little kids, and there was another one in the oven, or I think that is what you say when another baby is on the way. Now Mrs. Reuther was a nice old lady who lived next door on the other side of our house. She would check in on us from time to time during the day. Whenever I saw her coming over, I would quickly comb my hair, grab my catechism book, and act like I was studying. "There you are, studying God's words," she would say to me.

"Yes, ma'am, I am trying to improve my spiritual life," I would reply with my most solemn, innocent smile while looking toward heaven.

"You're such a good boy," she would always say.

And I would always say that I was always trying my very best to be a very good boy.

It was always a special treat when she would bring over her cornbread pancakes. They were the best. I was usually the one who met her at the door, because I always had a good idea when she would be making one of her rounds. She always had six cornbread pancakes—two for each of us. That meant that once she left, it was up to me to divide them. One for Marie, one for Sam, and four for me. Hey, I am a growing boy!

I glanced up to read the note Mom had left hanging on the refrigerator. *What is this?* I thought. What I now had in my hand was a job list. A job list on my first day of summer vacation! *This is not fair! Let's see:*

1. Wash The Dishes (Scott, you are the eldest, so you must set an example for your little brother and sister who always look up to you. Remember you need to do your chores with a smile.)
2. Pick Up The Clothes In Your Room
3. Dust Your Room

She must have meant it, because she used capital letters for each word. She always uses capital letters for each word when she really means it. Darn it and darn it again!

"Let's see that," Marie, my little sister, said.

"Me too," called out Sam, my little brother.

"Oh, you have to do the dishes so you can set a good example for us," Marie stated with an evil grin.

"Yes, we're too little to do dishes," blurted Sam.

"Remember to smile, Scott," Marie chimed in.

"And set a good example for your little brother, who always looks up to his big brother," Sam smirked.

I hated it when he smirked. He knew that if I laid a hand on "Mommy's precious baby," I would be in big trouble and end up getting grounded. I wished that I could sell both of them to pirates. I would give the pirates a "buy one get one free" deal. With my luck, the pirates would return them the same day for a refund and probably sue me for damages.

"I think that I'll have scrambled eggs and oatmeal," Marie said with a look that told me that it was going to end up with some seriously dirty pots and pans.

I told them both that I thought that would be a great breakfast menu, and as soon as they got dressed, they should start breakfast. Surprised by my gracious attitude, they retired to their rooms to change out of their pajamas and into their play clothes.

I had to act quick. The refrigerator was my first stop. The eggs—I had to hide the eggs where they wouldn't be found. Ah, the potato bin was perfect, and they would never look for eggs there. Now where could I hide the Quaker Oats? The flour canister would be the perfect spot! I quickly emptied the box of oats into the flour canister and then returned the empty box to the pantry. Upon their return to the kitchen, I had graced my face with the most innocent and compassionate look that I could give.

"We're out of eggs and oatmeal," Marie exclaimed as they rooted around for the missing breakfast items.

"What a shame," I said, "and I guess that means that you all will have to have cereal for breakfast."

I think that they were suspicious, but where was the proof? And I was not about to clue them in. "Perhaps you all would like toast instead today," I offered. They bit on my suggestion, and my cleanup was reduced to washing a couple of knives.

Okay, Job 1, CHECK! Job 2 would require a little more work. All of the clothes got shoved under the bed. *Must be careful not to have any loose ends sticking out.* Now, Job 2, CHECK! Job 3 would be a breeze, literally. I made sure that the bedroom window was open and turned on the window fan to high for about a minute. Instant dusting and mission accomplished. Job 3, CHECK! Just like that, I had quickly and efficiently attended to all of my daily jobs.

Well, it seemed like it was time to head out for the day. *I'll just call Ran and see what he wants to do today.* Wouldn't you know it, Marie was on the phone. "Marie, get off of the phone, because I have to use it!"

Marie just gave me that obnoxious sister smile and continued her conversation without even coming up for air. Sisters are such a pain in the … well, they are a pain! I think that every older brother should get a special pass into heaven for having to deal with a goofy, dumb sister.

Ten minutes later, she was still on the phone. She had not even started on the tiny job list that Mom had left for her and Sam. "Marie, I need to use the phone for a second," I implored. This time she didn't even look up but continued her non-stop blathering to one of her blathering friends. I could hear the combined blathering, and it was sickening. It didn't make one lick of sense. Of course, when they blathered, it never made any sense.

A few minutes later the exact scene was repeated again with the same results. This act of pure meanness was going to require payback and quick action. Okay, the paybacks came first. I quietly slipped into Marie's room and went straight for her dresser. She loved to wear ribbons in her hair and always kept a supply of ribbons on her dresser. There they were, right where they belonged, in her ribbon box. Well, a little bit of Elmer's Glue liberally applied to the middle of the bundle of ribbons should work just right. After returning the ribbon box to the dresser, I went to her closet. I knew that I had better not do anything really bad, so I decided to tie all of her shoes together by the shoelaces and then tie them to the register grid in her room. That should put a bump in her road as she tried to get dressed to go out today.

After sneaking back out of her room, I called to her, "Marie, I need to use the phone!" She just grinned at me and then turned her back to me. That did it, and now it was time for action! I went down to the basement and headed straight for the telephone connection. It didn't take long for me to spot the connection. *Let's see, if I just disconnect this one little wire, then ...*

"Jessica, Jessica, are you there?" I could hear my sweet little sister calling into the telephone receiver upstairs. That was music to my ears. Once I heard her slam the receiver down, I quickly reconnected the telephone wire and then proceeded upstairs to make my call. "Hey, Ran, whachawanna do today?"

Marie heard me on the phone and stormed back into the hallway. She blurted out, "Is that phone working now?"

"What are you talking about?" I replied. "It always works." I smiled at her and then turned my back to her. Sisters, what a pain in the ... neck! Anyway, I was about to leave for Ran's house when Sam came up to me and said that his job list stated that he was supposed to pump up the air in the tire of his new bicycle. He told me that he didn't know how to do that. I told him that was an easy job and all he had to do was to first let the bad air out of his bike's tire by opening the valve and then put fresh air in by blowing into the tire valve with a straw. He thanked me and then I finally left for Ran's house.

Randall Seebows was my very best friend in the world. I called him "Ran" for short. We were friends through thick and thin, whatever that meant. He lived two blocks over from my house, and we spent most of our free time together working on all sorts of things. Well, we didn't really work on things, but we spent time together or just plain hung out. Ran's little brother, Mortie, hung out with us a lot of the time too. We were always looking for neat things to do to pass our time.

"Hi, Ran, Whachawanna do?" I asked.

"I dunno. Whachawanna do?" he answered.

"I got it," I said. "How about we go down to Shady's and get an ice cream cone?"

"That costs twelve cents, and I don't have any money," Ran murmured.

"Not a problem," I said. "You know that old Shady cashes in empty soft drink bottles for ice cream cones, don't you?"

Ran and Mortie both agreed, but Mortie said that they didn't have any empty soft drink bottles.

"Come with me," I said, and we set off for Shady's.

Shady had a little corner bar, but he also dipped ice cream from a freezer under the bar and sold soft drinks. It was a small place, barely ten feet wide and not too deep. Shady was a big old guy who always looked like he was mad and always wore a bartender's apron, just like the ones that all of the bartenders wore in the *Tall Texan Cowboy Show* that we watched on TV every Saturday morning. The Tall Texan was our hero.

Once we got to Shady's we went around back. "Presto," I said. There in front of us were several rows of neatly stacked cases of empty soft drink bottles. We each picked out four empty bottles and then went around to the front of the store to visit Shady. A few minutes later, the three of us left, each with a twelve-cent chocolate ripple ice cream cone. Nothing to it, and we were off to a good start to our day.

"What are we gonna do this summer, Scott?" Ran asked.

"Already got that planned out," I replied. "Did you know that the *Tall Texan Wild West Show* is coming to the State Fair this year?"

"Really? The Tall Texan is coming here?" exclaimed Ran.

"Yup, and his trusty sidekick, Wang Chow KaPow, is coming with him."

"Wang Chow KaPow is coming too! That's gonna be really cool," replied Ran. "That will be great, except for, how are we gonna be able to get there and then get enough money to pay to see him, unless he's appearing for free? You know, they're gonna be charging about four dollars for a ticket, and that's a bunch of money."

"Not a problem," I said. "I already have it planned out. You know that spot in the fence behind the drive-in next to the fairgrounds? Well, it might still be there, and that's where we always used to sneak in," I bragged with all of the confidence in the world.

But Ran interrupted. "How are we gonna pay to see his show?" He thought a minute and finally said, "I might be able to get my big brother to drive us to the State Fair, but we're gonna hafta to pay him something, and that will cost money too."

"Not a problem," I went on. "This summer we'll just go over to the ballpark and shag softballs for the ball teams. They pay fifty cents a game to shag and return the foul balls and home run balls that fly out of the ballpark. It's an easy job, and you get to watch three games per night for free."

"Hmm." Ran was thinking. "What about Stubby?"

Stubby was the bossy, chubby guy who lived down the street from the ballpark. No one liked Stubby... well, mostly no one. Stubby was "in" with the ballpark manager, Steve. That meant that he was buddies with Steve, and he had locked up the job of shagging balls for all of the games for the entire summer. It was a good deal for him. He got to watch the games for free and then get paid fifty cents per game to shag balls. He used some of the little kids that lived across the street from him to help him.

I needed a super big enticement to get Stubby to agree to let me and my friends have a couple of nights each week when we could get paid to shag foul balls that were popped up outside of the ballpark. I had figured this problem out in advance. I knew what Stubby's weak spot was. "Just leave him to me," I said. "Stubby is crazy about this little blonde-headed girl who lives a couple streets over. I'll tell him that if he convinces Steve to let us shag balls four nights a week, and let him have the other three nights to work the scoreboard, I'll get that blonde-headed girl to invite Stubby over for ice cream. He'll do anything to be able to spend time with her. I can tell him that the invite won't come until the end of the season, so we'll be able to shag balls all summer, and old Stubby won't dare butt in on our business."

"How are you gonna get the blonde-headed girl to invite Stubby over for ice cream?" Ran asked. "She can't stand Stubby."

"Don't worry," I replied. "I'm not even gonna ask her."

"What?" Ran exclaimed.

"Nope, I'll tell Stubby that a condition of the deal is that he not even hint to the blonde-headed girl anything about the ice cream get-together, or the deal is off. Then after the season is over, I'll just tell Stubby that she changed her mind, because she heard that he bragged about getting a date or whatever you want to call it, with her. It's in the contract and he broke the deal, or so I'll tell him. Besides, Stubby is such a bragger that he's bound to slip up and say something about it during the summer. I guarantee it!"

"Yeah," Ran said. "Stubby does like to pop off all of the time. I guess you're right."

"Nothing that he can do at that point," I proudly proclaimed. "It cannot fail!"

"Yeah, I think that just might work," thought Ran aloud. "This will be the best summer ever!"

Chapter 3
A BUMP IN THE ROAD

"Hello Scott, this is Sister Mary Holy Flower, and I am glad that I was able to reach you."

I just knew that I should not have answered that phone call! I must be in trouble for something that they forgot to deal with before school let out. I knew I should not have replaced all of my classmates' pens and pencils with old broken crayons last week after everyone had left school for the day. It did almost get us out of taking that dumb math test. You can't answer math questions with broken crayons. Of course, that grumpy Miss Pennyberry just happened to have a bunch of extra pencils in her desk. I knew that I should have checked her desk too. I could have done it while she was on lunchroom duty. She never locks her office, and Miss Bunch would have been in the teachers' lounge. I was only half mad when Miss Bunch came to our class and gave out new pencils to everyone. I could never be mad at Miss Bunch;

she was so pretty. Well, at least I did manage to pass the test. It was helpful that Peggy Prepinham always checked and rechecked her test answers. I could easily see her answers, and if they looked promising, they would appear on my test answer sheet.

"Scott," Sister Mary Holy Flower continued, "you do remember that as an altar boy, you're required to serve weekly Mass during the summer, don't you?"

"Oh yeah, I guess that I do," I said. I had forgotten that Sister Mary Holy Flower was the altar boy commandant. She was short, squat, and as mean as a snake. Worse, she never liked me, and she always gave me the bad Mass assignments. I had to get her in a good mood. "Oh Sister Mary Holy Flower, I was just reading my catechism book when you called. You know that I really miss your catechism class over the summer."

"Well, bless you, my son," Sister said. "My news will make you very happy. You have been assigned to serve the 6:30 a.m. Mass all next week! I am sure that this will brighten your day, Scott."

Brighten my day, I thought. *It will brighten it all right, as I'll get to see the sunrise seven straight days when I should be home still sleeping.* "I cannot find the words to describe just how this makes me feel," I told Sister Mary Holy Flower.

"Good. Now remember, the altar boy picnic is just one month away, and you do want to make sure that you're in good standing so you will be able to attend the picnic, don't you?"

"Oh yes, Sister, I do. I plan to be so good that you will be tempted to see if I am walking around with a halo and angel wings."

"Yes, Scott, that sight would truly be a miraculous vision. Now don't forget, and goodbye. Oh, by the way," she added, "if you would like me to tutor you on your catechism this summer, I can arrange for you to come by the convent a couple of days each week to say the rosary with us, and then we can study your catechism uninterrupted."

Uh oh! This is a trap! I thought. "Oh Sister Mary Holy Flower, there is nothing that I would rather do, but I volunteered to cut the grass in all of the old widows' yards on my street all summer long, free of charge," I said. "I also help them clean their dentures on those days too, so I really do not have any extra time, although there are few things that can compare to saying the rosary and studying catechism with you." At least the last part was true.

"Well, that is very generous of you and something that I would never have guessed about you. Well, have a nice summer," she said, and she hung up.

Whew, that was a close one, I thought. Ugh, you're not supposed to have to get up early during summer vacation unless there is something important to do, like help Ran deliver papers or something. Oh well, with the altar boy picnic so close by, I had no choice but to serve my sentence on the altar.

"You have to what?" asked Ran as we climbed up the fire escape to sit out on our favorite perch atop the roof of the Cherokee Park Baptist Church. You had a great view up and down the street from up there. You only went up there at night, because it was too hot during the day, and people would also notice you sitting up there during the day. Night-time, it was cool, peaceful, and no one ever looked up there.

"Guess that you won't be helping me deliver papers next week," he said.

"Nope, but I'll make it up, sometime."

The next week rolled around, and I found myself serving Mass with my friend Meatball. Frank was his real name, but everyone called him Meatball. Meatball was a good guy, and I was happy that we were assigned to the same shift. He didn't much like the assignment either. Now my classmate Hudge was serving the 7:15 a.m. Mass along with Lex. I liked both Hudge and Lex. They were both okay guys. However, Hudge was Sister Mary Holy Flower's favorite everything. He could never do anything wrong according to her, so that made him a good target for me. Besides, Hudge was always a good sport. I think that Sister Mary Holy Flower was already trying to fit Hudge for a set of angel wings and a matching halo. I mean that I would never think of doing anything that would hurt him or anything, but maybe a small prank or two would be reasonable.

Well, Hudge was almost always late for everything. On Tuesday, after my Mass shift, I hid all of the altar boy cassocks and surplices in the church. Of course I told Lex where I had hidden them, since he did have to go with Father Cheese, as we called Father Limberger, to start the Mass. Lex said that you could hear Hudge tearing up the altar boy dressing room looking for the missing cassocks and surplices, finally joining Mass ten minutes late. We don't think that Father Cheese even noticed.

On Wednesday, I just felt that I had one more prank to pull on Hudge. He made it so easy because he was a nice guy, and as I said, he never got mad. After my six-thirty Mass, I quietly returned to the altar with Scotch tape in hand. Then I quickly went over to the altar boy kneeling bench where the altar bell was kept, and I taped the clapper of the bell so it wouldn't ring. I then taped the bell to the inside of the altar boy kneeling bench. Of course, I had told Lex to make sure that Hudge would be the altar boy to ring the bell.

When it came time to ring the bell, Hudge couldn't get the bell out of the stall. By the time he got it out of the stall, it was the most important time of the Mass to ring the bell. As Father Cheese held up the Host, Hudge tried to ring the bell, but no sound was made. Knowing that this was the most important time for a bell to be rung during Mass, Hudge called out "DING-A-LING-A-LING!"

Lex said that Father Cheese never even knew the difference. It turned out better than I had hoped.

Then the roof fell in on me. Sister Mary Holy Flower must have radar or something. Barely fifteen minutes after Mass, I received a telephone call from Sister, summoning me to the nun Mother House for an urgent meeting. Meatball was already there, and he didn't look very happy.

"Well, Mr. Stiles," Sister Mary Holy Flower started, "I guess that you and Frank thought what you both did was pretty cute, don't you? I strongly suspect that you, Mr. Stiles, had more to do with this than Frank, but as far as I am concerned, you both are equally guilty! This is one of the most sacrilegious acts ever performed against the Catholic Church. Indeed, it borders upon excommunication from the church!"

Meatball seemed taken aback by Sister's rantings, but I knew that they were only the rantings of a nun who had been wearing her nun habit too tight for too long. It had choked off the blood that was supposed to be circulating in her brain.

"Mea Culpa," I uttered under my breath.

Wrong thing to say. That really set Sister Mary Holy Flower off. I thought that her eyes were going to pop out clean through her rimless glasses! She seemed to get ahold of herself and then very coldly stated that as a result of my action's on God's holy altar, Meatball and I were no longer to be counted among the exalted ranks of the parish altar boys. "I can't excommunicate you from the Catholic Church, but I can excommunicate you from the holy ranks of the parish altar boys. This is your official notice that the both of you have been excommunicated from serving as altar boys," she mightily proclaimed.

"Does that mean that we don't have to serve the remainder of this week's altar boy Mass assignment?" I inquired. I thought that all in all, it had ended up in a pretty good deal for me, and it would be even better if we didn't have to finish out the week serving the six-thirty morning Mass.

That did it for sure. Sister Mary Holy Flower seemed to explode! "No! You are no longer altar boys, so you will not be serving the six-thirty Mass, and therefore since you are no longer altar boys, you are not permitted to attend this year's altar boy picnic!" she shouted.

What? Whoa ... hold on! I thought. The altar boy picnic was one week away. I had endured a year's worth of bad altar boy serving assignments, countless hours of altar boy training under Sister Mary Holy Flower, and the memorization of Latin, a dead language that I still cannot understand. It had been torment, torment, torment! Now this was bad news, very bad news!

I apologized to Meatball as we left the convent. Meatball was pretty good about it, especially since his family had already planned to vacation in Florida at the same time that the altar boy picnic was being held. He had not even planned on going to the altar boy picnic anyway.

I was not in a good mood when I got home. I decided to take it out on Marie and Sam just for good measure. After rummaging through the medicine cabinet, I found what I had been looking for. I broke off two big chunks of chocolate-flavored Ex-Lax and then offered one each to Marie and Sam. I had a friendly big-brother smile on my face, and I told them that they were the last pieces of my chocolate candy bar that Sister Mary Holy Flower had presented to me as a reward for giving special attention to my altar boy duties. I told them that I was full and couldn't eat anymore.

They figured that if the chocolate came from Sister Mary Holy Flower, it had to be safe to eat. Later, they were to learn another meaning for the word RUN.

A little later, Ran stopped by, and I shared the bad news with him. He said that he would give some Ex-Lax to Mortie if it would make me feel better. I told him no and that I liked Mortie, even though he acted goofy at times. About that time the phone rang.

Since Marie and Sam were outside, I answered the phone. "Hello, is this Scott Stiles?" the caller asked.

"Um, yes, it is," I replied.

"Well, this is Father Allgood, and I have a couple of words for you."

Oh no, Father Allgood was the pastor, and now I was really going to be in for it. No Purgatory for me now. I was going straight to hell. When the pastor calls your house, it is all over with. My rosary, my Saint Anthony medal, my confirmation scapular, my holy card collection, and a gallon of holy water all combined together couldn't get me out of this one. I was doomed! By the time he got finished talking to my mom, I would be grounded for the entire summer! Goodbye, Tall Texan and Wang Chow KaPow!

"Well, Father Allgood, let me explain," I blurted out.

"No need for explanations, Scott, as I already know everything that I need to know," he said.

Here it comes, I thought as I lowered my head for the boom. The angel of death was about to ring my doorbell.

"That was about the funniest thing that has ever happened in this church—ever!" blurted out Father Allgood.

I couldn't believe my ears. They must have turned deaf, or I was hallucinating or something. "I'm sorry, Father," I stammered out.

"DING-A-LING-A-LING! Now that is funny! I only wish that I had been there to see it and hear it. Funniest thing ever, Scott. I couldn't believe my ears. We can talk about this more next week at the altar boy picnic," he chuckled.

Redemption was drawing near, and I had to play my cards just right. "Oh Father, I am so terribly sorry, but I won't be there," I said.

"What do you mean, Scott?"

"Well, Sister Mary Holy Flower said that I should be excommunicated, but since she is not the pope, I have been excommunicated from the altar boys and can't go to the altar boy picnic."

"Nonsense, Scott," was his immediate reply. "I am exercising the power handed down to all pastors from none other than Saint Peter to absolve you from any blemish on your altar boy record and return you to your active status as an altar boy. In other words, I outrank Sister Mary Holy Flower according to Canon Law, and that comes straight from the pope!"

"Sister Mary Holy Flower said that I was not going to be serving the six-thirty Mass the remainder of this week, so should I show up for Mass tomorrow morning?"

Father Allgood replied that since Sister Mary Holy Flower had discharged me from my service for the remainder of this week, it was up to her to find my replacement for the six-thirty Masses.

Bingo, bingo, and bingo! I was still an altar boy, I didn't have to serve any more six-thirty Masses this week, and I was going to be going to the altar boy picnic! "Thank you, Father Allgood, and I'll offer up special prayers for all of your important intentions this week."

"Thank you, Scott, for adding a little levity to this church," Father Allgood replied. "You know that things can get a little stuffy at times, and a good laugh helps clear out the fog," he added.

Just like that, the prospects for my summer vacation had gone from good, to awful, to great. "Thanks for everything," I said. I had to tell Ran!

Chapter 4
BATTER UP

The day to finalize my deal with Stubby to shag balls at the ballpark had arrived. When I said that the little blonde-headed girl was Stubby's weak spot, I meant that she was his major weak spot, even more so than candy, and that was saying a lot. No way that I could have afforded to keep him in candy anyway. He was head over heels in love with this little blonde-headed girl. He reminded me of a rhino who was longing for a girl rhino. Well, I don't think that he was in love with her, but he liked her a lot, and she never ever even gave him the time of day. "Hey, Stubby," I called. "I have a deal for you!"

Stubby could barely contain himself when I promised him an ice cream get-together with the little blonde headed girl. "Are you sure that the little blonde-headed girl will go out with me?" Stubby asked.

"Yup, for sure," I replied.

"Do you promise?" he asked.

"You can count on it," I said. "Stubby, you're not questioning my honesty, are you? Maybe I don't want to do this deal with you."

"No, no, no, no, no!" he exclaimed. "Scott, you're about the most honest guy that I know, and I agree to this deal," he said, not wanting to miss out on a chance to get together with the little blonde-headed girl.

It was too easy. Bam, the deal was done, and we had ourselves a summer job. Just like that, it was done, and we were on our way to earning money to go see the *Tall Texan Wild West Show* at the State Fair.

According to my deal with Stubby, tonight was his night to shag balls, so Ran, Mortie, and I decided to watch the game from behind left field. It was our special spot, which was in a wooded area and gave us a bunch of privacy while still providing us with a good view. I noticed that Stubby's little-kid ball shaggers were standing nearby, getting ready for the game to start.

I overheard Timmy, one of the little kids, fussing about Stubby with the other little kids. I decided to find out what they were fussing about. "Hey, Timmy," I called. "What's the matter with you all?"

"I think that Stubby is cheating us again," he replied.

"Whacha mean?" I asked.

"Well, Stubby told us that he has to pay taxes on what he gets paid and then he pays us," Timmy explained.

We already knew that Stubby would usually give some little kids twenty-five cents to shag the balls and then keep the remaining twenty-five cents for himself. When you added in the twenty-five cents that he kept from the little kids to the money that he got for keeping score on the scoreboard, we felt that he was making pretty good money. We also felt that he was taking advantage of those poor little kids by doing this.

Timmy continued, "Now he's taking ten cents off of the twenty-five cents that he pays us so that he can pay the taxes. That leave us to split fifteen cents per game between the three of us."

"Just tell Stubby that you all aren't gonna shag balls for him then," I said.

"We tried," Timmy said. "Stubby told us that we have a contact with him and we can't get out of it because it is unbreakable."

"You mean a contract," I said. "Is it a written contract?"

"Nope, Stubby said that he is a certamafied member of the American Association of Softball Shaggers. According to their mylaws, written contacts, I mean contracts, are not allowed," sighed Timmy. "They all have to be talked contracts. Stubby told us that if he didn't hold back the extra ten cents per game from our pay, we would all have to go to prison for tax rotation."

"You mean tax evasion," I said.

"Yeah, that," Timmy said. "Stubby also told us that since the college owns the field and the college is a Catholic college, then we also would have to answer to the pope if we didn't pay our taxes. Stubby said that it is a mortal sin not to pay the taxes and that the pope would excommunibake us from the church, and I am supposed to make my First Communion next year. My parents would really get mad at me if I got excommunibakeded and didn't get to make my First Communion. To make things worse, Stubby told us that the pope likes softball a lot, because he even has softball games in the middle of Vacation City in Italy, where he lives. He would not be happy with us for not paying our taxes."

"You mean Vatican City, Italy. That's where the pope lives," I said. "Well, I have had many reasons to study mortal sins, and I can tell you that not paying taxes for shagging balls is not on the list. You also mean excommunicated, and you can't be excommunicated for not paying taxes. Maybe eating meat on Fridays will get you excommunicated, but definitely not for refusing to pay the

Stubby tax. As a matter of fact, the pope does not even have a soft-ball park in Vatican City. It is all concrete in front of Saint Peter's Church, and when the people are not standing around watching the pope, the trainee popes get to come out and roller skate on the concrete. Well, you kids just go on and shag the balls, and we'll see if we can't change Stubby's mind about how to handle the taxes."

The Fourth of July was about a month away, but Mortie had already managed to get his hands on a bunch of fireworks. "What are you gonna do with all of that stuff?" I asked Mortie.

"Well, I need to spread them out and see what I have here," Mortie answered.

In the meantime, Ran pointed out that Stubby was perched up on the scoreboard by center field. He must have hired the little kids to shag balls and decided to work the scoreboard, because the guy who normally did the scoreboard was off for something or sick.

"Just watch," I said. "Stubby will work it out so he gets to keep that job plus the ball-shagging job, just because he butters up Steve."

"You can count on that," Ran replied.

"Anyway, look at Stubby sitting out there eating a malt cup. He could buy three of them with the money that he's taking from those little kids for just this game," I said.

"He's a creep, and I never did like him," Ran chimed in.

"I wish that the scoreboard would cave in under him," I said.

"Yeah, he would see a bunch of fireworks then," Mortie said.

Just then it hit me. It was a stroke of brilliance. "Hey, Mortie, how many packs of regular firecrackers do you have?" I asked.

"Oh, about thirty, and they were really cheap this year," Mortie replied. "I have a bunch more at home that I'm saving for the Fourth of July."

"I've got an idea, and you and Ran need to come with me," I said.

We scampered through the woods to a point just behind the center field scoreboard. There was Stubby, snacking away on his malt cup. He also had a bag of popcorn, a couple of candy bars, and a soft drink lined up on the scoreboard platform right next to him. We were only a few feet away from him but hidden by the trees and woods that were located between the garages and the ballpark fence. I whispered to Ran and Mortie that at the end of the inning, we should all light firecrackers and start throwing them at Stubby from both sides and from behind the scoreboard. It would be like shooting ducks in a barrel or something like that. He would only be able to see shadows from where we would be standing, so he wouldn't be able to recognize us.

Ran and Mortie both agreed with the plan. We divided up the firecrackers and a few books of matches and then took our posts around the scoreboard. The inning finally ended and Stubby settled back with his soft drink and popcorn. He never saw it coming. At my signal, we all began lighting our firecrackers and started throwing them at Stubby. At the first loud POP, Stubby threw his bag of popcorn into the air while spilling his soft drink down his shirt and onto his pants.

We continued our bombardment of Stubby. Since he was facing the ballpark lights, it was difficult for him to see outside of the fence, especially by the woods. He never did see us. It became difficult to keep a good aim while laughing at Stubby's dilemma. Anyway, Stubby was too busy ducking the firecrackers to even notice who was throwing them at him. Before we knew it, he had fallen off the scoreboard and onto the ground, about four feet below. He got up and ran straight for home plate while the other team was taking the field.

We laughed and laughed until Mortie pointed that Steve, the ballpark manager, was heading across the field straight to the scoreboard. It was time to make a quick, stealthy retreat.

By the time Steve made it to the scoreboard, we had made it back to our normal viewing spot in the woods down the left base line. Since I worked at the ballpark shagging balls, I was permitted to enter the park for free to visit the concession stand. Nearby, I saw Stubby getting chewed out by Steve. He was blaming Stubby for the firecrackers! He told Stubby to go on home for the night, and he would get someone else to manage the scoreboard.

Being the helpful person that I am, I walked up to Steve and offered my services in his time of need. "Hello there," I said. "I couldn't but help overhear your conversation with Stubby. He should know better than to be playing with firecrackers. Seems like you need someone to keep score on the scoreboard, and you're halfway through the game. Tell you what, since you haven't paid Stubby yet, and because I know that you never pay until the end of the game, I'll take over and finish the work on the scoreboard for you. Then you can just pay me."

"You want the full rate for half of the game?" Steve asked.

"Well, I was thinking that I needed Stubby's rate plus an extra fifty cents, as there are possibly more unexploded firecrackers at the scoreboard, and I would be risking my life and limb."

"Come on, Steve, let's finish this game," came the calls from the two teams on the field.

Steve finally said okay, and I dashed off to the scoreboard for the next three innings and a full game's pay plus a small bonus. "Don't forget that I'm taking care of the ball shagging too," I called out to Steve as he ran back across the field.

"You just have to have a good technique," I explained to Ran and Mortie as we left the park later that night.

After the game, I found Timmy and his two friends. "Hey, you guys," I called. "Here's seventy-five cents for the three games that you all did tonight. It seems like Stubby had an enlightening experience, so I decided that you all deserved the full promised amount."

At the same time, we were well on our way to saving up enough money to get to see *The Tall Texan Wild West Show* at the State Fair.

A couple of nights later, we were back at our perch behind left field. There was not much going on, and it was Stubby's night to work again. Just like the other night, Stubby was back on the scoreboard, and some little kids were shagging balls at Stubby's discounted rate.

"Stubby is sitting there like he owns this place," Ran observed.

Stubby must have thought that he was a king or something. Just the way he sat there seemed to get under my skin. "Never did care for him much," I heard myself say. "Hey, Mortie, you got any of those firecrackers left?"

"Nope, just a few smoke bombs," he answered.

Hmm, I thought. *Just a couple of smoke bombs.* "I guess that, we'll just have to make do with smoke bombs," I said. "Mortie, Ran come on over here. When I give the signal, each of you light up one smoke bomb on either side of the scoreboard."

They quickly took off for their assigned posts. Right between batters, I signaled Mortie and Ran to light off their smoke bombs. I had waited until the second batter of the inning was up to bat. It was a thing of beauty. Very quickly a big orange cloud began to cover the scoreboard. Seconds later, Stubby came running and coughing away from the scoreboard. "The scoreboard's on fire," he called out, but no one could see the flames.

Then the cloud began to drift straight for the infield. "What is that crappy smell?" someone complained. Moments later, the orange cloud reached the stands, and the crowd began to leave the ballpark. Steve was going crazy. The teams had left the field, and the fans were leaving the ballpark. Finally, one of the ball players, who had gone out to center field, called out that the scoreboard was not on fire after all. Steve quickly got on the PA system and announced that all was clear, there was no fire, and the game would resume in two minutes.

About that time, Stubby appeared. I watched as Steve chewed out Stubby for starting a fire on the scoreboard. As I walked up behind Stubby, I held up a burned-out cigarette for Steve to see as I pointed to Stubby from behind. Steve told Stubby to go on home and that if he ever showed up to work and was caught smoking again, he could be fired for good.

I quickly seized this opportunity to earn a little extra money. "Hello, Steve, what a mess old Stubby made for you. Smoking is such a nasty habit. Anything that I can do to help out? Maybe keep score for you?"

"Okay, Scott, get out on the scoreboard and let's finish this last game of the night."

"Same financial arrangements as the other night?" I called out to Steve with a big grin. "Remember, I'll also be making sure that all of the balls get shagged."

We both heard the umpire call for "batter up." Finally, Steve said all right. Later that night I would leave the ballpark with Stubby's regular per-game pay, plus my fifty-cent bonus pay. Once again, I met up with Timmy and paid him and his pals the full seventy-five cents that Stubby had originally promised them. I left the ballpark after the game, found Ran and Mortie, and reminded them that you have to have a good technique. "Stubby," I said, "has a sloppy technique."

After dividing up our pay, we all headed home, content in the knowledge that we had enjoyed a fun night at Stubby's expense, and while we were at it, we had managed to make a little bit of money in the process. Our *Tall Texan Wild West* show savings account was starting to grow! It had definitely been a good night and a good start to our summer adventures.

Chapter 5
THE ALTAR BOY PICNIC

The day of the altar boy picnic had finally arrived. For once, I was happy to get up early and head to school. Now don't get me wrong—I never like going to SCHOOL school. It was just that we all had to meet at school to board the school bus that was taking us to the altar boy picnic. However, my sendoff was not perfect. Standing there with her altar boy clipboard was Sister Mary Holy Flower. When she saw me, she immediately called me out: "Mr. Stiles, I told you that you had forgone your privilege of attending the altar boy picnic when you committed the semi-mortal sin of upsetting the Holy Mass."

"I have come on the orders of a higher authority," I replied.

"Well, I am the highest authority around here, and I said that you couldn't go," she pronounced.

I told her that she had better check the chain of command, because I was pretty sure that Father Allgood outranked her in the parish, and he had both reinstated me as an altar boy in good standing AND said that I could go to the altar boy picnic. "Now, I can walk right over to the rectory and ask him to have a talk with you," I said.

"That will not be necessary," said Sister Mary Holy Flower, "because one of my vows was a vow of forgiveness, and I choose to forgive you for that act of holy desecration."

"Great," I said. After boarding the bus, it occurred to me that nuns do not take a vow of forgiveness, but I was not going to worry about it.

The altar boy picnic was everything that I had expected. We went to a park way out in the country. There was a lake with a float and slide. We got to canoe and ride paddleboats. The adult sponsors grilled hot dogs and hamburgers, and you could have as many as you wanted. They even had soft drinks and chocolate milk for us to drink! Best of all was that there were no teachers, nuns, or girls. Well, I would have kinda liked it if Lori Ann Lake was around, because she was about the only girl that I kinda liked. Nope, not at the altar boy picnic. It was the promised land, or so I thought. That meant that you couldn't have any girls hanging around, even if they were pretty like Lori Ann.

Ran had managed to stay in Sister Mary Holy Flower's good graces, even though she knew that he was my best friend. She would tell him that he should be careful because people would judge him by the company that he keeps. We decided that he didn't keep or even work for a company, so she must not even know what she was talking about. We ate and swam and then ate and swam some more.

After lunch, it was time for the annual seventh-grade altar boys versus the eighth-grade altar boys tug of war.

"I really don't like the look of this match," Ran said.

"Don't worry, the fix is in," I said.

"What do you mean?" he asked.

"The red end is our end, and the blue end is the eighth-graders' end. You know how they always put their biggest guys on the end of their rope?" I asked.

"Yup, just like a bunch of bulls," Ran answered.

"Well, watch what happens this time," I said.

When the whistle to start was blown, both sides began to tug. At first it was pretty even, but finally our side started to give way, inch by inch.

"My hands are starting to sweat," Ran said.

Well, everyone's hands were starting to sweat. However, the eighth-graders were having problems holding on to their end of the rope. They began to lose their grips, and we began to pull them our way. This year, the eighth-graders had changed the rules a little. While the sponsors were occupied elsewhere, a few up them scooped up some cow poop from the pasture by the lake and put it right in the middle of the tug of war area. They planned to drag us through the cow poop this year.

Soon, the eighth grade big guys on the end seemed to lose their grip on the rope and fall away. They would quickly get back up and grab the rope, but they had to grab it in the front, where they couldn't use their strength as well. One after another fell down and the rope began to move in our direction. Soon, we were pulling the eighth-graders across the cow poop. Finally, the eighth-graders at the end of the rope let loose and gave up, not wanting to join their classmates in the cow poop.

"I can't believe that we beat them fair and square!" yelled Ran.

"We beat them, sorta fair and square," I replied.

Ran gave me a funny look and then said, "What did you do, Scott?"

"I just lubricated their rope for them," I said. "I figured that a little hamburger grease spread on their rope would enhance their grip, and it did."

"I didn't hear you, and I don't know anything about it," Ran replied.

A little later, we decided to try out the paddle boats. After paddling our paddle boat out to the middle of the lake, Ran and I decided to rest up a bit.

"It would sure be nice if we could float around the lake without having to paddle," Ran said.

"Yup, that would be nice," I agreed.

There were a number of paddle boats out where we were. All of us were just floating around. Then it hit me! "I've got an idea," I said. "When I get into the water, hand me that long rope that they use to tie this boat to the dock."

Ran pitched the rope to me as soon as I was in the water. Up ahead of us was Hudge's paddle boat. Hudge and Slim had paddled out and were resting before paddling back to the dock. I tied the rope to the back of their paddle boat behind the paddle cover, so they wouldn't be able to see it if they looked back. I then swam back to our paddle boat and climbed back aboard with Ran's help.

Finally, Hudge and Slim started to paddle back to the dock, which meant that we were now headed that way too. I noticed that Hudge and Slim appeared to be working extra hard to paddle back. I called out to them that Ran and I were having a difficult time paddling too, in order to throw off any suspicion that we were the cause of their difficulties. Hudge glanced over his shoulder and acknowledged my call. I then yelled out that it must be because we were paddling upstream against the current.

Ran whispered to me that there was no upstream or current in that lake.

"I know," I said, "but I don't think that Hudge or Slim knows that."

When we got to the dock, I quickly hopped off our paddle boat and told Hudge that I would tie up both paddle boats. Hudge and Slim both thanked me, and I was able to untie my rope from their boat, and no one was the wiser... except for Ran.

As we sat on the dock, Ran and I struck up one of our serious conversations. "How do they make holy water?" Ran asked.

"Well, that is a long process," I said. "First, they have to boil a big pot of water, because holy water has to be clean in order to be pure. You're not allowed to have impure holy water. Then the nuns have to look at it."

"Why is that?" Ran asked.

"You know that the nuns cook the hosts that the priests use in Mass, don't you?" I asked. "Well, they have to holy up the holy water too, before they give it to the priests."

"How do they do that?" he asked.

"Well, in order to make sure that it is pure, they have to dip their rosaries into the pot of water. If the water does not turn a different color, then it's pure," I said. "Next, they put the water in a holy water holder jar to carry over to the church. Once they get there, the priest has to come out and dip his elbow into the holy water holder jar to make sure that it is not boiling hot. Next, he has to say the holy water prayer and bless the water in the holy water holder jar. Finally, they pour out the water from the holy water holder jar into the holy water holder font. It is now officially holy water."

"What do they do with it next?" Ran asked.

"They hafta divide up the holy water between the baptism fountain, the holy water bowls, and the Saint Blaise jars."

"What are the Saint Blaise jars?" Ran asked.

"You know how they celebrate Saint Blaise day at church by sticking a candle under your chin?" I asked. "Well, if you have a really bad sore throat and it's not Saint Blaise day, you go to church and ask to get some holy water from the Saint Blaise jars and you gargle. It fixes a sore throat just like that."

"How come you know so much about church stuff?" Ran asked.

"Well, I gotta uncle that's a priest and an aunt who's a nun," I said. "It just comes to me naturally, kinda like in my blood."

About that time, we heard the adult sponsors call all of us back to load up on the bus for the ride back to school. It had been a perfect day. Heck, the altar boy picnic had been all that I had hoped for, and a little more!

Chapter 6
HELLO, BISCUIT

The ballpark had provided us with a source of entertainment, and it was a personal source of enrichment for me, so naturally we ended up watching one of the women's league softball games a couple of nights later. I liked watching the women's softball games. The Peachtree Baptist Church had a team that was made up of beautiful blondes. Even the older women—you know, the late twenty or early thirty-year-old women—were, if not beautiful, very attractive in an older lady kind of way.

Well, the Peachtree Baptist Church had the most beautiful pitcher in the whole world. Her name was Marlene Modelle. She was a very good pitcher and a real good batter too. I could watch her for hours. Her windup and deliveries were enough to ... well, it was a really good windup that I never grew tired of watching. I would try to get Marlene to notice me before and after games, but I think she thought that I was just some local kid who liked to hang around the ballpark. Who am I kidding? She didn't even know that I existed. Well, that could be due to the fact that she was about a year older than me, or maybe two years, or three years, or, heck, she was just an older young lady. If I was only a few years or so older, then she would have noticed me. Well, probably not. She was just plain out of my league, but I could dream, couldn't I?

Marlene was the only girl—no, the only young lady—who could give Lori Ann Lake a run for the money, in my heart. Truth be told, I didn't stand a chance with Marlene or Lori Ann. Well, I could dream, couldn't I? That seemed to be the only answer that I could ever come up with when it came to Marlene or Lori Ann. On this particular night, me, Ran, Mortie, and Biscuit decided to watch Peachtree Baptist Church play another church team from across town.

Oh, Biscuit was one of our best friends. His real name was not Biscuit. His real name was Allison Johnson. He got the nickname "Biscuit" from … well, I don't know how he got that nickname, but that's what everyone called him. He was a good guy and we all liked him a lot. It seemed like a black cloud hung over him, though. If something bad was going to happen, it almost always happened to Biscuit. I was glad that this was not one of my nights to be shagging balls, because it was a whole lot more fun watching a game that I did want to see, plus I got to watch it with my buddies. It was a bonus night because the Peachtree Baptist Church team was playing and, of course, my beautiful Marlene Modelle would be pitching.

We had been scheduled to work tonight's games, but Stubby had buttered up the ballpark manager, Steve, and gotten him to give us the night off and let Stubby and his helpers take our places. We didn't much like that. Stubby always shagged the foul balls on the street side of the ballpark, if he wasn't working on the scoreboard. If he was working the scoreboard, he went back to getting the little kids to cover the street side of the park for him. Although we liked to mess with Stubby, we never bothered the little kids. They were all a bunch of nice little kids, and we didn't like the way Stubby took advantage of them. They were just too young to realize that he was taking advantage of them.

Stubby got Steve to unlock the service gate at the end of the wall next to left field. That way he didn't have to sit on top of the wall and then hop down to retrieve the foul balls that were hit into the street, like the rest of us did. He would just run through the service gate out into the street and retrieve the ball. We decided that since Stubby had cost us the money that we would have earned that night for our *Tall Texan Wild West Show* and the State Fair admission, we would have to find another way to make up the loss of income.

After a brief planning session together, we came up with an idea. The service entrance gate that Stubby used would only swing open in the direction of the street. Stubby was doing his normal goofing off, eating popcorn and candy, when the first foul ball popped over the fence and into the street. When Stubby went to retrieve the ball, he found out that the gate had been tied closed, and he couldn't get out. Climbing over the wall was out of the question for Stubby. I think it had something to do with gravity.

Biscuit ran out into the street, retrieved the ball, and then disappeared into our special hiding place in the woods behind left field. Stubby was pretty mad about not retrieving the ball, but it was understood that some balls just couldn't be found. He finally was able to unwind the rope from where we had tied the gate shut. When he returned to his post, he resumed his routine of sitting down, eating his popcorn and candy, and giving scant notice to the game being played.

Not too long after that, there was a loud SMACK, and another foul ball popped back over the wall by the street. This time when

Stubby got up to run out the gate, he found the gate was closed again and blocked by some concrete blocks. There had been a pile of these blocks across the street at the junior high school's new wing that was under construction. Somehow, several of those concrete blocks had mysteriously gotten moved from the construction site across the street and then ended up getting piled in front of the service gate that Stubby used. Of course, I didn't have any idea how they got there.

Biscuit had been out by the parked cars on the street, and as soon as he saw the ball bounce on the street, he ran over, picked up the ball, and then disappeared into our hiding place in the woods by left field. Stubby had now lost two balls in the first game. Steve would be getting mad at him pretty soon if he didn't start shagging balls.

This time Stubby began to watch the service gate. I knew that this was going to cause us a problem, so I had to come up with another idea.

I climbed over the wall and walked up to Stubby. "Looks like you're having some problems shagging balls tonight," I said to him.

"Yup, someone keeps locking the gate on me, and I can't get out to get the balls," he said.

"Well, that is just awful. What happened?" I asked as innocently as I could.

"First, someone tied the gate shut and I couldn't shag the first foul ball. Next, someone piled some concrete blocks in front of the gate so it wouldn't open. I couldn't shag the next ball when that happened," he said. "Steve is going to be getting pretty mad at me soon."

"That's just terrible," I said. "Who would want to mess around with you, Stubby? Well, I'm your friend, and I'm here to help you out. I'll just stay here and help you for a little while. That way we can keep an eye on the gate."

After a few minutes, I noticed that Stubby had finished off all of his popcorn. I knew that he was still hungry. He was always hungry. Time to strike!

"I can smell that fresh popped popcorn at the concession from all the way over here," I said. "It smells especially good tonight."

That did it. That was all the prodding Stubby needed. "I sure would like some of that freshly-popped popcorn," he said. "But it will probably be all gone except for the kernels by the time this inning is over."

"Well, Stubby, why don't I watch for the foul balls here long enough for you to go and get some of that freshly-popped popcorn?"

"Would you do that?" he asked.

I knew that I had him. "Sure, if you buy a malt cup for me, I'll be glad to do it."

He said that it was a deal, and he ran straight for the concession stand. That had worked out just as I had planned. Then, almost on cue, there was another loud CRACK, and another foul ball popped over the fence into the street. This time Ran retrieved the ball and ran back to our hiding place in the woods behind left field.

Stubby came running back with a bag of popcorn in one hand and a malt cup in the other hand. "I heard a CRACK and a foul ball hit out in the street," Stubby exclaimed.

"Yup, you sure did, that's for sure," I said, while taking the malt cup from Stubby's hand.

"Well, why didn't you get the ball?" he asked.

"I told you that I would watch for foul balls, and I did. There was a foul ball that went out into the street just a minute ago. I didn't say that I would go get it, and you didn't ask me to do that. I would have had to charge you extra to do that. You need to go get that foul ball. After all, a deal is a deal," I said as I started to walk off. I had done my part.

Then I stopped and turned around. "Stubby, you said that someone keeps locking this gate on you, and you can't get out to shag the foul balls."

"Yeah, that's right," he said.

"Well, I have a deal for you. Me, Ran, Biscuit, and Mortie will sit over here and watch the game from in front of the gate. You can't tell Steve we're here, or he'll make us pay or leave. We'll also watch the gate to make sure that no one locks the gate shut on ya. Best of all, we're gonna do that for a mere twenty-five cents a game, for the next two games. A bargain!"

"I only make fifty cents a game," Stubby said.

"Yeah, but someone is messing with you tonight, and you may end up getting fired if you don't start shagging foul balls," I said. "How about it? Is it a deal?"

"Okay, it's a deal," Stubby said.

"Payment in full in advance," I said.

"But I haven't gotten paid yet."

"Dig into your candy fund that you always keep in your front pocket."

"Okay, it is a deal," he said, and he handed over the fifty cents that we had bargained for.

Stubby went back to his station near the gate, and Ran, Mortie, Biscuit, and I sat back to watch the game. "Oh, by the way, don't forget to look for that last foul ball that went out into the street," I called to Stubby.

"Well, we shagged three balls tonight that we could sell back to the teams that play tomorrow night," I said to Ran, Mortie, and Biscuit. "That should get us about three dollars, plus the fifty cents that we made from Stubby tonight. That means that we made about two dollars more than we would have made if Stubby had not gotten Steve to change tonight's schedule. Yup, it was a good night."

It was even a better night because I got to watch my very favorite women's softball team, the Peachtree Baptist team, clobber the other team. Of course, beautiful Marlene was the star of the game, especially in my eyes.

Chapter 7
LAYING THE GROUNDWORK

Ran and I were sitting on the roof of our favorite place to just hang out and talk. Yup, we were back on top of the Cherokee Park Baptist Church. This place gave us a great view of Bardstown Road and the neighborhood around it. Plus, it was just a great place to hang out. No one ever looked up on the roof after dark, and it always had a cool breeze blowing in the summer. Don't know what it was like in the winter, because we just never seemed to go up there when it was cold outside. Besides, during the winter, we had school during the week, so we wouldn't be out very long on "school nights."

"I can't wait for the State Fair to roll around," I said.

"Me too," echoed Ran. "I can't wait to see the Tall Texan in person. He must be about seven feet tall. And his horse, Firestorm, is the best and smartest horse ever. He's so smart that he can not only add numbers but can multiply them too. I saw him do it in one of the Yummy Flakes commercials on TV."

The Tall Texan was just about the coolest cowboy I had ever seen on television. They had even started running commercials on television about his appearance at the State Fair, and that was about two months or so away. I said to Ran that I thought that maybe they were going to have the Tall Texan's friend, Chief Thunder Belly, appear too. That would be so cool. The Tall Texan and Wang Chow KaPow, his trusty sidekick, had rescued Chief Thunder Belly's daughter, Princess Running Summer Snowflake, from a band of mean outlaws who had captured her while she was fetching a bucket of water from the riverside for all of the old squaws in the tribe. The Tall Texan had Wang Chow KaPow dress up in an Indian girl's outfit to lure the outlaws into their ambush. Wang Chow KaPow is a little guy, so it was much easier for him to dress up as a little girl than the Tall Texan.

Ran jumped in. "I remember that episode! When the bad guys tried to grab little Wang Chow, he surprised them with a bunch of his mean judo hops and knocked them down."

"Judo chops, not judo hops," I said.

"No!" Ran exclaimed. "They were judo hops!"

"Ran, they're called judo chops, because he chops the bad guys."

"Well, he had judo hops too," Ran said.

"Hmm," I said," I guess when he hops around real fast, then those must be his judo hops."

"Yeah, that was what I was talking about," Ran responded.

"Makes sense to me, I guess," I concluded.

"The bad guys were so surprised that they didn't hear the Tall Texan ride up behind them on his faithful horse, Firestorm," Ran went on.

"Yeah, the Tall Texan had both of his six-shooter guns out and pointed at the bad guys, and he made them return Thunder Belly's daughter, Princess Running Summer Snowflake. Chief Thunder Belly was so happy, he and the Tall Texan became blood brothers, which meant that Chief Thunder Belly would always be there to help the Tall Texan, and the Tall Texan would always be there to help Chief Thunder Belly," I finished.

"Yeah," Ran said. "They smoked a peace pipe and ate fried chicken together to seal their friendship. Chief Thunder Belly gave the Tall Texan his own pair of bass moccasins, like the ones they sell at the shoe store."

"You know, that's where the shoe store gets their bass moccasins from to this very day," I said.

"From Chief Thunder Belly?" Ran asked.

"Nope, I think that Princess Running Summer Snowflake is in charge of all of the Indian squaws that make the bass moccasins. They put them on the Wells Fargo train, which then brings them to Louisville. The Tall Texan had Wang Chow KaPow give Chief Thunder Belly a bozo tree."

"What's a bozo tree?" Ran asked.

"You know, one of those little tiny trees that they grow in Japan, and you can even still see them in Chinese restaurants today," I said.

"Oh yeah, I know what you're talking about," Ran said. "I bet that Wang Chow Kapow brought bozo tree seeds when he came over here from China or Japan. I wonder if the bass moccasins had a penny in the front of them like the ones that we have today."

"They could have, since Lincoln is on every penny, and he was already dead by the time the Tall Texan and Chief Thunder Belly met," I deduced. "They invented the Lincoln penny the day after President Lincoln died. They say that the Tall Texan always has a shooting contest when he appears. Maybe it will be a contest between him and Chief Thunder Belly."

"I bet that the Tall Texan will have his trusty rifle, the Texas SureShot," Ran said. "I remember that once the Tall Texan pulled out the Texas SureShot, he never ever, ever misses his target. I remember that if someone tossed a silver dollar into the air, the Tall Texan could shoot the silver dollar dead through the middle so that when it landed, it was turned into four quarters."

I looked at Ran with a puzzled look on my face.

Ran went on. "That's why they call quarters, quarters. The Tall Texan shot them into four equal pieces back in those days."

"I never thought about that, but I guess that it makes sense," I said. "Won't be much longer till State Fair time." We both agreed.

"What are we gonna be doing tomorrow?" Ran asked.

Well, I'd heard that the Fraters over at the seminary had found a bunch of wild puppies back in the woods behind the church. The puppies' mother had died or something like that, and the Fraters had found them and were supposedly trying to find a home for them. The Fraters were seminary students. I didn't know why they were called Fraters. I guessed that it was because they had not been ordained yet, and since you couldn't call them Father such and such, you had to call them Frater such and such. I think that it was Latin for Father trainee or priest trainee or junior Father.

"Do you think that your mom will let you keep a puppy, Scott?"

"I'm sure that she will when she sees the puppy's cute face and the puppy licks her on her face. Mom has a soft spot for puppies and little brothers and sisters. I mean, if she thinks that Marie and Sam are cute … ugh … then she has to think that a little puppy is a whole lot cuter."

"Where will you keep the puppy?" Ran asked.

"Hmm, Mr. Gagel doesn't have his dogs anymore, and he still has their old doghouse."

Mr. Gagel and Mrs. Gagel were a couple of our neighbors who were always really nice to us. As a matter of fact, they were the best neighbors in the whole entire world.

"I bet that he would even pay me, I mean pay us," I said, "to move the old doghouse out of his yard. It's a really cool doghouse. It has some type of ceramic shingles on the sides to help keep dogs warm in the wintertime."

Hmm, I would have to get some straw for the doghouse, to make the puppy comfortable, I thought.

"They've been spreading straw on the grass over at the college gym that they're building a couple of blocks away," I said. "I bet they wouldn't even miss a bundle of straw. What do you think?"

"I think that it's a great idea, and then we could name him Biscuit Jr.! It would be fun. Here, Biscuit; here, Biscuit," Ran said with a loud laugh.

"I don't think that the real Biscuit would like it, and maybe the puppy will need a real dog name."

"Not a stupid dog name," Ran begged.

"Nope, I'll name the puppy after us."

"Oh, like RanScott! Here, RanScott," Ran called while laughing.

"Ran, slow down now. I want a real dog name that when people hear it, they'll think of us. I've got it—TROUBLES," I said.

"Not bad, not bad at all, and it certainly would fit in with our little group. Then Troubles it will be. What do you think your grandmother will say, Scott? You know that she's always coming by to check in on you all while your mom is at work."

"No problem," I said. "Grandma loves dogs. Heck, I think she loves dogs more than Marie or Sam."

"What about you? Does she love dogs more than you, Scott?"

"Nope, I'm her favorite, and there's nothing that will change that fact."

"Okay, then tomorrow we go get a puppy and bring it … him … her, or whatever, home," we agreed.

"Ran, since you're my very best friend in the entire world, I'll want you to be the puppy's godfather."

"Wow, that is neat, but I thought that you could only be appointed godfather when someone gets baptized."

"Not a problem," I said. "We studied baptism in catechism class, and there's nothing to it. You just pour a bottle of water over the puppy's head and then say that it is baptized. She shouldn't be hard to baptize. Heck, we're getting the puppy from the seminary. It may already come pre-baptized."

"What about a godmother?" Ran asked.

"Nope, I am not gonna have some dumb girl involved with my dog. She would probably want to put ribbons in its hair or something dumb like that," I replied. "Besides, dogs don't need a godmother to be baptized. They only need a godfather, because I read it somewhere in my catechism book last year. This will be a manly dog," I proclaimed.

"Can a girl dog be manly?" Ran asked.

"That's not what I mean," I said. "I mean that he or she will be a tough dog, who is strong and faithful and not afraid of nothing. Seems like we have taken care of the planning. Now all we hafta to do is to put our plan into action tomorrow morning. What else can we take care of tonight?"

"I don't know," Ran said. "You know that we havta get up early in the morning to deliver papers."

"Yup," I agreed. "I've decided that it's easier to get up early and deliver papers in the summertime, because you don't have the heavy burden of having to go to school later hanging over your head."

When I helped Ran deliver papers on school days, I always got sleepy after lunch. Sister Mary Wackenhammer used to love to sneak up behind me when I was nodding off and then whack me in the back of the head with a dirty eraser.

"We should have gotten a special permission pass from the bishop that since we were working men, the nuns wouldn't be allowed to sneak up behind us and whack us in the back of the head if we accidentally nodded off," I said. "We should be able to get a pass to come into school late too."

"I think that you're right," Ran said.

"We should be able to show up for school an hour later than everyone else, because we need to have time to unload the stress of going to school after delivering papers."

"Yeah, and the nuns would have to not be able to mouth off to us because we're late," Ran said.

"The nuns hafta do what the bishop says or they would get demoted to a novice nun."

"What is a novice nun?" Ran asked.

"That is a nun trainee, and all they can eat are loaves and fishes until they get promoted to nunhood," I said. "I think that I should have time to stuff extra newspapers into the seat of my britches before I go to school and get sent to see Miss Pennyberry and her yardstick, anyway. Seems like she's always lurking around the halls, waiting for me to commit an innocent infraction, so she can swoop in like an ugly buzzard wearing glasses and then drag me to her office for a quick trial, condemnation, and a punishment that is administered by a giant yardstick."

"She's so mean," Ran said.

"I think that she wears a corset that is way too small that causes her brain to not get enough blood floating around in her head. It puts her in a bad mood, and she just looks for someone to take it out on, like poor little innocent me," I said. "Seems like it's always me."

"Well, Scott, you're the one who placed thumbtacks on her desk chair seat, and the one who poured glue on her desk chair seat, and the one who let all of the air out of her car tires in the school parking lot, and the one who loosened all of the wheels on her desk chair so they would fall off, and the one who put dog poop in her potted plant that sat in the sun on the window sill behind her desk," Ran said. "That really stunk up her office, and it got even worse when you sprayed stinky pine-scented disinfectant on it. The darn thing up and died! I can sort of see why she seems to think of you first when something happens around school."

"Those are all minor offenses, and she just doesn't have a sense of humor. She needs to learn to relax," I said.

"Yeah, someone should snip her corset one day," Ran said.

"How do you know what a corset is?" I asked Ran.

"Oh, I was over at Stubby's, and he had gotten a hold of one of his mom's corset books, or whatever you call those books, and he showed me one. Funny thing is that all of those pretty women in the corset book, well, none of them looked like they even needed a corset."

"Maybe she isn't wearing a corset," I said. "You know, I think that only pretty women wear corsets, and Miss Pennyberry is too mean to be pretty. She probably wears a girdle, and it is probably three sizes too small. You know only pretty women wear corsets, and the rest of them wear girdles. I think that after squeezing into a girdle and wearing it around school all day, she must hafta stay in a bad mood all of the time. Yup, those girdles are pretty strong. I mean that I think that you have to use something that works kinda like a shoehorn to even squeeze into one."

"Nope, I think that they grease up their bodies with Crisco shortening so they can slide in a little easier. I saw some mannequins wearing girdles when my mom was shopping at Kaufman's.

Why do they always put girdles on skinny mannequins anyway?" Ran asked.

"They come from the mannequin factory that way, so the salespeople don't have to grease them up with Crisco," I said. "They would make for great sling shots, but I don't know where we could find used girdles that we could cut up for slingshots."

"I don't think that I would want to use a used girdle from Miss Pennyberry," Ran said.

"Yuck, I hadn't thought about that," I said. "I bet that if the buttons on her girdle ever popped off, she would just burst out of her clothes!"

"Oh gross!" Ran said. "I don't even want to think about that. Even the thought of that makes my eyes water and hurt. Do you think that the nuns wear girdles too?"

"Kind of," I said. "Their girdles are heavy duty. That's why they wear those long, black nun uniforms. They need to make sure that their girdles are covered up and also protected from the rain and snow."

"Why's that?" Ran asked.

"Well, I have it on good authority that the nun's girdles are made out of cast iron and have a lock on the front of them. If it ever got wet, it would rust."

"Why do they wear iron girdles with locks?" Ran asked.

"I think it's because they took a vow of chastity, which means that they can't ever get married," I said.

"What is chastity?" Ran asked.

"Oh, that means that if a nun ever breaks her vow, then the pope comes over and chastises her. Then she gets demoted to a nun novice. A nun novice is a nun trainee, and they only get to eat loaves and fish sandwiches until they get promoted back to a nun. If a priest or a brother wants to marry them, then they can't, because only the head mother nun has the key to the iron girdles, and she took a vow of Holy Orders that meant that she was under orders never to unlock any nun's girdle."

"Can a priest or a brother date a nun?" Ran asked.

"Oh sure, just as long as he takes the nun to a bingo or to see a church movie like *The Ten Commandments*," I answered. "Maybe that's why all of the nuns are always in a bad mood. How would you feel if you had to walk around wearing a miniature pot belly stove for a girdle?"

"How do they go to the bathroom?" Ran asked.

"You know that the pot belly stove over at Biscuit's house has a latch door on the bottom to clean out the ashes. I think that the nuns have a latch on the bottom of their iron girdles too," I said. "It works the same way."

"Makes sense," Ran said. "Well, time to head in for the night."

"See ya, Ran."

"See ya, Scott."

Chapter 8
TROUBLES

The next morning came quick. Right after delivering papers with Ran, we headed off to the seminary. The Fraters were always fun. They were really nice. I wondered that if once they were made priest, they would turn mean or grumpy like Father Taurman. I had heard that once there were a couple of the Fraters who got ordained and turned into priests and then never smiled again, ever! The Fraters were always nice to us, though. A couple of them even took us up the winding staircase in the bell tower all the way up to the top. It was really neat. You could see all the way to downtown and to Southern Indiana from way up there. The Fraters told me that on a clear day, you could see all the way to the Vatican, if the lighting was just right.

We did learn a lesson, though. Never, ever go up to the top of the bell tower when the bells were supposed to ring. We were up there one time and the bells started to ring. It was so loud! I thought that my ears would explode! It was spooky when the bells began to move. You could hear a little motor sound, and then the bells started to sway back and forth. Before you had time to get back down the stairway, G-O-N-G, G-O-N-G, G-O-N-G!

Other than that, it was a lot of fun. Anyway, when we got to the seminary, we were told that the Fraters were in class but that they would be finished soon and would be coming out for lunch. Ran and I decided that we would wait out back. The priests and the Fraters had a swimming pool down the hill by the woods. It was a neat place, and we used to sneak down there for a swim when no one was around. No harm, no fowl, as they said. I always wondered how fowls figured into that saying. I mean, what did chickens have to do with swimming pools?

We sat around the pool talking about just where the litter of puppies might have been found in the big woods that wrapped around the church and seminary. Lunchtime finally rolled around, and that meant that it was time for us to see the Fraters. We quickly found the Fraters, who had just gotten out of their Frater classes. They even had to go to Frater school during the summer, when everyone else was out of school. Frater Eric told us that they had two puppies left, but they were going to be keeping one as their Frater mascot. They kept the male puppy and named him Bosco. I got the girl puppy. After a brief disappointment, I picked up the girl puppy and held her in front of me. She immediately gave me a big lick on my face. That was it! We were now immediately the best of friends. I showed her to Ran and said that I would like to introduce him to Troubles.

It soon came to pass that Troubles was a perfect name for this cute little puppy. We wrapped Troubles up in a burlap potato bag, put her in the front basket on my bike, and then headed for home. I had a few hours to figure out just how I was going to introduce Troubles to Mom.

I thought over my plan of action. First, we had to take a detour and stop by my grandmother's house. She liked dogs, and I was still her favorite grandchild. I'd tell her how my fondest dream had come true by getting this adorable puppy. She would love on the puppy and then, since I'd pour on all of my charm, she'd be sure to take up for me and make a strong case when she talked to Mom.

Next, our plan called for taking Troubles home to meet Maria and Sam. They would be a pushover, and I'd tell them that they were allowed to play with Troubles, although I planned to limit their playing time to between two and three in the morning. Next, we'd go to visit Mrs. Reuther next door. She and her husband had a couple of beagles, so we knew that they already loved dogs. I'd tell her to remind Mom how safe it makes her feel to have dogs, because they are always ready to let her know if a prowler is around.

Next, we'd show Troubles to Mrs. Holloway. She was a really nice lady, but we would start with her little kids. Little kids always like puppies, and we would let them get attached to Troubles and then let Mrs. Holloway see them playing with Troubles. She would be a pushover.

Next, we'd run down to Mr. and Mrs. Gagel's house and negotiate a deal with Mr. Gagel to let him give us money to move the doghouse from his house to our back yard. His dogs had died, so he didn't need the doghouse anymore. We would need to call Biscuit and Mortie to help move the doghouse, because it was pretty heavy. Then we'd run down to the college gym and gather up some straw for the doghouse. It was important that we make the doghouse look happy and inviting ... kinda like a den. Finally, we would take the money that we got from Mr. Gagel and buy a couple of dog dishes and some dog food and then put water and some of the dog food in the dishes. At that point we would have the table set for the main course—Mom!

The plan was immediately put into action. "Why, Scott, Troubles is such an adorable puppy," my grandmother announced. "I never knew how much you wanted a dog of your own. I am sure that your mother will just love her."

Next it was a quick visit to my house to see Maria and Sam. They were in their normal annoying mood until they saw Troubles. It took all I had to be nice to them. Ugh! They fell for Troubles just like I thought they would.

After my sickening display of brotherly and sisterly love, my next stop was at Mrs. Reuther's house. "I think that she will be a fine little dog," she announced. "We can always use another dog around the neighborhood. It helps keep things safe, you know. I'll mention that to your mother, Scott."

Then we took Troubles to meet the little kids next door. Just like I had predicted, the little kids immediately took to Troubles, and when Mrs. Holloway looked out of her kitchen window and saw what was going on, she immediately came out to see Troubles. I had decided to let her oldest little girl, Linda, hold Troubles. That was all that it took.

"Mommy, see Troubles … I just love her. Don't you, Mommy?" That cinched it. Mrs. Holloway was in the bag, and she was going tell Mom just how much she liked Troubles and how her kids were attached to Troubles.

At that point, Mortie and Biscuit had shown up. We quickly marched down to Mr. and Mrs. Gagel's house. Just as I predicted, Mr. Gagel was happy to get rid of the doghouse and paid us ten dollars, to boot, just for moving it. We somehow managed to load the doghouse onto Biscuit's wagon and drag it to my house. As we moved down the street, you could hardly see the wagon under the overhang of the doghouse.

Once we got the doghouse set up in our back yard in an out of the way but comfortable spot, we were ready for the next step.

I tied a light rope around Troubles' neck, and we ran down to the college gym construction site while pulling Biscuit's wagon. Instead of each of us gathering a handful of straw, we decided to take one of the straw bundles that the landscaper had conveniently left lying on the grounds of the building site. Now the doghouse had enough straw for the next couple of months, and the leftover straw was stored in the garage.

We still had a little time left before Mom was to get home. We ran over to the pet store up at the Loop. Just as planned, we had just enough money for two bowls, a collar, a leash, and some dog food. We then dashed home just as Mom was walking up the street from the bus stop.

Mrs. Reuther happened to be on her front porch and called out to Mom that she loved my little surprise and she just knew that my mom would too.

I had Mortie summon Marie and Sam out and let them hold Troubles. The way that they loved over Troubles almost made me puke. Nevertheless, I put on my most innocent smile as Mom walked up the driveway. A chorus of "Hello, Mom" and "Hello, Mrs. Stiles" came from me and Ran.

"Mom, you look extra pretty tonight," I said with the best, most innocent face that I could come up with.

"Oh, hello there," Mrs. Holloway called out to Mom. "We absolutely love your addition."

By then, Mom was on guard but totally confused.

"We love her, Mom! Can we keep her?" begged Marie and Sam. "She's a girl dog, and I can dress her up in cute little girl ribbons," Marie said.

"Aren't they just two of the cutest little kids you have ever laid her eyes upon?" I asked Mom, knowing that I had set the stage for them to pull Mom's heart wires, or heart rope, or heart strings— whatever it was called.

Even though I had planned for their reaction, that last statement from Marie was sickening to me. My dog would never wear ribbons—period! I could feel the bile working up from my stomach to my throat. I just had to force it back down and smile. I hated to play the role of the good big brother, who was lovingly smiling at his bratty little sister and his dopey little brother, but I did it with a smile.

Oh well, my plan was starting to work as I watched my mom listen to the two little goofballs, even though she was still confused about the entire goings-on. "Scott, something tells me that you have a hand in all of this," Mom said.

"Who, me?" I replied with the most innocent face I could come up with.

Before anything else could be said, the phone rang and I dashed off to answer the call. "Mom, it's Grandma, and she wants to talk to you."

Mom looked at Troubles and then at Ran, Mortie, and Biscuit, unsure at this point just what to think.

After several minutes and many "But Mother" remarks, Mom returned to the back porch, where we were all gathered.

I think that Grandma had done her job on Mom. Mom looked straight at me. "Scott, somehow I cannot help but believe that you're behind all of this."

"Who, me?" I asked again, as innocently as possible. I used my last, best, most innocent face and tone of voice for this last accusation.

"Who else? If you had wanted a dog, don't you think you should have asked me first?" she asked in a not-too-motherly voice.

"Well, Mother, I wanted to show you that I could act in a mature fashion and handle the situation myself. I wanted to make you proud of me," I said with a smile. "Mom, Troubles was a gift from God, anyway."

"What are you talking about?" Mom asked.

"God wanted me to have Troubles and to bring her home to live with us," I said. "I couldn't tell God no, or I could end up in hell or having to spend extra time in purgatory. Sister Mary Wackenhammer, I mean Sister Mary Wackenmeister, said that I must always do what God commands me to do. Anyway, Mom, I am just trying to follow God's will."

"Wait a minute; wait a minute," Mom interrupted. "What do you mean God's will?"

I was ready for this question, and I had my well-rehearsed reply all ready. "The Fraters at the seminary gave her to me, and since she came from a church and seminary, then God had to have been the one who came up with this idea, and who am I to ignore God's divine will?"

Well, that reply worked about as good as I had planned, which means that it left Mom temporarily speechless. She finally said that she would have to have a word with the Fraters when she next saw them. Not quite finished yet, she asked, "And where do you suppose that we are going to go to get the shots for this dog?"

"They have a free clinic from time to time by the fire station on Bardstown Road," I said, as I knew this from seeing it in the newspaper.

"And where will the dog sleep?" Mom asked.

"Look over in the corner of the yard. We already have a dog-house, and it was donated for free," I replied.

She had to admit that it was a very nice doghouse. Mr. and Mrs. Gagel had really liked their dogs and taken very good care of them, keeping them in a deluxe doghouse.

"Look, Mom, she already has a collar," I said.

"And what is HER name?" Mom asked.

"Troubles," we all replied.

Mom said that somehow that name was fitting and might prove to be prophetic, whatever that means. I think that is some kind of poetry. Come to think about it, I think that Mom was wrong on that last part, because I have never heard of a dog who liked poetry.

"And what is Troubles supposed to eat?" Mom asked.

"We already have a bag of dog food, and we know that you're friends with the butcher and that he would probably give you fresh meat scraps from the butcher shop for your loving son's sweet little puppy."

At this point, Mom looked down at the floor and closed her eyes. I knew that I had won!

"I guess that you can keep Troubles, but you will be responsible for her, and you will have to clean up the yard after her when she goes to the bathroom."

"It's a deal!" I exclaimed. "But only number two droppings and not number one."

We all let out a cheer of joy. Of course, my cheer was more of a cheer of victory. As I have said many times before, you have got to have a good technique if you want to be successful.

Chapter 9
TROUBLES FOR STUBBY

It was made clear from the get-go that Troubles was MY dog. Mom made me let Marie and Sam play with her, but she was my dog. I really didn't have any problem letting Sam play with Troubles, because she usually got the best of him. She was able to bite his pants leg and pull him down. It was funny to see that little puppy pull Sam around the back yard, and he couldn't do anything about it except call for help. She never hurt him.

Marie was okay most of the time. However, when she tied ribbons on Troubles, I really got mad. I was not allowed to beat Marie up, so I had to think of other ways to get back at her. My favorite way was to put some of Troubles' fresh dog poop in Marie's shoes. She never caught on because I pushed the little doggie tootsie rolls way up into the toes of her shoes, and by the time she pulled her shoes on, it was too late. That really made Mom mad too. Marie tried to blame me, but I was quick to point out that

Marie often ran out in the yard in her socks, which really made Mom mad. I asked Mom why in the world would I want to pick up dog poop and put it in my little sister's shoes. Mom seemed to always believe me on that one. Marie never seemed to remember to look inside her shoes before she put them on. Seemed like she would, after having to wash out her socks so many times. But everyone knows that girls are not as smart as boys, not even close.

Even though Troubles was a girl, she was very smart, and I was able to teach her many tricks and commands really quickly. She would sit, stay, and come on my command. She also liked to play fetch. I started playing fetch with a softball. It was really funny to see her grapple with a softball until she could get it in her mouth to the point where she could carry it. I could even point to a softball and tell her to fetch it, and she would run off, grab the ball in her mouth, and bring it back to me. She was as proud as could be when she presented me with the softball. It quickly became apparent to me that I would be able to use this particular skill that I had taught Troubles. As a thought appeared in my mind, Ran walked in from the alley.

"Hi Ran, whachawanna do?" I asked.

"I dunno. Whachawanna do, Scott?" he answered.

"You know, our pal Stubby has a little racket going. He thinks that he's the most important person at the ballpark after Steve."

"That's for sure," Ran replied.

I continued, "He has a way of taking advantage of the smaller kids that hang around the neighborhood. I think that he does boss some of them a little bit, but mostly pops off around them about what a big guy he is. They always fall for his act, and then he uses them to his advantage. You know, I have the left-field side of the ballpark locked down as far as the shagging foul balls goes, and Stubby knows that he should not mess with me. I mean, I never threatened him or anything, but he just leaves me alone, other than to pop off about something in order to make himself seem big or important. Well, he's responsible for shagging the foul balls on the right-field side of the ballpark. Now remember that we are always paid fifty cents a ball game to shag the balls. That's a lot cheaper for the teams than replacing the foul balls, because they all foul a lot of balls out of the ballpark."

"Yup, I know that," Ran said.

"Well, tonight, ole Stubby had talked the little kids into shagging the balls on the right-field side of the ballpark again. As usual, he was paying them twenty-five cents a ball game out of the fifty cents a ball game he was getting paid. In addition to that, he was working the scoreboard. I mean, that's a bunny job. He just sits out there on the scoreboard and watches the game and eats whatever he brings out from his visit to the concession stand. The only time that he gets up is to change the score or update the score at the end of the inning."

"Yup, I know that too," Ran said.

"Well, Stubby has a crooked scheme going," I said to Ran. "Every night, he has one of his little ball shaggers say that someone ran off with the ball, or it couldn't be found, or it rolled down the drain or something. This happens once in every game. Now you know that there are a lot of foul balls hit in every game. That means that the kids are returning three almost-new softballs to Stubby every night. The real reason that he wanted to cut the grass by the scoreboard is because he has hidden a box behind the scoreboard where he hides the new balls that the little kids don't turn in, but give to him. Now, these teams rotate their schedules and only play at the ballpark once a week. So Stubby gets to the ballpark early the next night and offers 'almost new' softballs to the team managers for an 'almost new' price."

This was a scheme that was begging for me to bust it up and maybe make a little money or get a reward in the process. I called together my war council of Ran, Mortie, and Biscuit to tell them about my plan, and it was a pretty good plan.

The next night, we showed up at the game. Mortie took up his position outside the fence on the left side of the scoreboard, and Biscuit took up his position on the outside of the fence on the right side of the scoreboard. We waited patiently until, finally, in the third game of the night, one of the little shaggers snuck a third fouled-out softball night to Stubby, who was on his normal perch on the scoreboard. They ran it out in a popcorn bag so anyone who saw them would think that they were just running a bag of popcorn out to Stubby. That definitely was not out of the ordinary, because everybody knew that Stubby was always eating. Stubby then placed the softball in the little box that he had hidden behind the scoreboard to retrieve later. The box didn't have a regular lid because Stubby used the lid to sit on while keeping score, so it was going be easy pickings.

Once Stubby returned to his post on the scoreboard, we put our plan into action. Mortie and Biscuit were busy keeping Stubby occupied by asking him to tell them about some of his exploits. Stubby always liked to brag about himself, so this was an easy job for them. In the meantime, Ran, Troubles, and I snuck up behind the center field scoreboard. The fence was pretty loose near the ground there. I had taught Troubles how to fetch a ball by saying, "Ball." I held Troubles up in the air and pointed toward the box of softballs and said, "Ball." She saw the softballs and immediately started to squirm. I put her on the ground again, and Ran lifted up the fence for her. I said "Ball" again, and Troubles took off straight for the box of softballs. She grabbed the first one that she could get a hold of and proudly walked back to me and Ran. I picked her up, petted her again, and said "Ball" again. Same path again with the same results. We repeated this one last time until the final ball was retrieved. I petted Troubles, and she must have been as proud as a little dog could be.

We then signaled Mortie and Biscuit that we were done so they could leave their posts. It was really funny to watch Stubby climb down from his perch on the scoreboard and look all over the place for the missing softballs. He even held up the empty box and turned it upside down, expecting the softballs to magically reappear and drop to the ground.

The next night when I was working left field, I decided to meet Ran, Mortie, and Biscuit early before the game. We returned the balls to Steve, claiming that we had found them that day in the brush near right field. He was happy to get them back and treated all of us to a malt cup for being so honest to return them. Off and on, we continued to swipe the softballs from Stubby, who had previously swiped them. He never caught on, and we made a little money by selling the softballs back to team managers at a steeply discounted price, courtesy of the Stubby Appropriations Company. We were well on our way to saving enough money for all of us to be able to get in to see *The Tall Texan Wild West Show* at the State Fair.

Chapter 10
FISHING

One particular night, Ran, Mortie, Biscuit, and I were all sitting on the roof of the Cherokee Park Baptist Church, watching the cars drive up and down Bardstown Road. It was a good night for some serious guy-talk about anything that we thought might be important. It just so happened that one of our favorite topics came up. That was the subject of tormenting Stubby. It is not that we didn't like Stubby. He was … he was … well, he just was Stubby. There are just some people in the world that have an "I am asking for it" air about them, and Stubby was that kinda guy. His "I am asking for it" was about the size of a billboard that was hanging over his head wherever he went. The thing was that since he was such a jerk the way he treated anyone smaller than him, it just made you want to give it back to him double.

Biscuit said that we had just about run out of ways to mess with Stubby. After some discussion, Mortie and Ran kind of came up with the same thought. I thought to myself that we were not even halfway through with our summer vacation, and certainly there had to be more things that we could do to tease Stubby. He deserved our best efforts, even if he didn't realize that he did. Then it hit me! I had a flash of brilliance, or that is what I told the guys anyway. I reminded them how Stubby was so "in love" with that blonde-headed girl. They all remembered that, but they said that she was not interested in Stubby, and they were almost positive that she would never go in with us on a prank that we would play on Stubby. I said that she didn't have to participate. She would be an unaware participant.

"Not sure where you're going on this one, Scott," Ran said.

I told them that we were all going fishing on this one.

Ran, Mortie, and Biscuit all looked at me with puzzled looks on their faces.

"We are going Stubby fishing," I said.

"What do you mean?" came a question from the bunch of them.

I told them that we were going to attach the bait and then throw the hook and fishing line out to Stubby. I guaranteed them that Stubby would bite on this one and not let loose for anything.

"I bet that he would let loose for a candy bar," Biscuit said.

"Nope, not a chance," I said.

"What is the bait?" Ran asked.

"The bait is the blonde-headed girl."

"She won't help us," they all said together.

"Oh, she will, and she won't even know that she is doing it," I told them.

"How are you gonna do it Scott?" Biscuit asked.

"You all know where she lives, don't you?"

They all said they did.

"Well, when you start talking about the blonde-headed girl to Stubby, you can see him getting all excited."

"Yup, that's the truth," Biscuit said. "He looks like his eyes are about to pop out of his head, and he starts to slobber and drool."

"Yeah, I don't even like to be close to him when he gets like that," Mortie added. "I might catch a Stubby germ or something, and that would be worse than having to spend a week hanging around with the goofy girls and their Goofy Girls' Yippity Yappity Club."

"Here's what we're gonna do," I said. "Well, we casually let him overhear us talking about looking into the cute little blonde-headed girl's window at night."

"You can't see into her window from outside," Ran said.

"You and I know that, but Stubby doesn't know that," I said. "By the time I get finished talking to him, I'm sure that he'll be interested. Yup, that will get his attention real quick. I guarantee that he will automatically become our best friend and want to hear more."

"If he starts to slobber, I want a raincoat and an umbrella with me," Biscuit chipped in.

"I even think that we can make a little money off of him on this deal," I concluded.

"Okay, we're all interested," Ran said. "Tell us more."

"Just leave it up to me," I said.

The next day at the ballpark before the games, I started up a conversation with Ran, Mortie, and Biscuit as Stubby neared us. He had his usual grumpy, arrogant look on his face, and he would have avoided us completely if there had been another route to the concession stand.

"Yeah, that little blonde-headed girl is a real cutie," I said as Stubby drew near.

Stubby's ears immediately perked up.

"Do you think that she saw us looking in at her?" Ran asked.

"No, it was too dark outside, and her window was lit up. You know when your room is lit up and you look outside in the dark, you can't see nothing," I said.

"Yup, I guess so," replied Ran.

That was too much for Stubby. "What did you see? Whose room? What did you see?" he panted.

"What are you talking about, Stubby?" I asked.

"The beautiful little blonde-headed girl last night, in her window, in the dark, what did you see?" Stubby panted.

"Who me? I didn't see anything, Stubby," I replied.

"Yes, you did, you liar! Now tell me what you saw!" he demanded.

"Now Stubby, what makes you think I saw anything at all?" I asked.

"Ran asked if you thought that she had seen you," Stubby blurted out.

"Oh, that," I said. "Well, we might have accidentally seen the blonde-headed girl in her window last night while she was … well, she was … in there."

"What did you see? What did you see?" Stubby exclaimed.

"Well, that is a classified secret, and I cannot share that information with anyone other than Ran, Mortie, and Biscuit, who were with me. We are all sworn to secrecy."

"How did you see in her window?" Stubby asked.

"Well, that is also a secret, and it would take something special to get us to tell anyone that secret."

"Something special? Like money, candy, or something?" Stubby begged.

"Well, my mom said that I've been eating too much candy," I sighed.

"How about money? You can't be eating money," Stubby said.

"W-E-L-L," I said, looking at Ran, Mortie, and Biscuit.

Looking over at Ran, Mortie, and Biscuit, Stubby said, "It's money! How much? Come on, Scott. I got money! I gotta know about that little blonde-headed girl. She is so cute. I need to know what you did and what you saw."

Biscuit looked at me and said, "We could use some extra money in order to go see *The Tall Texan Wild West Show* at the State Fair."

Mortie chimed in, "Yeah, we could."

"I'll pay," Stubby exclaimed. "Just tell me how you were able to see inside her window."

"Well, let's see. I guess for five dollars we could tell you and maybe even help you."

"Five dollars!" Stubby choked out.

"Yup, five dollars each," I said. "The State Fair will be here soon, and the Tall Texan is bringing his Wild West Show to the State Fair this year. You know we'll each need a buck and a quarter just to get into the fairgrounds, and that's not counting the price of admission to *The Tall Texan Wild West Show*."

"Hey, that's also not counting paying someone to take us there and to get something to eat," Mortie said.

"Take it or leave it!" I said.

Stubby thought for about two seconds and then his lust or yearning got the best of him. "It's a deal," he said.

"Five bucks each?" I asked.

"Yes, five bucks each," he said. "Now tell me how you saw her in her bedroom, and you have to help me see inside her window."

"S-c-o-t-t, he's starting to slobber," Biscuit whispered.

"Money first, Stubby," I replied.

Ole Stubby fumed as he dug five one-dollar bills out of his front-right pocket candy fund and three five-dollar bills out of his left front pocket. "Here you go, along with some complimentary pocket lint," he said as he handed the money over to me. "Now tell me everything."

Stubby's face was as red as a tomato, and I thought that he was going to have a heart attack right in front of us. He would be foaming at the mouth next.

"I think that he's in heat, and if he comes near me, I'm gonna deck him real quick," Ran said.

"Have you ever been over to the blonde-headed girl's back yard?" I asked.

"Nope, only by her front yard. I ride my bike past it every day a couple of times a day. I thought that she might notice my English Racer, because it's a three-speed bicycle and has a light on the front handlebars."

"Well, you have to go into her back yard—that's where her window is located," I told him.

"Is it on the first floor?" Stubby asked.

"Nope, it's on the second floor."

"Then how do you see inside of her window if it is on the second floor?"

"Easy," I replied. "They have a big tree in their back yard, and all that you have to do is shimmy up the tree, climb out on this limb, and there you are, sitting right outside of her window. You can see EVERYTHING."

"Oh wow, oh wow, oh wow," Stubby panted out. "Everything— you can see everything. How did you get up the tree? With my manly build, I'm not suited for tree climbing, you know."

"You mean that you're too fat," Biscuit blurted out.

"Come on now, Biscuit," I said, "Stubby here is pursuing the girl of his dreams. Give him a break. Stubby, they have a little ladder that they keep by their garage. You can get it and lean it against the tree."

"Yeah, I can lean it against the tree and then climb out on that limb," Stubby agreed. "And she won't be able to see me?"

"Not a chance," I said.

"Not unless we shine a light on him," Mortie whispered to Biscuit with a grin.

Stubby was really getting wound up by now. *I should have asked him for more money up front,* I thought.

"When can we do it?" he asked.

"There are no games at the ballpark tomorrow night, so we can do it tomorrow night."

"What time? What time?" Stubby asked, almost panting again.

"About nine, because it gets dark around nine."

"Great, I'll meet you in the alley behind her house."

"Stubby, don't be late or chicken out, because there are no refunds."

"Not a chance," Stubby called back as he ran to the concession stand. He was actually singing to himself as he ran away.

"That is one weird guy," Ran said. "Scott, do you know which room is hers?"

"Nope, don't have a clue, but it has to be one of them, don't you think? It could be one on the front of the house, for all we know."

"If we're lucky, it'll be one of her brothers' rooms back there," Biscuit laughed.

"From the tree limb, even if you can see someone, you couldn't tell who it was or what they were doing," Ran said.

We all met up the next night in the alley behind the little blonde-headed girl's house. I asked Stubby if he was ready and he said that he was. I noticed that he was wearing a bright-yellow tee shirt. So much for blending in with the green leaves.

We moved the ladder from the garage over to the tree and raised it up to the branch that Stubby would have to climb up on. "That's pretty high up there," Stubby said.

"The greater the risk, the greater the reward," I said. Actually, I had heard the Tall Texan say that in "The Tall Texan versus Hombre Howard and the Hombre Gang" on television.

Stubby said, "Okay," and slowly climbed up the ladder. "I can't see anything," he called down.

I said, "You have to climb out on the limb a little bit more."

"I still can't see anything," Stubby called down in a whispered call.

"Climb out a little bit more," I said.

About that very same time, two lights came on, both on the second floor near Stubby. "Which room is hers?" Stubby whispered down.

"The one up there," I said.

"There are two rooms up here. Which one?" he asked.

"The one over there," I called up.

"Which 'there?' That 'there' or this 'there?'" he asked.

"The one with the lights on," I said.

"Both of them have lights," he said.

"Yeah, that one," I called.

I heard him say that was not such a good answer. Then we saw a shadow flash by just inside of the window. "I think that I saw her," he said. "But I'm not sure."

"Climb out farther on the limb," I said. I could tell that Stubby was completely overcome with whatever people get overcome with at times like this. "A little bit closer and you'll be able to see everything."

"Yes, closer, I must get closer," he said. "Hey, little blonde-headed girl, your dreamy boyfriend is coming to see you."

When I heard that, I thought that his dream was going to turn into a nightmare if he wasn't careful.

As he climbed farther out on the limb, we all heard a C-R-R-A-C-K, and suddenly the limb and Stubby came falling down. Ran, Mortie, Biscuit, and I immediately dashed out back into the dark alley where we could see what was going on without being seen.

Stubby had fallen directly on their back porch and landed on some buckets or something. It caused a loud commotion. The back porchlight switched on immediately, and the little blonde-headed girl's father came out carrying a baseball bat. Even from where we were hiding in the alley, we could tell that he was really mad.

"What is going on here?" he asked as he looked down at Stubby, who was trying to get untangled from the mess that he had fallen into. Then the little blonde-headed girl's father saw the branch and looked up and noticed the nearby windows, where the lights were still lit. "Why you little warped snot, I ought to …."

"Herbert, no!" screamed the man's wife.

"What were you doing up there you little piece of …?"

"Herbert!" his wife screamed again.

"Uh … uh … I was out chasing lightning bugs, and I saw a big one up there, and I was trying to get it so I could add it to my lightning bug collection for Boy Scouts!" Stubby exclaimed.

"Lightning bug collection my… "

"Herbert!" his wife interrupted again. "Come with me right now, young man. We are going to take a drive over to your house and have a talk with your parents right now."

The last that we saw of Stubby was him being grabbed by the ear and shoved into the little blonde-headed girl's dad's car as it headed over toward Stubby's house.

Well, this had turned out better than we had even thought that it would. Heck, every one of us was five dollars richer than when we started out that night, and we had been entertained by a great show to boot. We then all agreed that we would call it a night, and all of us headed home.

Chapter 11
POOL HOPPING

We were definitely in the middle of a very hot summer. Even Troubles thought that it was hot. When we would go over and look at the new gym they were building over at the college a couple of blocks away, Troubles would run down into the creek and flop around in the water. That seemed to cool her off, but it didn't make her smell very good. Funny thing though, as much as Troubles liked to flop around in the creek and get all wet, she really didn't like it when I had to put her in the big tub in the back yard and give her a bath.

One time, Marie thought it would be cute to give Troubles a bubble bath, so she slipped bubble bath into the water while I was going to turn off the hose. When I came back to bathe Troubles, I found her covered with bubbles, and Marie was laughing her head off. I quickly washed off all of the bubbles before any of Troubles' dog friends could see her, because I knew she would be embarrassed. In the process, I also "accidentally" managed to wash all of the bubbles off of Marie, about three times or so. She was pretty mad about that, but she got even madder when she discovered that she had managed to put her stocking feet into dog poop that had somehow managed to work its way into her shoes again after the bubble bath episode. I remember telling Marie that I couldn't imagine how she managed to always be getting her shoes full of dog poop.

One of those hot nights, Ran, Mortie, Biscuit, and I were sitting around and sweating together. "Sure is hot tonight," I said.

"It's hot enough to boil an egg in a swimming pool," Ran said.

"It's hot enough to sweat a sumo wrestler down to the size of a pygmy wrestler," Biscuit said.

I had never heard of a sumo wrestler, so I asked what one was.

"He's a big fat guy who wrestles other sumos," Biscuit said.

"Never heard of sumos," I said.

"They come from a country called Sumo-Matre-A," Biscuit went on. "Everyone over there is really big and fat, and they have to wrestle for their dinner. I saw them on TV once. They really dress kinda strange."

"Whacha mean?" I asked.

"Well, you know when you play sports and you gotta wear a jock strap for protection?" he asked.

"Yup, so what?" I said.

"Well, these sumo guys don't wear anything but their jock straps when they get out in their wrestling rings, and there are a lot of people watching them. They even have girls watching them," Biscuit explained.

"Why don't they put on some swimming trunks over their jock straps?" I asked.

"They don't make swimming trunks big enough for sumo guys. They are really, really big," he said. "Anyway, some skinny old guy throws some rice on the floor in front of two of them, who are really hungry. They bow down at each other to act polite, but they're really just sizing up the other sumo guy. Then the old skinny guy waves a stick at them. After that, they run into each other, and the one who doesn't get bumped over wins and gets to go out to eat at a Chinese restaurant, and the loser has to gather up the rice that the skinny old man threw on the floor and then take it home and cook in into rice cakes or Rice Krinkles."

"I didn't know that," I said. "Did you know that, Ran?"

"Nope, did you know that, Mortie?"

"Nope, I didn't know that either," he replied. "Does that mean that Rice Krinkles are made by a bunch of sumo guys?"

"I guess so," replied Biscuit.

"I don't think that I want to eat any more Rice Krinkles," I said.

Well, we talked for a while and sweated some more. Then we talked a little bit more and sweated a little bit more. Finally, Biscuit had an idea what we could do to cool off. "I know," he said. "Let's go pool hopping!"

"What are you talking about?" Ran asked.

"Pool hopping! You know, we find a swimming pool that's not being used and we go there and hop into the water for a swim."

"And just where are you gonna find a swimming pool that's not being used tonight, and do you think that the people who live there will just say, 'We are not using our swimming pool tonight so just hop in'?"

Biscuit thought about that for a second and then Mortie chipped in. "I've got it! We can go over to Jessica Kramer's house and use her swimming pool. It's on the other side of the college campus, so we could just cut across the campus and climb the fence around her back yard and hop into the pool. You see, she's on vacation with her cousins, so the pool will be empty."

"Are you sure about that?" I asked.

"Yup," Mortie replied. "I heard Jessica and her cousins talking about this vacation last week."

"Okay," I said. "Sounds good to me. Lead on, Mortie, since you know the way to get there."

It was not that long of a walk to get to Jessica's house. As we stood in the woods behind her house and looked over the fence, I said, "Looks like they are on vacation. Doesn't look like anyone is home."

"Swim time," Biscuit said as he climbed over the fence. He ran over to the chairs next to the house and dropped his shirt, shoes, and socks. Mortie and Ran did the same. I thought that I would be a little more cautious. I put my shirt, shoes, and socks next to the fence in case I had to make a quick getaway.

We were having a great time, and it really did cool us off. We had been there for about forty-five minutes. About that time, Mortie threw Biscuit's shoes into the deep end of the pool, and Biscuit had to keep diving down in the dark to find them. One of those times while Biscuit was down at the bottom of the pool, we saw headlights of a car that was pulling up the driveway and heading back toward the pool. It looked like Jessica's parents had not gone on vacation with her.

I had stayed near the back part of the pool all night, just in case. Now my caution paid off. "Someone is here!" I yelled. "We need to get out of here!"

Ran and Mortie heard me, but Biscuit was still under the water trying to find his shoes. I was first over the fence with my shirt, shoes, and socks in hand. Ran was right behind me. About the time that Mortie grabbed his stuff, Biscuit came up from the water. He was laughing, and then he grabbed Mortie by the ankle and tripped him back into the pool. Biscuit had no clue that the party was coming to a quick end. "I got my shoes, you guys," he loudly bragged. It became a loud commotion with Biscuit laughing and

Mortie trying to yell at him to tell him that someone had gotten out of their car in the driveway and was headed their way.

By the time Biscuit figured out what was going on, it was too late. Mr. and Mrs. Kramer stood in front of Biscuit and Mortie. I could hear them yelling at Mortie and Biscuit for a long time.

Ran and I had put on our shirts, socks, and shoes and were listening to the conversation from the other side of the fence. It was very dark where we were hiding and listening, and we knew that Mr. and Mrs. Kramer couldn't see us. We were relieved that Mortie and Biscuit didn't rat us out. They said that they had been chasing a stray cat into the back yard and had thought that the cat had fallen into the pool and was going to drown. Biscuit told Mr. and Mrs. Kramer that they just dove in and risked life and limb to save the poor little kitten from a "watery grave." The cat had transformed to a kitten by now.

That was a pretty dumb excuse, but when you're under a whole lot of pressure, I guess that's about the best you can do. I think that Biscuit said a couple of other things, but I couldn't quite hear what he said. I don't think that Mr. and Mrs. Kramer believed Mortie and Biscuit for one single minute, but when Mortie said that they went to school with Jessica and were real good friends and volunteered at the animal shelter, Mr. Kramer eased up, at Mrs. Kramer's urging. In exchange for one day of working around Mr. Kramer's yard under his direct supervision, he agreed to let them go home, and he would relent from telling their parents about the incident.

Mortie and Biscuit quickly agreed and even more quickly grabbed their shirts, socks, and shoes and took off. We met up with them a little later, and all of us had a good laugh. Biscuit said that he was never worried one bit about getting in trouble, because he had mentioned to Mr. Kramer that his dad beats him with a stick from the hickory tree in the back yard every day, just for good measure.

I said, "You don't even have a hickory tree in your back yard, and your dad never lays a hand on you."

"I know," Biscuit replied, "but I was playing up to Mrs. Kramer, and it worked."

We all decided to call it a night and went our separate ways until a new day that would present new adventures.

Chapter 12
FOURTH OF JULY

The Fourth of July finally arrived, and we were going to celebrate. The only problem was that none of us had any firecrackers or fireworks … period. Biscuit had already set off his supply of firecrackers that he had stashed for the Fourth.

We were sitting out on my front porch steps, wondering what we could do. Ran and Mortie's parents had threatened them that if any fireworks were found, they would be grounded for the rest of the summer. Ran's mom had heard about some kid getting his hand blown off by a firecracker, and she was all shook up about that. The problem was that she got Ran's father all fired up too, so they lowered the boom on Ran and Mortie about the fireworks, which meant that they had lowered the boom on the rest of us too. None of us wanted to get grounded for the rest of the summer and risk not getting to see *The Tall Texan Wild West Show* at the State Fair. Well, in all honesty, and I am always sorta honest, I had managed to get my hands on a few packs of firecrackers, but my stupid sister, Marie, had ratted me out. I would fix her for that, but I just had not quite figured out just exactly how to fix her yet. This was going to go way beyond the dog poop in the shoe punishment.

To make matters worse, when Mom confronted me about my firecrackers, Sam showed her where I had stashed them in the garage—the little troublemaking snitch. Sam was going to be getting some payback too. Ran and I had been talking about coming up with some type of plan for revenge against Marie and Sam. As we sat there talking, we snacked on a bag of homemade cinnamon candy that Ran's mom had cooked.

"This is pretty good cinnamon, but it's not very hot," I said.

"Yup, my mom doesn't like to make it very hot," Ran replied.

"Well, I like it when it's really hot, and you have to get a drink of water with every bite," I said.

"Yeah," Ran said, "like atomic hot!"

Then it came to me! "Ran, you've come up with the perfect revenge."

"Whacha mean, Scott?"

"Is anybody home at your house?" I asked.

"Nope, everyone's gone swimming except for me and Mortie."

"Let's head over to your house. I've got an idea," I said.

When we got to Ran's house, we found a bowl full of the cinnamon rock candy that Ran's mom had made. "Do you all have any Tabasco sauce over here?" I asked Ran.

"Yeah, but it's the really hot stuff," Ran said. "My dad really likes that stuff, but none of the rest of us do because it is atomic hot. Your eyeballs will almost fall out if you eat something that has that stuff poured on it or mixed in with it." Then Ran just grinned at me.

I fished a pan out of the cabinet and then put some of the cinnamon candy into the pan.

"Mom already cooked the candy," Ran said.

"I know, but hand me the bottle of Tabasco," I said.

"Oh, I'll get it," Ran replied with an even bigger grin.

As we melted down the cinnamon candy, I started mixing in Tabasco.

"That's gonna ruin the candy, or at least make it firehouse hot," Ran commented.

Fortunately, the mix still kept its cinnamon smell. We poured this almost-lethal mixture of cinnamon candy and tabasco into a plastic tray. We needed to let it cool off and get hard.

"Do you still have that old freezer in your basement?" I asked Ran.

"Yup, still there."

We hid the tray in the back of the freezer and decided that we could check back in an hour or so.

A little later, we returned to the freezer and discovered that the cinnamon-Tabasco mix had hardened like a rock. It even still looked like the original cinnamon candy, except that it was a little bit darker red.

I dumped the mix onto a cookie sheet. Ran then got a hammer and broke the hardened mix into little pieces. "Okay, here's what we do," I said. "We pour this mix into a bag. Then we put a little bag into the larger bag and put some of the good cinnamon candy in that bag. You and I will just casually reach into the bag, take cinnamon candy from the little bag, and eat it in front of Marie and Sam, but we won't share it with them. Then we'll make an excuse to put the bag down and "accidently" forget about it, but when we do that, we'll have to make sure that we take the little bag out without them seeing it. When we get caught up in whatever distracted us, Marie and Sam will steal the bag and eat the Tabasco cinnamon candy, or at least one piece of it."

"Oh, that's great," Ran said.

Well, we went straight over to my house and sat down to talk on the front porch. We made a show of eating candy so that Marie and Sam would see us. As predicted, they came out and decided to be nice to us in hopes of getting us to share some of our candy. "What are you all eating?" Marie asked.

"Some homemade cinnamon candy that Ran's mom made," I answered.

"We love homemade cinnamon candy," Marie said. "Can we have some?"

"After ratting me out to Mom about the firecrackers? No way and get lost!" I answered.

"Mom said that you were supposed to share," she said.

"Well, Mom can share when she is here, but right now she's not here, so bug off," I said.

About that time, Ran sat up straight. "Is that Troubles? I think that I hear Troubles, and it doesn't sound good."

We both jumped up and ran around the house toward the back yard, "accidentally" leaving the bag of Tabasco cinnamon sitting on the porch. We didn't really run to the back yard, though. Once we rounded the corner of the house, we ducked behind the bushes and peeked around at Marie and Sam. "I got the little bag out of the big bag," Ran said.

Marie looked around and then said, "Look what I have found! A bag full of cinnamon candy! Finders keepers. Quick, let's take it in the house before Scott comes back. He's got to get up pretty early in the morning to outsmart me."

"Yeah, early in the morning," Sam laughed.

"I knew that they would head for the kitchen," I said, and Ran and I quickly took up a spot where we could peek into the kitchen window without being seen. Sure enough, they had just dumped out the Tabasco cinnamon candy on the kitchen table. We tried not to laugh as both Marie and Sam each grabbed a large handful of the "candy" and started stuffing it into their mouths. As they bit into the stuff, they each began to make terrible faces. About two seconds later, they ran to the sink and spit it out. "My mouth is on fire! You're murdering me!" Sam yelled at Marie. "I'm too sweet and innocent to die!"

"My mouth is on fire too!" Marie exclaimed. About the same time, both of them yelled out, "WATER!"

Marie knocked Sam out of her way and then quickly filled up a glass of water and drank it straight down. Sam just stuck his mouth under the faucet and drank and drank and drank. "My mouth is still on fire," he yelled.

Marie said, "Quick! We need to get to the bathroom and drink some Pepto Bismol straight down. Quick! Let's go before we blow up or something."

"I don't want to explode!" Sam cried.

As they ran to the bathroom, I quickly and quietly dashed into the kitchen, swept the Tabasco cinnamon candy into a grocery bag, and then dashed back out the back door. "Got to destroy all of the evidence," I told Ran." I think it's about time that we head out."

"Yeah, I guess our job is done here, and we should move on to something else," he replied.

Later on that evening, Ran, Mortie, and I sat on the street curb all bummed out because everyone else in the world was setting off firecrackers on the Fourth of July, and we sat there not even allowed to light a dumb little sparkler. About that time we saw Biscuit walking down the street toward us. "Hi, you guys, whacha doing?" he called.

"Just sitting around doing nothing," I said.

"Hey, it's the Fourth of July, and we're supposed to be lighting firecrackers and stuff, just like everybody else," Biscuit replied.

"Can't do that," I called back. "Ran's mom and dad threatened Ran and Mortie that if they light off any firecrackers, they'll be grounded for the rest of the summer."

"Yeah, our mom is all fired up about some kid who blew his hand off lighting firecrackers," Mortie said.

"They say that every Fourth of July," Biscuit said. "Well, I have a bag full of fireworks that my brother gave me this afternoon, and I was hoping that we could go out and light them off tonight."

"Hmm," I murmured. "Well, technically, if the fireworks are yours and only you light them, well then, Ran and Mortie couldn't possibly get in any trouble for lighting them off," I said.

"Yeah!" Ran and Mortie said together.

"I mean, they would just be innocent bystanders," I continued.

"Yup, one thing that you can always say about me and Mortie is that we're the innocent types," Ran laughed.

"Great, what do you have there?" I asked Biscuit.

"Well, this is one that I've really been wanting to try out, because I've never had one like this before," Biscuit replied. "It's called a chaser, and you put it on the street or on some flat parking lot, aim it at someone, light it, and it will chase the person that you aimed it at. It's best to aim it at someone you're not particularly fond of, like Stubby. Watch and I'll show you."

We all watched as Biscuit carefully set the chaser in the middle of the street. He told Mortie to run down the street a couple of houses and then wait.

"I thought that you said that you had to aim it at someone that you don't like," Mortie said.

"Well, Stubby doesn't like you, does he?" I asked.

"No, I guess not," Mortie replied.

"So that will work, because the chaser is being aimed at someone who is not liked," I explained.

"Oh, yeah, that makes sense," Mortie agreed.

When Mortie had run down the street as instructed, Biscuit aimed the chaser straight at him and lit it. A bunch of sparks flew out of the back and it started to move straight toward Mortie. However, after moving about five or six feet, it suddenly turned around and started to go back straight for Biscuit! Biscuit's eyes got as big as baseballs when he saw the chaser coming after him. He yelled out and then threw his bag of fireworks into the air and started to run down the street in the opposite direction, screaming with each step. I think I heard Biscuit yell out a couple of words that he'd have to tell Father Taurman about. The faster he ran, the faster the chaser moved, and it seemed to keep following him no matter which direction he ran. We were laughing so hard, we could hardly breathe, and our bellies began to ache.

Finally, as the chaser got almost about a foot away from Biscuit, it exploded with a BOOM! Biscuit about jumped out of his shoes, and we fell on the ground, laughing our heads off.

Biscuit returned down the street to where we were standing. We were still laughing. "I wasn't scared," was the first thing he said.

"Oh no, you weren't scared," we all said, laughing. "We could tell by the way that you held your ground when it started to chase you."

"It was an act, and I knew that it was going to do that. I was just trying to provide some entertainment for you all."

"Yeah, sure it was, and sure you did," I said. "Come on, let's pick up all of these fireworks that fell out of the bag when you didn't panic and you weren't a bit scared." I told Mortie and Ran that it was okay to pick up the fireworks out of the street. We couldn't leave them lying in the street for some little kids to pick up. Heck, Ran's parents would be proud of Ran and Mortie for being such good SumoMarians, or whatever the "do good" guys were called. We all gathered up the fireworks and returned them to Biscuit's bag.

We walked down the street until we ended up out in front of Players Field. Timmy and the other little kids were hanging out there too. They didn't seem to be in a good mood. "Hey, what's going on, guys?" I asked.

"That dad-gum Stubby," Timmy replied.

"Whacha mean?" I asked. "What did he do this time?"

"Well, we had pooled our ball-shagging money together to buy some candy. I don't know how Stubby knew about it, but he did."

"He's got candy radar," Ran said.

"Well, anyway, when he saw us with our bag of candy, he said that he had to inspect it for safety reasons," Timmy said.

"You all didn't have to let him inspect anything," I said.

"Stubby is a lot bigger than us, so we didn't have much choice," Timmy sighed.

"What happened?" I asked.

"Stubby said that by us bringing in our own candy to the neighborhood, we were hurting the concession stand and the gas stations that have candy machines. He said that there was a 'Fair Business Tax,' and he was the local tax guy for our neighborhood. He even had a badge to prove it, but I couldn't really tell because he flashed it at us so quick and then put it back in his pocket. He said that he had to take one-half of our candy and give it to the ballpark and the gas stations so that they wouldn't go out of business. He even said that it pains him to have to be the one who enforces this tax."

"The only thing that pains him is his stomach when he's eaten too much candy," Biscuit said.

"Well, we'll see if we can get even for you guys," I said.

"Hey, I saw Stubby camping out in the tent in his back yard as I was coming over here," Biscuit said.

"Camping out? Why is he camping out?" I asked.

"Some of the younger little kids had been over there and told me that he has his big sister's diary in his tent, and he ran them off so he could look at the diary all by himself."

"Yeah, we heard the same thing," Timmy said.

"Where did he get the diary anyway?" I asked.

"The little kids didn't say, but Stubby didn't want them hanging around, so he ran them off," Biscuit said. "I think that he must know where she hides it in her bedroom, and his parents don't let them lock their bedroom doors. I bet that she's spending the night out, and Stubby just snuck into her room and grabbed it."

"Why does he want to look at her diary anyway?" Ran asked. "Seems like it would be pretty boring reading."

"Nope," I said. "I heard him say that he looks through it for stuff that he can threaten to rat her out on to their parents. She either has to pay him off in candy or money. If she doesn't pay, he rats her out. I think that she refused to pay him one time and he ratted her out, so now she always pays up. He doesn't want any company tonight, anyway that you look at it ... but maybe we could stop in for a visit to see our good ole buddy Stubby tonight."

"Hey, what do you have in mind, Scott?" Ran asked. "You know that Stubby isn't exactly best friends with any of us, and there's no way that he's gonna invite us over for a campfire get-together."

"I wasn't thinking of a social type of visit. Maybe a 'passing through the neighborhood and thought that we would look in on him' type of visit," I grinned. "I mean, it is the neighborly thing to do, checking to make sure that ole Stubby is okay and all of that. Heck, he doesn't even hafta know that we stopped by to check on him." I smiled. "Hey, Timmy, you all might want to head over to the Ramser's back yard where you can watch what happens but you won't be seen. The Ramsers are away on vacation until next week. I can't get your candy back, but this might make you feel a little bit better. In the meantime, we'll walk on down to Stubby's house and peek in on him. I bet that his parents don't know that he's looking at his sister's diary out there. Maybe we should try to draw their attention to his new reading interests and see what they think. You know that Sister Mary Wackenhammer always tells all of the boys that they will go blind and have diarrhea every day for the rest of their lives if they look at stuff that they're not supposed to be looking at."

"She said that you would have diarrhea for looking at your sister's diary?" Biscuit asked.

"Oh yeah, that's a big one," I said. "I think that it's a special diarrhea disease that you have to go to the doctor and get penicillin and tetanus shots for, or something like that. Or at least that's what I heard."

"Well, what are you thinking about doing, Scott?" Biscuit asked.

"Biscuit, my man, I think that you can play a major part in tonight's visit to see good ole Stubby."

We quietly walked on down the street to Stubby's house. Then we quietly snuck around behind the garage next door to his back yard so we could see what he was doing. We could see the pup tent real clearly because Stubby had his dad's camping lantern, which lit up the inside of the tent. It was one of those fancy ones that had a gigantic battery. You could even see Stubby's outline through the tent because the lantern was so bright.

"He's got the flaps on the tent closed," Ran said. "Must be darn hot inside there with the flaps closed."

We could also hear the music from Stubby's transistor radio. It was not playing real loud or anything, but it did give me an idea. "Hey, you guys," I said, "I think I've got an idea, and Stubby's transistor radio can help us out. Biscuit, I'll need one of your firecracker packs. Ran, Stubby always keeps a couple of cans of motor oil under his back porch. He keeps them for his lawn mower. Run over there and sneak a can out and bring it over here. Mortie, over in the corner of the back yard is a bag of fertilizer that Stubby's father uses for his garden. It really stinks. Grab it and bring it over here."

When Mortie returned with the fertilizer, we very quietly spread all of it out in front of Stubby's pup tent so that when he got out of the pup tent to head for the house, he would have to step in it for several steps.

"This stuff really stinks," Ran whispered.

"Smells like a cow barn. Where do you think they get this stuff from?" I said.

"Probably from cows," Ran said. "How do they get the cows to poop in the bags?"

"Don't know and I don't care," I said.

"I wouldn't want to be the guy holding the bag under the cow's tail when he poops," Biscuit said.

Mortie now slowly spread out the motor oil on top of the fertilizer and tried to make it as slippery as possible. I then got one of Stubby's yard rakes off of his back porch and went back to the tent. I used the rake to spread the fertilizer and motor oil around the front of Stubby's tent, so he couldn't possibly get out of the tent without slipping on the stuff. I then returned the rake to the back porch. As we sneaked back past Stubby's pup tent and returned to our vantage point on the other side of his backyard fence, I could hear Stubby say, "Something stinks out here tonight."

Once we got to our lookout position, I told Biscuit that I needed him to pull out two fuses from a couple of firecrackers and tie them end to end. Then I told him to tie the long fuses to one of the firecrackers that was in the pack of firecrackers that we were going to use. I wanted the whole pack to go off. Lastly, I told him to sneak up to the very back of the pup tent and light the fuse and then run back to where we were hiding. The longer fuse would give him the time to make it back to our hiding place before the firecrackers went off.

Things worked just like I planned. Biscuit lit two packs of firecrackers that he had placed right next to the back of Stubby's pup tent and then sprinted back to our hiding place. The next thing that we all heard was BANG-BANG-BANG-BANG-BANG-BANG-BANG! It was really loud because the regular Fourth of July noise that you hear at night had died down.

We could see Stubby's outline through the pup tent. He let out a loud Y-E-I-I-I-I-I-I as he scrambled to get out. At the very same time, the kitchen lights in the back of his house came on. When Stubby went to run out of the pup tent, he slipped on the oiled-up fertilizer and fell flat on his face. When he tried to get up again and take off, he slipped again and fell back down on his face.

About that time, Stubby's father was running out the back-door yelling, "Stubby, what's going on back there?" As he got close to Stubby, he slowed down and said, "What is that nasty smell?" Then he saw Stubby, who was by then on all fours and trying to crawl away. Stubby's dad stepped forward and reached down to help Stubby up, but as he did so, he slipped on the oiled-up fertilizer, and with the added weight of Stubby trying to pull himself up, both of them fell down into the mess. "What is going on here?" he yelled at Stubby. Stubby's dad was so annoyed by the music coming from the tent that he reached toward the pup tent to shut off the transistor radio.

"I'll get it," Stubby said, but he slipped and fell on his face again.

When his dad looked into the pup tent to get the radio, he saw the diary. "What in the world?" he shouted.

"This is where it gets good," I told Ran.

"Stubby, what are you doing with your sister's diary?" we heard his dad demand.

"Um … um … I was reading some very interesting stuff so that I could learn how to be a better little brother, Father," we heard Stubby stammer.

"Better little brother my hat!" yelled his father. "I'll bet that you learned a lot snooping on your big sister! Give me that diary, turn off that lantern and radio, and then you and I are going inside to have a talk with your mother, young man."

We could barely contain our laughter as we watched Stubby's father pulling him toward the house by his ear.

"Before we can go in to talk to her, I guess that I'll have to hose you down with the garden hose," his father complained.

"Mission accomplished," I said. "Look, Ran and Mortie, we all got to enjoy a really neat fireworks display, and you never had to touch a single firecracker all night, except for picking up the loose firecrackers out of the street so some little kids wouldn't find them and blow their hands off. I think we can all agree that we behaved very well tonight."

About that time, Timmy and the other little kids ran over from the Ramser's yard, where they had been hiding. "That was great, Scott," Timmy said, laughing. "It was worth giving up some of our candy to see Stubby get in big trouble."

"Glad that you all enjoyed the show," I said. "However, it's getting late and we have another day tomorrow, so I think that we should all head back home now." We all agreed that it had been a great night and we were getting tired, so we all headed home and called it a night. We were one day closer to seeing the Tall Texan in person!

Chapter 13
MR. PEPPERCORN

When we were home, we would let Troubles run loose because she always stayed around the house. If I didn't see her, I would call her, and she would come running to me. One day, I saw Troubles heading between the houses directly across the street from my house. I kinda wondered where in the world she was going, so I decided to follow her. She continued straight ahead and ended up on the back porch of a house one street over. As I was walking over there, I saw a little old lady come out, speak to Troubles, pet her on the head, and give her a treat or something.

I went into the lady's yard and said hello. The little old lady was very nice and smiled at me. I told her that Troubles was my dog, and that my name was Scott. She told me that she was pleased to meet me, and her name was Miss Reeses. She said that Troubles had been coming over for a couple of weeks, and she and her sister, who lived with her, had become fond of Troubles. They didn't know Troubles' name, so they called her Pebbles. Troubles must have been okay with the name, because she seemed to like Miss Reeses.

Miss Reeses asked me to wait a second as she went back into her house. She returned with a plate of chocolate chip cookies and offered some to me. They were the best chocolate chip cookies I had ever tasted. Well, I knew from that moment on I was going to like Miss Reeses too.

Miss Reeses and her sister were retired schoolteachers. Well, they didn't act like any schoolteacher that I had ever met. They were really nice. I had never in my entire life met a nice teacher. I always thought that they taught teachers how to be extra mean when they went through teachers' school. That was not normal for me to like any schoolteachers, but I liked Miss Reeses and her sister.

We talked for a while and then the grocery delivery guy came by. Miss Reeses said that he was bringing some groceries and some fresh tomatoes. She said that she loved fresh tomatoes. I guessed that she had that small grocery store down at the other end of the street deliver groceries because she was pretty old, and I didn't see a car in her drive, so I guessed that she didn't drive. My grandmother said that grocery store was way too expensive. Well, this was the start of a friendship between me, Miss Reeses, and Troubles, and of course that made Ran, Mortie, and Biscuit her new friends too—she just didn't know it yet.

Ran lived two streets over from my house. We would cut through the alleys and yards to get to each other's house. There was one grouchy old man the next street over, and his house was located right in our cut-through path. His name was Mr. Peppercorn, and he really was a big grouch! He was very particular about his house and his yard. We really never bothered anything until he started griping at us about cutting through his yard. It's not that we made a habit of cutting through his yard ... well, maybe his yard just happened to be the most convenient cut-through that we liked to use. That wasn't our fault.

Mr. Peppercorn always kept everything in its place. He had a real nice flower garden and a real nice vegetable garden, and he used to manicure his yard and bushes. One day when he was watering one of his gardens in the back yard, he "accidentally" watered me and Ran as we were walking down the alley. He thought that "accident" was very funny, especially since the accident lasted about ten seconds as we tried to get out of the spray from his hose. It seemed like the spray from the hose was accidentally following us down the alley as we tried to get away. Mr. Peppercorn laughed and laughed and then yelled at us: "Serves you boys right, and stay out of my yard!"

He didn't know it, but he had just declared war. I was just an innocent bystander that was now being drawn into a war that I had not sought out but was happy to take part in

As I was cutting through Mr. Peppercorn's yard a couple of days later, I noticed that he had vegetables growing in his garden. An idea came to mind. Perhaps I could repay Mrs. Reeses's kindness toward Troubles with some fresh tomatoes from Mr. Peppercorn's garden.

Later that evening, Ran and I decided to visit Mr. Peppercorn's "vegetable market." Mortie and Biscuit were with us as usual. We had to come up with a way to distract Mr. Peppercorn, because he liked to sit on his back porch and look at his garden. We talked about it and then came up with a plan. Mortie would run up and ring Mr. Peppercorn's front doorbell. Biscuit was stationed next door where he could see when Mr. Peppercorn answered his front door and also warn us when he was on his way back. When Mr. Peppercorn went to answer the front door, Ran and I ran across the back yard straight for the vegetable garden. We really didn't have a lot of time to be choosy, so we grabbed the first couple of tomatoes that we saw. All of a sudden, Biscuit whistled to us that Mr. Peppercorn was on his way back. We didn't have time to run back out into the alley, so we dove behind a couple of bushes in the yard just as Mr. Peppercorn returned to his chair on the back porch. We signaled Biscuit to have Mortie ring Mr. Peppercorn's doorbell again. Once again, Mr. Peppercorn got up and went to answer the doorbell. This time we were quick to pick several really plump tomatoes and quickly made our getaway to the safety of the alley.

We signaled Biscuit that we were clear and to come on back. He then signaled Mortie, who rang Mr. Peppercorn's doorbell one last time. We watched as Mr. Peppercorn got up, grumbling the whole time, and headed inside toward the front of the house. Mortie and Biscuit used this time to run between the houses and meet us in the alley. The next day, we presented Miss Reeses with a bag of fresh tomatoes. She was so happy to get them. When she asked me where we had gotten them, I told her that they came from a nearby garden that we liked to work in from time to time. She smiled and then offered us a plate of chocolate chip cookies and thanked us.

Mr. Peppercorn was one of those kinds of grumpy old men that you just had to aggravate. We used to get together to come up with things to do to make him mad. He cut his grass at least twice a week, whether it needed it or not. One evening when he had left his back porch for the night, we slipped into his garage, emptied all of the gas from his lawn mower, and put it back into his gas can. We watched the next day as he tried to start his lawn mower and it refused to start. When he finally looked into the gas tank, he saw that it was empty. He scratched his head, grumbled something, and then got his gas can and filled up the lawn mower.

That night, we again emptied the gas tank out of his lawn mower. True to form, a couple of days later, we happened to be within earshot as we heard him trying to start his lawn mower again, without any success. We ran down the alley and peeked into his back yard. He finally looked into the gas tank and saw that it was empty again. He scratched his head, grumbled something again, and then went back and got his gas can to fill up the lawn mower gas tank.

We repeated this trick two more times, all with the same result. I think that Mr. Peppercorn was suspicious, because he began to glance around to see if anyone was watching, so we decided stop this prank. That didn't mean that we were finished with Mr. Peppercorn, though.

One day we were watching him water his gardens. We had been trying to figure out what we could pull on him next. Biscuit was playing with a couple of little ball bearings in his hand while we were talking. Then I had an idea. The ball bearings were just small enough to fit into Mr. Peppercorn's garden hose.

That night we snuck into Mr. Peppercorn's back yard after he had gone inside for the night. He always kept his garden hose neatly wound up on its rack next to the spicket. I unscrewed the hose from the spicket and then inserted about four little ball bearings. They were just small enough to fit into the hose, but not too fat where they would get stuck until they reached the point where the hose connected with the hose nozzle. I screwed the hose back onto the spicket.

Now, every morning at ten o'clock sharp, Mr. Peppercorn would water his gardens. We all knew his routine, so we gathered out in the alley behind his house to watch what would happen. Since he liked to spray us with the hose, we made sure that we were hidden from his view. Mr. Peppercorn was humming a little song to himself as he opened the spicket for the hose. As he walked the hose out, the water pressure began to force the ball bearings through the hose to the point where the hose connected with the smaller hose. The water stopped at the nozzle that Mr. Peppercorn was holding. He fooled around with the nozzle but didn't seem to notice the bulge that was beginning to grow in the hose because the ball bearings had stopped it up. We could hear him grumbling as he began to turn to look back at the spicket. He then spotted the hose with the very, very big bulge. Before he could do anything … B-A-N-G! The hose exploded and water went everywhere.

It went off better than we had hoped. It was all we could do to keep from being seen or heard by Mr. Peppercorn as we laughed our heads off. Every day seemed to bring a new opportunity to torment Mr. Peppercorn. One day we placed a sign out in front of his house. He couldn't see it from inside his house because we placed the sign in front of the big bushes next to his front porch. The sign said:

FREE HOMEMADE COOKIES FOR
NEIGHBORHOOD CHILDREN
RING DOORBELL

That worked real good, because he was inundated with about every kid in the neighborhood asking for free homemade cookies.

Mr. Peppercorn liked to go out for coffee every morning. He would drive his prized 1935 Chevy pickup truck. It was a beauty. As a matter of fact, he called it his Blue Beauty, and he also kept it in perfect shape. One day when he drove home after his coffee at the coffee shop, he left Blue Beauty parked on the street. Now, we would never do anything to damage such a nice truck, but we could still have fun with it. We placed a FOR SALE sign on the front and back windows. We put a price of $500 on each sign. It didn't take long for people passing by and seeing Blue Beauty and the FOR SALE signs to stop and start ringing Mr. Peppercorn's doorbell. That was fun!

I think that the last thing we did was to place a sign on his front yard again that said: FREE ROSES—PICK YOUR OWN ROSE. Mr. Peppercorn had a bunch of rosebushes in his front and side yards, and he was always working on them. He was very particular about his prize roses. When he came home from another morning visit to the coffee shop, he found his rose bushes surrounded by people who were clipping his roses. He almost had a heart attack as his prize roses were being snipped and carried away. It was another stunning success for us!

Chapter 14
MOOSE GOES TO THE MOVIES

Today was the day that we were going to the movies. The Uptown Theater was playing *The Tall Texan and The Despicable Desert Desperados*. This was going to be The Tall Texan's greatest movie yet. They also had a cartoon carnival, or at least that is what they called a bunch of back-to-back cartoons, plus some goofy movie called *The Pony Princess* that was made mostly for goofy girls. Why in the world do they even make movies like that? It probably didn't have a single bad guy in it. Yuck!

It was a matinee, so I knew that I would be staying there for the whole afternoon. Of course, my buddies Ran, Mortie, and Biscuit and Biscuit's little cousin, Moose, were coming too. Moose got to hang around with us from time to time when he was spending the week over at Biscuit's house. We didn't really know just how Moose got his name. He was our age, but he was a real little guy. He had a good sense of humor and fit just right with all of us. Lew and Stacey, Moose's parents, thought that Biscuit was a good influence on Moose. If they really knew Biscuit better, they may have thought otherwise. Nope, they *would* have thought better!

Anyway, Mom had given twenty-five cents each to me, Marie, and Sam for admission. She also gave each of us five cents for the concession stand. All of the good candy and the popcorn costs ten cents and up, but we did the best that we could with the cheap candy that only cost a nickel. Since it was going to be a long day at the movies, Ran, Mortie, Biscuit, Moose, and I knew that we had to pack something to eat and manage to sneak it into the theater. The doorman would make you get rid of any candy or stuff outside if he saw you trying to sneak anything in. He was a mean hombre. That's cowboy talk for "bad guy."

I made a balogna sandwich and stuck it in my pocket. I had several catsup packages stuffed in my pocket too. The other guys had packed their snacks into their pockets too, except for Moose. Biscuit had hidden Moose's sandwich under his hat, and the plan was for Moose to distract the doorman, who took the tickets and watched for kids sneaking in candy and stuff. He would act like a little kid asking the doorman where to restroom was while we quickly walked by as we handed him our tickets. It worked like a charm. Moose should grow up to be an actor, he did so good.

Once we got into the theater, we got our favorite seats, which were located near the back of the theater. There was no use in drawing attention to ourselves. It was not time to start eating yet, so we just sat there talking. It was not long before I saw Marie and her friend Charlotte prancing in. Charlotte was just as goofy as Marie, and I really didn't like her much anyway. Any girl who wanted to be friends with Marie just had to be plain goofy or something.

Marie also had Sam in tow. Mom had told her that she needed to look after her little brother and let him sit with her. I bet Mom also told her that if Sam had to use the bathroom, she would have to take him into the women's restroom. Sam was a goofy little brat too. How in the world could I have ended up with such goofy relatives? Ran said it was because my mom must have eaten sauerkraut and spaghetti when she was pregnant. It was a proven fact that when you mix German and Italian food together, it makes you goofy. I didn't know that, but it did make good sense, and Marie and Sam were really goofy.

Sam always sided with Marie against me. Both of them were always trying to get me in trouble. Mom always felt that she had to believe Marie on everything because she was the "only girl." Yuck, and thank goodness that she was the only girl, because I don't know if I could have stomached having two sisters. Then there was Sam. He was the youngest and the "baby" of the family. Give me a break! He was a sawed-off, half-pint, walking pile of trouble that only knew a few phrases like "I'm going to tell Mom," or "Scott did it," or "Scott did this or did that," or "Scott hit me," or "Mom always believes me because I'm her favorite." The little twerp was pretty right on that last one, although I think it was a toss-up between the baby and the only girl. Needless to say, I was never in the running for most believable, even though I thought that I always sounded real believable, or at least my stories did, and I was actually innocent sometimes.

I often wished that I could figure out a way to sell Sam and Marie to pirates, but I knew that would have made Mom sad. I thought that she might be able to get over it, but I decided not to chance it. By the time that the cartoons had finished playing and the previews were done previewing, I was getting pretty bored. The cartoons were dumb reruns of reruns that I didn't even like before they became reruns. Unfortunately, *The Pony Princess* was the first movie to play. Not only did they not have any bad guys in this movie, but it was supposed to take place in some country called Pony Land. They had fairies and singing flowers and all kinds of stupid stuff in Pony Land. They should have called it Pukey Land. The princess was some goofy-looking girl who wore a long ponytail, as you might have guessed. Well, she was kind of cute, but she acted like a regular goofy girl riding her goofy pony around the goofy Pony Land. The way that she acted made her un-good-looking. I think that's a word. I just sat there in misery, wondering what I could do to pass the time until the real movie, *The Tall Texan and the Despicable Desert Desperados* came on.

I could see Marie, Charlotte, and Sam sitting up near the front of the theater with their eyes glued to the screen. My brain was hurting from having to listen to all of the goofy pony songs. Everyone knows that ponies do not sing! If any bad guys would show up in this movie, I would cheer for them to rustle off the goofy ponies and sell them to be turned into dog food. Marie, Charlotte, and Sam looked like they were actually being entertained by this dumb, goofy movie.

An idea finally hit me. I got Ran's attention and then he got the other guys' attention. We had to sneak past the doorman and go up the stairs to the balcony. I don't know why he was called the doorman, because he worked all over the place and never just stayed in one place taking tickets. Anyway, they always kept the balcony closed on Saturday matinees. Guess they didn't want to worry about some dumb kids climbing up into the balcony and falling over the railing.

Once we got up there, we were safe. Since the balcony was roped off, and everyone knew not to go up there, no one ever checked the balcony. Heck, we had our own private viewing seats away from everyone else. The only thing that we had to watch out for was to make sure that the guy in the projection room couldn't see us from the window that looked out into the theater from inside his little room. Once the movie started, I don't think that he ever looked out until the end of the movie, when it was time to start the next movie, or preview, or the dumb concession-stand commercial.

We all huddled together. I had noticed that Marie and Charlotte and Sam were all sitting together next to the aisle. It was Sam, Marie, and then Charlotte. I didn't really care about bothering Sam today, but Marie had tried to rat me out to Mom on something, and I wanted to pay her back. I pulled out the three catsup packages from my pocket. Since neither Sam, Marie, or Charlotte knew Moose, we decided that he would be the one to pull off our prank. If you added in the fact that Moose was such a little guy and he would probably not be noticed by anyone, it was perfect. Moose was to slip downstairs and into the row behind Marie and Charlotte. Once he got there, he was to open the catsup packages and spread the catsup out on their arm rests. This was going to be pretty easy, because the dumb movie had all of the dumb girls laughing and waving at the ponies on the screen all of the time.

Moose slipped down there and got in position right behind Marie and Charlotte. A couple of seconds later, something dumb happened to the dumb Pony Princess and all of the dumb kids started laughing and waving their hands in the air. Moose was really good. As I watched from the balcony, I was impressed at just how fast he spread the catsup on the arm rests without being noticed by anyone and then quietly slipped out of his row of seats and headed back up the aisle for the balcony. He had not even made it up the aisle when Marie put her arm down into the catsup. I couldn't hear what she was saying from so far away, but from the look on her face, she was not happy. Then Charlotte put her arm in the catsup on her arm rest. Same result for her. We were all quietly laughing at their problem. Sam just sat there unaware and seemed to be hypnotized by the dumb movie on the screen.

When Moose made it back to the balcony, we all congratulated him on a job well done. We told him that we were going to have him appointed as a member of the Rotten Tomato Society. I had just made up that name, but we all agreed that it sounded good. Marie and Charlotte got up to go to the women's restroom to wash off the catsup. Marie dragged Sam with her, so I guess that I was right in saying that she would take him into the women's restroom. She couldn't blame me on this one, because I was nowhere to be found, and she never dreamed to check the balcony.

It was getting near the end of the dumb Pony Princess movie and we were all getting super bored. We had already eaten our sandwiches and stuff. Then I had another idea. I sent Moose down to the concession stand to get some straws and paper napkins. The concession stand was always busy, and no one would notice a little kid reaching up and grabbing a bunch of straws. Moose returned with a handful of straws.

I looked at the guys and simply said, "Spitball time." Everyone grinned. I said that we needed to sit low in our seats so we couldn't be seen behind the rail of the balcony if someone looked up. We all picked out an area of the theater for our quiet attack. By that time, Marie, Charlotte, and Sam had returned to their seats. Of course, my first target was Marie. First shot was dead on and hit her in the neck. She immediately looked at Sam, who just happened to be laughing at something on the screen. That made him guilty in her eyes, so she whacked him on the back of his head. I don't know what was said, but Sam looked unhappy and Marie looked mad but satisfied that she had taken her revenge.

I waited a minute and then repeated my shot with the same effect. Marie got mad at Sam and whacked him again, much to his displeasure.

I then took aim at dumb Charlotte. This time I missed her but got the guy sitting in front of her. He turned around and said something to her, but again I couldn't hear what they were saying. She just kind of held up her arms as she talked. When I shot at her again, I hit her square in the back of the head. She immediately turned around to yell at someone, but no one was sitting there. She was not quite sure what to do. I shot again and hit the guy in front of Charlotte again, and again he turned around to fuss at Charlotte. This time Charlotte got up and had Marie and Sam move to the empty seats right behind them that Moose had used. This was getting to be fun.

I took turns shooting at Marie, Charlotte, and the people behind them. I even hit Sam a couple of times, but he was too dumb to figure out what was going on, and I think that he was too afraid to accuse Marie because she might whack him again. In the meantime, the other guys were having just as much fun as me. Since we all picked separate areas of the theater to target, no one ever became the wiser about our prank. We kept this up until we ran out of spitball ammunition. Fortunately, it was time for *The Tall Texan and the Despicable Desert Desperados* movie. We all settled back in our seats for a real good movie.

I bet that the Tall Texan will win an Oscar this year for his movie. I never could figure out what an Oscar was, because I never saw a horse or anything called Oscar, but I was pretty sure that an Oscar would have to be something like that. It would probably be a new six-shooter or something. This movie was going to be even better than Tall Texan movies usually were, because each one of us knew that at the end of the summer we would get to see the Tall Texan in person, along with Wang Chow KaPow, Chief Thunder Belly, and FireStorm, the Tall Texan's big, powerful horse. Heck, we even looked forward to seeing Princess Running Summer Snowflake. That was okay, because everyone knows that an Indian princess can't be a goofy girl, so it was okay to like her. If the Tall Texan liked her, then we had permission to like her, and she was kinda cute, in an Indian princess kinda way. I thought for sure that this summer would end up being the very best summer in my life, ever!

And finally we heard the Tall Texan theme song: "Tall Texan, No Way to Disguise ... Tall Texan, Terror to Bad Guys!" There, right in front of us on the giant screen, stood the Tall Texan and Wang Chow KaPow. None of us moved or said a single word as we watched the movie and story unfold right before our eyes. It was almost like a spiritual experience seeing our hero up close. Well, it was kinda close and definitely a whole lot better than watching it on our little black and white TV. By the time that the Tall Texan had saved Princess Running Summer Snowflake from the Despicable Desert Desperados, we were super excited.

"Won't be that much longer before we finally get to see the Tall Texan in person," Ran said.

That was going to be the highlight of our summer vacation, all of us agreed. We could hardly wait for the State Fair to start. Well, we kinda needed to wait, because we still had not earned enough money to get to the fair, pay admission to the fair, and then pay for the show tickets. But we had definitely gotten a pretty good start.

Chapter 15
SCOTT'S DAIRY COMPANY

I hate getting up extra early on any morning. It is really a struggle for me to do so. I am one of those people who definitely does not shine when they rise. It's more like an adventure in sleepwalking until I can make it to the bathroom and splash some water on my face. After that, the world starts to slowly come into focus.

Now, Ran and I are the very best of friends. Anyone who knows us can easily tell that, because I have made the supreme sacrifice to get up before the crack of dawn and help my very good friend deliver his newspaper route that he took over from his big brother. Heck, dawn or nothing else has cracked or even made a peep that early when we make our way to the newspaper drop-off corner. We always glance at the headlines as we load up our newspapers into our newspaper bags. We need to check and see if there is any important news that we need to know about right away, like school being cancelled, or The Tall Texan visiting town sooner than the State Fair.

I have never been able to figure out just how the newspaper company can get all of this information together, print it, and get the newspapers out to the drop-off corner since the last run the night before, but they do. I heard that they have some type of alien intelligence that helps them, but I really don't believe in all of that. I mean, we, meaning the humans on earth, just recently shot up a couple of rocket ships into space with human spacemen. Heck, all they did was go up there, look around, and then turn around and come back. Now if there had been any super-intelligent space aliens up there, don't you think that the spacemen would have seen them while they were flying around up there? Any space aliens would have to have flown all the way over to the moon to hide, so the spacemen couldn't have seen them.

Nope, the process for getting the newspapers printed and dropped off at the drop-off corner will remain a mystery for a long time. Kinda like the lost continent of Atlanta. They haven't figured that one out too. Anyway, this morning was no different. When I got to the drop-off corner, Ran was already there. "Hi, Ran, whatcha doing?" I asked.

"Nothing. Whacha doing, Scott?"

"Nothing," I replied. "Well, whachawanno do?"

"Guess we had better get started delivering these papers now," he said.

"Yup, guess so," I said.

That's how we usually started just about every day. As we started delivering our papers, I noticed that the Park Dairy milkman was out delivering his milk and stuff. That was not anything new or unusual. We saw him a couple of times a week delivering milk and stuff. It was kinda nice to have the dairies sending a milk truck and a milkman out real early to deliver milk, orange juice, and a couple of other things before breakfast time. You never had to worry about running out of milk for your cereal or doughnuts in the morning. That is something that you don't wanna mess around with, and it is just the kind of job that was really important, as far as I was concerned.

It seemed to be an easy job too. The guy would just walk up to the milk box at the house, take the empty milk bottles, and replace them with full milk bottles. Everyone was happy. As we delivered our newspapers, we also saw the Farm Fresh Dairy milkman and the Green Family Dairy Company milkman too. None of it was out of the ordinary. However, this morning my stomach was growling ahead of time, and I was kind of thirsty. I had seen the milkman stop at a couple of houses as I walked up the street. Well, actually, I walked across everyone's front yard. It was a much easier throw to just pitch the newspaper up onto the porch if you were walking in the front yards right in front of the porches, as opposed to walking down the sidewalk and throwing the newspaper all the way to the front porch without hitting anything sitting on the porch or having the newspaper land near the porch. That was true, especially if it was raining! You always had to make sure that you were able to pitch the newspaper right up in front of the front door, just to keep it out of the rain. No one wanted a wet newspaper. Ran told me that if someone got a wet newspaper, they would call him and make him bring over a dry newspaper to their house. He said that wet newspapers brought out the grumpy in people. I bet that Mr. Peppercorn must have gotten a bunch of wet newspapers, because he was always super grumpy. Glad that we didn't deliver his newspaper.

Well, as I was saying, I was getting pretty hungry. My stomach alarm clock must have gone off early, and I was starting to hear my stomach let out a growl or two myself. I wondered if Ran could hear it from across the street. No, probably not. He usually listened to the transistor radio that he carried with him when he delivered papers.

Then I had an idea. When I passed one of the houses where the Park Dairy milkman had stopped, I walked over to the side door. Most of the houses had side doors and back doors with a small silver box for the milkman to put their milk in. Sure enough, there was a box at the side door. I walked up and opened the box lid. Looking back at me were two brand-new, half-gallon bottles of milk. *Hmm, this might work*, I thought.

I grabbed both bottles and put them into my newspaper bag. We were getting close to the end of our paper route, so I had a lot of extra room in my newspaper bag by now. Ran didn't seem to notice my short detour from my normal delivery route. When we finished, we walked over to his house to put up the newspaper bags. We always kept the newspaper bags at his house, because he said that he was responsible for them. He would bring my newspaper bag to the newspaper drop-off corner every morning for me.

Ran noticed that I had something in my newspaper bag. "What's in the bag?" he asked.

I proudly pulled out the two half-gallon bottles of milk.

"What's that?" he asked.

"Two half-gallon bottles of milk," I answered.

"Whatcha gonna do with them?" he asked.

"I'm gonna drink one and give the other one to you. I'm kind of hungry and thirsty this morning."

"Thanks," Ran said, and we sat down on the street curb and opened our bottles of milk. We took our fingers and fished out the cream that is always stuck in the top of the bottle. Don't know why they put this stuff in milk bottles anyway. It really tastes yucky on my cereal. If it fell out into my cereal bowl, I would scoop it up with my spoon and dump it back into the milk bottle. Let Marie or

Sam deal with the cream. If I was lucky, they wouldn't notice until they had a blob of the stuff in their mouths.

Ran and I sat there and enjoyed a couple of swallows of the milk. It was really good at first, but then I started to get tired of it real quick. "Wish that it was chocolate milk," I said to Ran.

"I've got an idea," Ran said as he darted into his house. A minute or two later, he came out with a can of chocolate syrup.

"Great idea, Ran!"

So there we sat, on the street curb in front of his house. We each poured a bunch of chocolate syrup into our bottles of milk and then held our palms over the bottle openings as we shook the bottles until we thought that the chocolate had mixed in real good. We ended up using that entire can of chocolate syrup. We drank chocolate milk until we couldn't drink any more. "It would be great if the milkman delivered chocolate milk," I said. Then an idea began to form in my mind.

A few mornings later, while we were making our morning deliveries of newspapers, I stopped and looked into the milk boxes on the sides of the houses and on the back porches. It was hard to keep up with Ran, who was delivering newspapers on the other side of the street, but I was on a mission. Box after box came up empty. Well, they weren't empty, but they didn't have any chocolate milk in a single one of them. I was getting to feel a little disappointed. However, a couple of mornings later, we were delivering the morning newspapers before the milkman had started his deliveries on the street. I knew this because on the first milk box that I happened to check, I saw the two empty milk bottles and something else. I had hit the jackpot! When I opened the milk box, there in front of me was the answer to my prayers. Well, maybe it was the answer to my hopes, because you cannot pray and ask God to help you out on something that … that … something that I should confess to Father Taurman about, but I probably won't.

Well, it was summertime, and I had all summer to try to frame this up just right for Father Taurman for when I had to start going back to the confessional when school started. That was if my conscience bothered me enough to come clean, and I was hopeful that I would have forgotten about the matter by then. You can't get in trouble for not confessing something that you forgot that you were supposed to confess in the first place. I figured that I could just offer up an extra Hail Mary and Our Father to act as a cover-all for anything that I had forgotten to confess to Father Taurman.

Back to the exciting story! There right in front of me, stuck into an empty glass milk bottle, was a note, and it had the milkman's name—Bobby! *Well, this is going to pay off big time*, I thought. I couldn't wait to share my plan with Ran, but it would have to wait until we were finished delivering this morning's newspapers. When you have something big going on, it is best to plan it out in advance.

"I know the milkman's name," I told Ran.

"So what, you know the milkman's name?" Ran replied.

"Well, Ran, think about it. What if you were the milkman? And, oh, his name is Bobby. Anyway, if you were Bobby delivering milk on your route and you saw a note addressed to you in an empty milk bottle, and that note was asking you to leave an extra half-gallon, or quart, or however they come, bottle of chocolate milk, what would you do?"

Ran thought over this for just about a second and then he lit up a big smile. "I would leave whatever you had asked for," he said with a big grin.

"Right, and I think that when Bobby makes his next bunch of deliveries on that route, we should visit a milk box in order to leave him a special note."

"Great idea!" Ran chimed in. "We'll just place an order."

"Now we just have to pick out which of his customers' milk boxes we want to use for our note."

"How about old man Collins?" Ran suggested.

Old man Collins was about as mean as Mr. Peppercorn. He was just mean and grumpy to everyone. He called kids a waste of our fresh air, because if we didn't have so many of them running around all over the place using up all of the fresh air, he would have more fresh air for himself. He was weird too, because he always had a cigarette in his fingers and coughed a lot. I bet he could even take a bath or a shower while holding his cigarette and not get it wet. We suspected that, somehow, he was behind the mysterious disappearance of the little kids' tricycles on his street. It seemed like every time one was left on the sidewalk near his house, it mysteriously disappeared. We suspected that he was selling them to the bicycle pirates.

"Yeah," I said, "old man Collins would be the perfect target for our plan."

The big important morning finally rolled around. I used my best crotchety old man writing to write a note to Bobby. It said:

Milkman Bobby. I want you to leave an extra bottle of chocolate milk in my milk box.
Signed Mr. Collins

I put the note in one of the empty milk bottles in old man Collins' milk box and then snuck back down the street to the newspaper drop-off corner and loaded up our newspaper bags with newspapers. Next, we hurried to make our newspaper deliveries so that we could get back to old man Collins' house and find out if our note had worked. I think we set a new world's record for newspaper delivery time.

I snuck up on his back porch, and lo and behold, there was a quart of chocolate milk! It was great, and I was tempted to open the bottle of chocolate milk right there. But then I thought that I was being dumb. If old man Collins woke up, he would catch me red-handed. I stowed the bottle of chocolate milk in my newspaper bag and snuck out to the street, where Ran was waiting. "Mission accomplished," I said. This was going to be fun, or at least until Mr. Collins received his milk bill.

I started leaving notes for extra chocolate milk on every other milk delivery day. Since the personalized note had worked so good at old man Collins' house, we decided to expand our operation to several more houses on the street. It didn't take long to learn that Bobby could also deliver more than chocolate milk. He had orange juice and potato chips and ice cream. The ice cream was going to be a problem, though, since it was summertime and it was still hot outside in the morning. We could only order the amount of ice cream that we were able to eat each morning before it melted.

We began to load up on anything Bobby had in his milk truck, and he never once caught on, at least for the short time that we did business with him. We also decided to bug old man Collins. We started taking his plain white milk, and we were pretty sure that he started to complain to Bobby about it. Then we started taking white milk from his neighbors and putting their milk into his milk box along with his milk. He either didn't receive enough white milk or he received too much white milk. We were pretty sure that he was probably all fired up and had to be crabbing at somebody about it. He always was crabbing. He was a natural crabber.

Things were going so good that we decided to expand our operation. Well, what we actually did was to slow down and finally stop the Bobby Custom Delivery Service and then start up a new one with the Farm Fresh Dairy milkman. It was a business decision. We were never able to find out the Farm Fresh Dairy milkman's name, but the old note in the bottle routine had worked so well with Bobby that we decided to try it without knowing the Farm Fresh guy's name. We started slowly, and things worked out according to plan. There was not anyone on his route that we didn't like, so we didn't pull any tricks on any particular one of his customers. We would just pick out a couple of his customers at random.

One morning we decided to go for broke. I wrote out a note asking for five extra quarts of chocolate milk and three extra quarts of orange juice. We placed the note in the milk box on the side of the house that we had picked out. Then we left another note in the milk box on the back porch of the house right across the street. That note asked for four extra quarts of chocolate milk and three extra quarts of orange juice. We watched from a spot in the bushes a couple of doors down. When the Farm Fresh Dairy guy showed up at the first house, he must have seen the note, because he went back to his milk truck and loaded up his milk-carrying thing and went back to the house. When he went to the house across the street, he returned back to the milk truck and loaded up his milk-carrying thing again and then returned to the house. That milk box was located on the back porch. He was back there a little while, and then he finally returned to his truck, but he didn't leave. After a minute or two, he went back to the back porch of the second house.

"He's onto us," Ran said. We watched as he returned to his milk truck and then left to continue his route. We quietly sneaked over to the first house, and there was everything that we had requested! We loaded up the five extra quarts of chocolate milk and three extra quarts of orange juice. Now we had to check out the second house, and we were pretty nervous about this one, because the Farm Fresh Dairy guy had made three trips to the back porch instead of two. Also, he had taken an extra-long time at this house.

We were extra, extra quiet as we went around the house to the back porch. When I opened the milk box, I saw three quarts of chocolate milk and one quart of orange juice. There also was a note from the Farm Fresh Dairy guy. It said, *"I am sorry to have to short your order, but I ran out of chocolate milk and orange juice this morning."*

I couldn't believe this! Of course I had to destroy the evidence, so I shoved the note into my pocket and then handed the quarts of chocolate milk and orange juice to Ran. Then we made our successful getaway. The note then made its way down the sewer. I didn't want to leave a trail or clue! I saw that trick on a Dragnet television show.

Once again, I thought that it would be best to close down another successful operation and move on. There was one other dairy company that made deliveries around the neighborhood. We were getting a little tired of chocolate milk and orange juice by this time. However, the Green Family Dairy not only delivered the milk, orange juice, and stuff, but they were also in the candy business, and they made the very best boxed fancy chocolate candy and fudge. This was a target that we just couldn't pass up. Everyone loves chocolate candy and fudge. We agreed that their boxed chocolate candy was the best because they had chocolate-covered cherries, chocolate-covered nuts, chocolate mints, and chocolate-covered caramel, plus a whole lot more. They had a whole bunch of different flavors of fudge, and some even had nuts! We didn't know what to order, so one day we went to one of their ice cream stores that was nearby. We made notes of all of the different kinds of boxed chocolate candy that they sold. They even had white chocolate, whatever that is. Ran said that they must have run out of regular chocolate and mixed flour or something into the mix. "Oh, that makes sense," I said. It had chocolate in its name, so it had to be good.

Anyway, we picked a nearby street that the Green Family Dairy guy took care of. We didn't want to stir up any more trouble on the streets that we had already used, so moving our operation was a good idea. Well, the notes worked like a charm. Soon we had all kinds of boxed chocolate candies stored up.

Then disaster happened. Do you remember that I said that Biscuit was a good guy but the type of guy who always seemed to have a black cloud hanging over his head? Well, we had told Biscuit about our new business. He immediately wanted to try it out for himself. We were not crazy about this idea. After all, we had turned ourselves into very successful businessmen, but he insisted, and he was one of our very best friends. We agreed to let him put a note in a milk box and even told him which note and which milk box would be the best. I told him that he needed to make sure that he picked up his order as soon as the Green Family Dairy guy left.

Well, on this particular day, the Green Family Diary guy was running a little late, but he did leave the box of chocolate candy that Biscuit ordered. Biscuit was super happy and ran straight across the front yard to get the box of candy, whooping it up the whole way. I had told him to sneak up to the side door where the milk box was and quietly get the candy. Well, Biscuit tripped over the bird bath that was in the front yard and ended up making a lot of noise. Just as he opened the lid of the milk box to get the box of chocolate, the side door flew open and an old lady looked down at Biscuit and started yelling. "Robber! Robber! Robber!" The old lady flew right out of the house in her nightgown and bathrobe and began to swat her broom at Biscuit! She was going to wake up everyone in the entire city!

Biscuit took off running down the street, while Ran and I decided to quietly sneak up the street in the opposite direction. If anyone had stopped us, we would have told them that we were on our way to church to serve the six-thirty morning Mass. Everyone knows that altar boys never get into trouble, ever!

We finally joined up with Biscuit. No one had caught him, and since it was not quite light yet outside, we didn't think that anyone would recognize him. As a matter of fact, none of us had ever seen Biscuit run so fast. We told him that he should try out for the Olympic hundred-yard-dash team. Ran said that Biscuit would only win if he had that little old lady running after him with a broom. After laughing at Biscuit's antics, we had a quick management meeting and decided that it was time for our dairy business to shut down.

Chapter 16
THE GOOFY GIRLS

Well, we were past halfway through our summer vacation, and one morning we decided to climb up in our favorite climbing tree and just hang out for a little while. Ran, Mortie, Biscuit, and I had packed a couple of peanut butter sandwiches, so we were set for the day. We liked this particular climbing tree because it was located in a great spot where we could see all up and down the street as well as the nearby busy street, so we always had something to look at. We were sitting up there looking over into the back yard of Margie Zaster, one of the goofy neighborhood girls' house. She had some friends over, and they were all just sitting around talking and acting goofy, like goofy girls do. The Goofy Girls' Yippity Yappity Club was in session. I heard that there were some guys that thought that the goofy girls were cute, but we thought that they were just plain goofy. When you grow up with the same goofy neighborhood girls, they never become cute. They always stay and act goofy looking.

We would have to think up something to do to them to make them mad. After talking about them for a good while, we started to think about the upcoming State Fair. The Tall Texan immediately took over from the talk about the goofy girls. "Yup, it's gonna to be real neat when the Tall Texan comes to town," Ran said.

"Just how tall is the Tall Texan?" Mortie asked.

I said that he was pretty tall, but it was a secret because the Tall Texan didn't want any of the bad guys to know much about him.

"He's almost too tall for his horse, Firestorm, and Firestorm is about one of the biggest horses in the whole Wild West," Biscuit said.

"I wonder how old he is," Mortie thought aloud.

"He's pretty old," I said. "I heard that he's around thirty or thirty-five years old. But he's a good old and not a bad old. I mean, he eats buffalo, corn on the cob, and apples because that's all that they have in the Wild West. Everybody knows that those things are healthy and they keep you young and healthy and keep your bones from breaking or squeaking. You never heard of a squeaky Indian, have you?"

"Nope, guess not," Mortie said.

About this time, Moose came by. He was too short to be able to climb up like we did, so we dropped our rope down to him so he could use it to climb up. We always kept special supplies like our rope, a flashlight, a slingshot, and spare peanut butter and jelly sandwiches stored in our tree. However, we suspected that someone else was climbing up our tree too, because we would find the paper wrappings for our spare peanut butter and jelly sandwiches on the ground all torn up the next day. If we ever caught whoever was eating our sandwiches, we would deal with him or them pretty badly.

Once Moose found a comfortable branch to sit on, he started burping. It was kind of funny listening to all of the different types of burps that he could come up with. He had a freight train burp, a dump truck burp, a house-rattling burp, and a couple others that he had not named yet. "Why ya burping so much?" I asked.

"Well, I ate some fried hot dogs and pancakes for breakfast, and they've loaded me up with a bunch of gas in my stomach, and now I feel kinda heavy," Moose answered.

"Heavy!" I said. "Moose, you're a little guy and not a bit heavy."

"I'm not heavy for you, but I'm heavy for me. Everyone knows that pancakes swell up in your stomach after you eat them, and when they swell up, you feel heavy."

"Yup, that's true," Ran said. "I ate a dozen pancakes before, and when I left the table, the pancakes just started to swell up right away. I know that I felt about thirty pounds heavier right then."

"Well, when you eat fried hot dogs with pancakes, your stomach changes the pancakes and fried hot dogs into burping gas," Moose said. "When that happens, you get real heavy."

"Wait a minute," I said. "How can you get heavier just because you have burping gas? You can't see it or feel it, because it's just air, and air doesn't weigh anything."

"That's easy," Moose explained. "You know when you have an empty camping jug of propane gas, and your dad takes it to get filled up and brings it home? Well, when it gets filled up with propane gas, which is almost identical to burping gas, it's heavier."

"Yup, he's right," Ran commented. "When my dad's propane camping tank is empty, you can toss it around because it's so light. But after he gets it filled up with propane gas, it's heavier."

"You know, I think you're right," I said.

"It's just simple science," Moose said. "The problem is that if I don't burp out the burping gas, it will build up a bunch of pressure in me, and I could explode or ignite if I get close to a fire or something."

"Well, burp away," I said.

As Moose continued his burping, we all started to add our own burps to show our support for him.

After a while, our talk drifted back to the Tall Texan again. "He sure is a good shot," Biscuit said.

Ran was sitting on one of the stronger limbs and shooting tree seeds, or whatever you call the little seed-like things that grow on trees, at the goofy girls. He was a really good aim with the sling-shot. "I bet that the Tall Texan is a good shot with the sling shot," Ran said.

We could hear the "ouch" from one of the goofy girls as he hit them with the tree seed. Goofy girls, they never ever looked over and up into the tree where we were sitting.

"The Tall Texan's legs almost reach to the ground when he's riding Firestorm because he's so tall," Ran remarked between shots.

"Betcha can't hit that balloon that they have over in their yard," Biscuit said to Ran.

We all watched as Ran took real careful aim and then let loose a shot from the slingshot. POP, came the noise, followed by a couple of goofy-girl screams.

"Did we have a bet on that, Biscuit?" Ran asked.

"Nope, I would have bet you if you had asked me, but no bets after the shot," Biscuit replied.

"I bet that the Tall Texan could have made that shot left-handed, turned around backwards, looking through a mirror, with one eye shut," I said.

Probably so, we all agreed, because we all knew that The Tall Texan was the best shot that the Wild West had ever seen. "I think that he was the guy who taught all of the other good guys how to shoot real good," I told everyone.

"I heard that Roy Rogers learned from him too," Moose added.

"Maybe Wang Chow KaPow will do some of his judo hops for everybody too," Biscuit said. "Where did Wang Chow KaPow come from?"

"No one is sure," I said. "They think that he came from Japan or China or somewhere over there. I think that he snuck over on a banana boat or a tuna boat, because the evil Lord Togaboga was mad at him for beating him in a judo match over there, and all of the geisha girls wanted to marry Wang Chow KaPow instead of evil Lord Togaboga. You know that old evil Lord Togaboga was a pretty bad guy over there. He was the king of the kingdom of Japan or China, but they didn't know how to pronounce king, so they called him lord. He was so mean that he kept all of the good food for himself and his buddies. Lord Togaboga and his friends got to eat hamburgers and fried chicken, and the rest of the people almost had to starve. That is how chop suey was invented. One day, when the people didn't have anything to eat, they saw that after the rain had stopped and the sun had come out, the rice noodle patties had dried up, and the rice noodles that had not been picked had gotten hard. When they gathered up the dried-up rice noodles, they put them in a pot with some tuna fish and then chopped it up to make chop suey. I think that they were able to buy rice at the grocery store, so they could serve the chop suey over rice. They put some real salty brown stuff on the chop suey when they eat it. It's called soil sauce, made from soil beans. They were able to get that at their grocery stores too. If you go to a Chinese restaurant today, you can still get the same chop suey that they made back then."

"I don't think that I would want to eat dried-up rice noodles." Mortie said.

"It's not so bad, because they give you fortunate cookies to eat to get rid of the bad taste from the chop suey."

"What is a fortunate cookie?" Mortie asked.

"It's a funny looking little cookie that has a little piece of paper in every one of 'em."

"What's the little paper for?" Mortie asked.

"Don't know, because I have never had a fortunate cookie, but I guess that it says, 'Made In Japan,' or something like that."

"Makes sense," Mortie replied.

"Anyway, I want to see Wang Chow KaPow do a bunch of his judo hops on a bunch of bad guys," Moose said as he finally climbed over to where we were sitting in the tree.

"I would like to pet Firestorm," Ran said.

"Probably won't be able to," I said. "You know that he's a very big horse, and he's called Firestorm because he has a stormy personality."

"Yeah, you're probably right," Ran said. "But I would like to give him a horse biscuit or something as a friend offering."

"Whachawanna do now, y'all?" I asked.

"Those goofy girls are still over there, and I wish that they would go somewhere else. I can hear their goofy yacking all the way over here," Ran said.

"Yeah, that's why we call them the Goofy Girls' Yippity Yappity Club," I said. Glancing over to where the goofy girls were playing or yacking, I noticed something. "Did you notice that all of those goofy girls rode their bikes over there?"

"Yup, they're all lined up in the alley behind the garage," Ran said.

"I don't think that they can see their bikes from where they are in the yard," I told the guys. "Come on with me and be real quiet." After climbing down from the tree, I ran to a nearby porch and grabbed a newspaper off of it.

"Whatcha doing?" Ran asked.

"Need it for something," I said. We made one stop on the way over to the garage where the goofy girls had parked their bicycles.

Mr. Benish penned his dogs behind his house, and they would provide something that we would need. The dogs liked us, and they didn't even bark as we went into their pen. I reached down and carefully picked up a couple of fresh dog poops with the newspaper. Then we headed for the bicycles. "Loosen up the air valves in the tires so they'll go flat," I instructed Ran, Mortie, Biscuit, and Moose.

While they were doing that, I applied the finishing touch. I very carefully smeared the fresh dog poop on each seat and every hand grip. All that I needed to do was to smear it so you wouldn't notice it until you gripped the hand grip or sat on the seat. I had to be real careful, because I didn't want to get the dog poop on my hands, because it was really stinky. I don't know what Mr. Benish fed his dog, but it made real stinky poop. I couldn't figure that one out. Mrs. Benish was a real good cook, and if she had leftovers and gave them to the dogs, then how could the dogs make such stinky poop? Then it dawned on me. Mrs. Benish is a real good people-food cook, but probably not good dog-food cook. Oh well.

After we were done, I told everyone that we needed to sneak into Mr. Helfrich's back yard next door. The Helfrichs had a tall wooden fence that you couldn't see through. "We need to bust up their little party," I said. "Mortie, bring me the garden hose, and Moose, you turn on the water when I signal you."

Once we were ready, I signaled for Moose to turn on the hose. I aimed the hose over the fence and into the yard, where I could hear the goofy girls yacking. The goofy girls immediately started screaming. It was perfect, because they were sitting in a corner of the yard. I had them pinned in, and they were getting drenched. It was hilarious! It was all that we could do to keep from laughing out loud.

I signaled Moose to turn off the water, and we ran across the alley into a yard that had a bunch of large bushes. From here we were able to hear the goofy girls fussing about being soaking wet. We could also see where their bikes were parked.

One by one, they came out into the alley to get on their bikes and go home and change into some dry clothes. About the same time that they gripped their hand grips and sat down on the seats to take off, they noticed that they all had flat tires. Then they noticed that they all had sticky hands that stunk real bad. They started screaming about the stink and ran back into the yard to wash their hands. I don't think that they had figured out that every one of them had sat in the dog-poop bicycle seats. Oh well, they would.

It was time for us to head back for the day and plan our next exploits. Later on, Ran and I saw a couple of the goofy girls. They asked me if I knew anything about the soaking or the flat tires or the dog poop. I looked and Ran and he looked at me. "Whacha talking about, you goofy girls?" I asked.

"We think that you dumb boys sprayed us with the Helfrich's hose and flattened our tires and put stinky stuff on our bikes," they said.

"Who, us? We all were at altar boy practice today, so it couldn't have been us," I said.

"They don't have altar boy practice during the summer," one of the goofy girls said.

"We're practicing on our own, so we don't forget our Latin over the summer," I said. "*Mea culpa*," I added.

"What does that mean?" one of the goofy girls asked.

"It means that you're goofy, in Latin," I answered.

"I think that you all probably got caught under the Helfrich's lawn sprinkler," Ran said. "You all probably ran over some glass in the alley that flattened your tires. Gotta be careful about where you ride your bike in the alleys around here."

"The stinky smell was probably some of your own goofy stinky perfume that you all like to play around with," I added.

Both of the goofy girls just put their hands on their hips and gave us goofy stares, and then they just finally walked off.

"Stupid goofy girls," I said.

"Yeah, stupid goofy girls," Ran replied.

Chapter 17
TRAFFIC JAM

"Been a pretty good day," I remarked to Ran. We had all gone home for dinner and decided to meet again up at the ball field to plan out our night.

"No softball games tonight," Mortie sighed. "I really do like watching the softball games, especially the girls' softball games."

"Yup, they're all fun, but the girls are r-e-a-l-l-y cute, and many of them play just as good as the men do," I said.

"They're good, but not that good," Biscuit added as he strolled up to meet us.

"Yup, maybe so, but they sure are a whole lot prettier to look at than the men's teams. It's a shame that there's not a game tonight … we could have messed with Stubby," Ran said.

I thought about it and said, "I think that Stubby is just one of those guys that was just asking to be messed with. You know, I wouldn't feel that way if he didn't always try to bully the little kids that are younger and smaller than him."

"Everyone is smaller than him," Ran laughed.

"You know what I mean. He's pushy to everyone that is younger and a lot smaller than him," I replied.

"Yeah, you never see him trying to mess around with someone his own age or size, because they would knock the snot out of him," Biscuit joined in. "As big as Stubby is, they could probably fill up one of those big trash barrels over by the concession stand with all of his snot."

"Ewww, that is gross just to think about," Mortie said.

"But it's true," Biscuit replied. "They would have to get a crane to lift it up."

"Shut up," Ran said. "You guys are grossing me out. Stubby is not even home tonight."

"Whacha mean?" I asked.

"Well, I had hopped the fence next to the ball field right before we came over here," Ran said. "I had to use the bathroom in a bad way, while no one else was using it."

Biscuit laughed. "The ball field is closed during the day! They could have announced that you needed to use the can on the PA and no one would have heard anything. But you can hear something when Stubby is in there."

"Yup, there ought to be a caution sign that says 'Enter at Your Own Risk' after Stubby has been in there," Biscuit said. "One time before a game, before a lot of people were there, I saw Stubby running down behind the stands and straight into the men's bathroom."

"It's not a bathroom … it is a restroom," I interjected.

"You know what I mean," Biscuit said. "Well anyway, he ran into the 'restroom' real fast. You would think that his pants were on fire or something. Come to think of it, they were probably going to be close to igniting if he had let one or had not gotten in there real quick. Since I was close by, I kinda ran over there and was outside just as he must have slammed the stall door closed. Then it happened, and it was terrible. It sounded like a major explosion or something in there. Kind of like an elephant exploding or something. It sure sounded like one. I was sure that the stall door had been blown right off of the hinges. I thought that I felt the ground shake. If that building had not been built out of concrete blocks, I think that it would have blown apart. Then Stubby let out a ... a...a ... moan—a moan of relief, I guess. Kinda sounded like a hippo's mating call. There were a couple of little kids walking up to the water fountain that is in the front of the 'restroom,' but when they heard Stubby's moan, they looked at each other, yelled, and then took off running back to the stands. That probably saved their lives, because I'm sure that any water that came out of that water fountain after Stubby's explosion was probably poisoned for a good five minutes. A few minutes later, Stubby came strolling out of the restroom with a big look of relief on his face. I watched him stop at the water fountain and get a big drink. I thought that he was bound to keel over from the poisoned water or something, but he just kept drinking and drinking and drinking. He finally walked back to the concession stand to load up on a bunch of candy and stuff before the first game. He probably had to fill up his candy supply in his candy hiding place on the scoreboard. I thought that I should put up a sign or something to warn people about the deadly gasses in the restroom, but I didn't. At least the women's restroom should have been safe, because it has a concrete brick wall between it and the men's restroom."

"Well, what has all of this got to do with Stubby's plans for tonight?" I asked.

"Well, before Biscuit interrupted me," Ran said, "as I was getting ready to hop back over the fence to leave the ball field, I heard Stubby talking to some of the little kids who live down the street. He was bragging that his parents were going to take him with them to see that new cowboy movie playing at the Bard Theater. Well, it's not real new, because it's already played at one of the movie theaters downtown, but it's still pretty new. Anyway, he was popping off that he gets to see adult movies, while they don't get to do anything but hang out around our neighborhood. You know, just like he always pops off."

"Hope that he spills his popcorn on the floor," Mortie said.

"Yeah, after spilling his Coke in his lap," Ran laughed.

"Wish that we could be there to make things miserable for him," Mortie said.

"I think that their movies start at seven o'clock tonight," I said. "Maybe we can mess around with Stubby tonight."

"Whacha mean?" Biscuit asked.

"Gotta idea, but we need to get moving because we need to get there about twenty minutes before the show stops."

So off we went as a plan was coming together in my mind. On the way, we ran into Moose. He was playing with his Boy Scout flashlight. "Hey, Moose, you doing anything tonight?" I called.

"Nope, you got something in mind?" he said.

"Yeah, I do. Come on with us," I said.

As Moose joined in, Ran said, "Whacha thinking about doing, Scott?"

"You know, Stubby's father always has to be the first to go somewhere, and then he has to be the first person to leave that somewhere," I said. "He never wants to wait around or be caught in traffic."

"Yeah, so what? We all know that."

"Well, I think that since he has decided to take Stubby with him, we can mess with him and Stubby both," I said.

"How are we gonna do that?" Ran asked.

"You know that no one ever leaves the Bard Theater going straight out onto Bardstown Road, because there is too much traffic coming from both directions," I replied.

"I know, they all take that little cut-through on that little alley that runs out of the parking lot and behind all of those stores and ends up at the street by the traffic light," Ran said.

"Yup, well you know where that little skinny alley dips down behind the stores and then comes up to the street?" I asked. "Well, I think that there may be a traffic jam there tonight."

"How are you gonna do that?" Ran asked.

"One of those stores is an appliance store that has a bunch of boxes that refrigerators and washing machines come in. The empty boxes get stacked out behind their building. Well, I have it on good authority that some of those boxes may appear in that alley where it dips down below those buildings."

Ran looked at me and then began to smile really big. "I think that I got an idea of what you're talking about now, Scott," he replied.

We got to the alley about fifteen minutes before the show was supposed to be over. Sure enough, a whole bunch of big appliance boxes were stacked up behind the appliance store. "Quick, everyone grab a box and drag it down into the dip in the alley," I called out.

Everyone grabbed a box, and then we dragged them all down. They were really not all that heavy, except for the wooden pallets in the bottom. We quickly arranged them so that when a car drove down the dip in the alley, it would run into a wall of boxes. You really wouldn't be able to see the boxes ahead of time because of the way that the alley dipped down below the streetlights. Well, the car wouldn't actually run into the wall, but it would be blocked by the wall when it got there, and it would definitely have to stop. As the car would pass the point where the alley dipped, we would push more boxes behind the car. We could just drop them down from the ledge above. Since it was just a single-lane alley, the car would be boxed in.

We were ready. "Moose, I need for you to stand near the back of the parking lot and act like a parking lot attendant and point the cars to the alley. As soon as Stubby's dad drives down the alley, you can take off. I bet that Stubby's dad will be the first guy out."

A couple of minutes later, just as I had thought, Stubby's dad came walking out of the theater, with Stubby close behind. They quickly got into their car and then headed straight for Moose, who was waving his flashlight just like a regular parking-lot attendant. Biscuit had given Moose his baseball cap to pull down over his eyes so he wouldn't be recognized. It was perfect.

Stubby's dad followed Moose's pointing and headed down the little alley. However, more people were starting to leave the theater and head for their cars in the parking lot. Instead of leaving, Moose continued to wave his flashlight to direct traffic toward the little alley.

As soon as Stubby's dad started down the dip in the alley, we pushed the boxes off of the ledge above the dip and watched them fall into the alley. Ran and I jumped down and pushed a couple of them further down the dip behind Stubby's dad's car. Then we all ran over into the neighboring yard and hid in the bushes to watch the show.

After directing a number of cars toward the little alley, Moose took off running between a couple of houses and joined us. We watched as Stubby's dad rolled up to the box roadblock and then stopped. After a minute, he decided to try to back out of the little alley. We all almost exploded in laughter as we watched. It was all that we could do to keep quiet. He backed into the wall of boxes that we had pushed in behind him. About the time that Stubby's dad backed up to the roadblock behind him, the cars that Moose had directed into the little alley began to stack up in the dip in front of the boxes behind Stubby's dad's car. Everyone was yelling and honking their horns. They couldn't just move the boxes aside, because the neighbors all had fenced-in yards, and there was a concrete ledge next to the dip behind the stores. The ledge was too high to push the boxes up and over the top.

Stubby and his dad ended up dragging the boxes in front of his car to a spot at the top of the hill. They just left them there. Stubby was whining the whole time, and his father kept yelling at him to just "grow up" and help move the boxes. The people in the cars by the other roadblock finally stopped yelling at each other and pulled the boxes back behind the appliance store. As we sat there, we watched everyone finally clear out the alley and empty the parking lot.

"Well, it has been a pretty entertaining night," I said.

We all agreed and then decided to call it a night and head home until tomorrow.

Chapter 18
FROM WORMY TO THE POPE PICKER

It looked like it was going to be another ordinary summer day. Ran had come over early after delivering newspapers on his paper route. " Whachawanna do today, Scott?"

"I don't know, Ran. Whachawanna do, Ran?"

"I don't know, Scott. What is that great smell that is floating in the air?"

"Oh, Mrs. Holloway is baking a big batch of her super cookies next door," I said.

"They sure do smell good," Ran said. "Do you think that she will give us some of those cookies?"

"Nope, they're for her kids and the birthday party that they are going to later on this afternoon," I answered. "I heard her talking to Mr. Holloway this morning as he was leaving for work. He wanted some cookies and she wouldn't even give HIM any of those super cookies. He even asked her a couple of times, but she shot him down each and every time. She's not even giving the kids any cookies before the party, although I saw one of them sneaking out the back door with one."

"Boy, she must be really tough to turn down her husband AND her kids," Ran sighed.

"Hey, I may have an idea just how to get a few of her super cookies for us!" I blurted out. "I think that I just had a flash of brilliance!"

"Sure that it wasn't a fart?" Ran laughed.

"Pretty sure it wasn't, and it is brilliant, if I do say so myself," I added. "Come on and help me find something in my room. We need to find the bait."

"Bait? Are we going fishing?" Ran asked.

"Nope, the bait is what I'll use to lure the little kids next door in, so that I can get them to smuggle out some super cookies for us," I said.

Ran looked a little confused but said, "Okay, I'm in, but what are we looking for?"

"Wormy," I replied.

"What's a wormy?" Ran asked.

"Wormy is Sam's hand puppet or mitt or something," I said. "It's like an oven mitt, but it's decorated. It's colored like a big mix of brown, white, and orange. When you put your hands into it and open and close the mitt end to grab something hot, it looks like a big red mouth. It has two green, fluffy balls sewn onto it that look like eyes. It also has two pointy cloth ears on top of its head that look like, well, ears. They're red on the inside, just like the mouth. It's really strange looking, but Sam really loves his Wormy."

"Never heard of a worm with ears and eyes," Ran replied. "Okay, we find Wormy, but how is a funny-looking Wormy gonna get us some of those super cookies from Mrs. Holloway?"

"First we find Wormy, then I'll explain the details."

We dug all through the room and through Sam's toy box. Wormy was not to be found.

"I can't understand it. Sam always has Wormy with him when he goes to sleep at night. That's it!" I shouted. I ran over to Sam's bed, lifted up his pillow, and there all safe and sound was Wormy. "I found Wormy right next to Lammy," I said.

"What is a lammy?" Ran asked.

"Lammy is Sam's stuffed little black lamb," I said. "He sleeps with Lammie and Wormy. Look, Lammy's eyes have fallen off and he has a little red mouth and a bump where his nose used to be. Sam loves Lammy a lot, so I usually don't mess with Lammy unless I am really mad at Sam."

"Okay, we have Wormy, but how is Wormy going to get us some of Mrs. Holloway's super cookies?" Ran asked.

"You know that toy radio transmitter kit that I got for Christmas a few years ago?"

Ran thought and then said, "Yeah, it was kind of cool looking, and you could listen to radio stations or transmit to a radio close by if you could line up the two frequencies together. Yup, I remember it all right, but how can we use that to get the super cookies from Mrs. Holloway?"

"Well, we are gonna use Wormy to get the little kids to go sneak into their kitchen, snatch some super cookies, and bring them to us," I informed Ran.

"Yeah, just like that. Wormy says 'bring me cookies,' and the little kids bring us cookies, I guess."

"Ran, you kinda have the right idea, but you're not quite there yet. We need one more thing, and I know just where it is," I said as I rummaged through my desk drawer. "Here we go. One little portable nine-volt battery-powered transistor radio is just what the doctor ordered."

We quickly set up the radio transmitter and microphone next to the bedroom window that faced the driveway next to the Holloway's house. "Now we turn on the transmitter and the transistor radio and tune them both into the same frequency. Okay, Ran, let's test the transmission. You take the transistor radio onto the front porch, and I'll try to transmit to you. If you can hear me, ring the doorbell once."

"Why don't I just answer you through the transistor radio?" Ran asked.

"Because the transistor radio only receives and doesn't transmit."

"Oh yeah, I forgot. I'll run out front right now," he said as he headed outside.

"Ran, Ran, Ran, can you hear me?" I said into the microphone. DING DONG, the front doorbell sounded. "Okay, great, now come on back in here," I said.

Once Ran had returned with the transistor radio, I carefully wrapped it inside of Wormy. We then very carefully took Wormy outside and placed it under a bush next to the Holloway's house. After making sure that it could only be seen if we drew attention to it, we ran back into the house next to the window facing the Holloway's house, where we had set up the transmitter, and waited for one of the little kids to come walking from their front yard to their back yard or vice versa. We didn't have to wait long until Loretta, the second oldest of the little kids, came walking by.

I nudged Ran and got ready to reel Loretta in. "Hello there, Loretta," I said in a disguised voice.

Loretta stopped dead in her tracks and looked around. She started to take a step, but then I called out to her. "Where are you going, Loretta?"

That got her attention, and she stopped dead in her tracks again. "Who are you and where are you?" she said. "Are you my guarding angel?"

"You mean your guardian angel, and no I am not," came the voice. "I am right here, Loretta."

I could tell that Loretta could hear Wormy, but she still had not seen him. "I am right here next to you," I said through Wormy.

She started to look around.

"Look down, Loretta," I said.

When she looked down, she saw Wormy laying under the bush. I could tell that she was confused. Wormy looked like a toy of some kind, but it was talking to her, and toys don't really talk to people. As she bent over to look at Wormy more closely, she started to reach out her hand to touch Wormy. "Don't touch me or I'll have to bite your fingers off," Wormy called out. Loretta immediately jumped back. "I am just kind of nervous around humans, and I don't like for them to touch me," Wormy said.

"Oh, okay," Loretta said.

"You see, Loretta, I am pretty hungry, and I guess that makes me nervous."

"Well, I was just going to pet you," Loretta said.

"Well, I might let you pet me behind my ears if … if … if …" Wormy replied.

"If what?" Loretta asked.

"Well, if you can find something for me to eat," Wormy replied.

At the same time, I pointed to an old shoebox that was in the bottom of the closet. Ran reached over and grabbed it. As I got ready to start talking again, I grabbed a crayon and wrote "Wormy's Lunchbox" on the lid. I pointed for Ran to slip out and put it on our back-porch steps.

"What do worms eat?" Loretta asked.

"We like cheeseburgers, but in the mornings, we like fresh-baked cookies," Wormy replied. "Do you know where any fresh-baked cookies are?"

I could see Loretta frown and then put on a big smile. "Yeah, my mommy has baked some cookies for the birthday party this afternoon. She baked a whole big bunch of them," she said.

"Well, if you can get me a few of those cookies, then I'll let you pet me behind my ears," Wormy said.

"Well, my mommy really does not want me to take any of the cookies, and she told me so herself," Loretta said.

"Well, okay, I guess that I'll just have to starve to death, and you will never get to pet me behind my ears," Wormy sighed.

Loretta looked pretty sad and then thought for a minute. "Maybe I can just get a few cookies when Mommy isn't looking," she said. "Do you want me to bring them out here so I can watch you eat them?"

"Oh no," Wormy answered. "Worms get very nervous when someone watches them eat. Have you ever watched a worm eat before, Loretta?"

Loretta frowned and thought. "No, I guess I haven't, but I have seen my dad catch them to take fishing so he could catch fish," she said.

"Oh no! Don't even talk about that!" Wormy cried out. "My best friend got taken fishing, and I never heard from him again! His name was Wilbur Worm."

"Oh, poor Wilbur Worm," Loretta sighed. "Yeah, I guess that worms don't like going fishing very much after all."

"Loretta, just sneak the cookies out of the kitchen and put them in my little lunchbox on the back-porch steps over at Sam and Marie's house. It says 'Wormy's Lunchbox.' Then I'll be able to find them and eat them without anyone watching."

Loretta gave Wormy a big smile, ran to the back of her house, and headed for the kitchen. Ran and I watched for a few minutes, hoping that she would be able to sneak out with some of the super cookies. At last she came out, followed by her little sister, Shirley.

She had the cookies, and she quickly ran over and put them into Wormy's Lunchbox, as I had instructed her. As soon as she was finished, she ran back over to Wormy. "Can I pet you now, Wormy?"

"I guess so, but who is that other little girl?" Wormy asked.

"Oh, she is my little sister, Shirley. She was going to tell Mommy on me, but I told her that you told me to get the cookies, so she wanted to come see for herself if you were real. Can I pet you now?"

"Okay, but very softly and only behind one ear so that I can still hear while you're petting me," Wormy answered.

"Oh, you're a cute little worm," Loretta cooed. "Can Shirley pet you too?"

"No, only you, because you were the only one that brought some cookies for me to eat."

I could see that this was going to work out great. Ran told me that Loretta had brought out four of the super cookies and put them in the box. Both Loretta and Shirley looked pretty sad.

"Well, maybe, just maybe, I might be able to let Shirley pet me behind my ear if she does something for me," Wormy replied.

"What does she have to do, get you a pile of dirt or something from the sandbox?" Loretta asked.

"No, nothing like that. If the both of you go back into the house and sneak out some more of those fresh-baked cookies and put them into my box, I'll let Shirley pet me behind my ear," Wormy said.

I could see Loretta and Shirley look at each other and frown. "What if Mommy sees us?" Shirley asked.

"She's in Dick's room getting him dressed, and that always takes a long time," Loretta said. "You know that he likes to wear suspenders. He won't go out without them."

"Okay, but we'll have to tip toe into the kitchen," Shirley said with a giggle.

Ran and I watched again as both of the little girls snuck back into their house to sneak out some more cookies for us. We didn't have to wait long until they both came sneaking back out of the house carrying handfuls of cookies. They ran over to Wormy's Lunchbox and put them in with the other cookies. Then they ran back to Wormy.

"Can Shirley pet you now?" Loretta asked.

"Okay, but just for a minute and real softly," Wormy replied.

Ran appeared carrying the Wormy Lunchbox, and it had twelve cookies in it! I said to him that we had better finish this before Mrs. Holloway noticed the missing cookies. I told him to make a lot of noise going out the back door and to head for Wormy.

As soon as Ran got up to leave, I moved back to the transmitter. "I feel big footsteps," Wormy said, sounding as nervous as I could make him sound. "Quick! Run into your house and I'll try to hide real quick."

Both of the girls got up and quickly ran around to the front of their house. I could hear their front screen door shut as they ran inside. Ran picked up Wormy and quickly brought him back inside my house.

"Okay, we put Wormy back, put the transistor radio away, and put the transmitter back into the box," I said. "Oh, we need to put Wormy back under Sam's pillow too." When we'd finished all that, I said, "All of the evidence has been taken care of, except for the super cookies. Ran, would you like to help me get rid of the rest of the evidence?"

"Sure would," he replied.

We dumped the super cookies into a bag and then headed down the alley looking for our next adventure while munching on Mrs. Holloway's super cookies.

It wasn't long before we ran into Biscuit. "Hey, guys!" he called out.

"Hi ya, Biscuit. Whatcha doin?" I replied

"Nothing much, just coming back from up at the Loop. The Woolworth store had this neat little gag thing, but I kinda wish that I hadn't bought it."

"Whacha mean, Biscuit?" I asked.

"Well, it looks like a big bug in an ice cube, but I don't have anyone that I can use it on," he said. "If I use it on my big brothers, they'll beat me up, and I can't use it on my parents."

"Show it to us," I said.

Biscuit reached down into his pocket and pulled out a little plastic cube that had a mosquito stuck square in the middle of it.

"It looks like an ice cube that has a bug frozen in it," Ran said.

"Yup, that's what it is supposed to look like," Biscuit replied. "Problem is that there's no one I can use it on without getting in trouble or getting beat up."

"I have an idea on how we can use it," I said. "Why don't you all come over today at lunch and hang out for a little while?"

"I dunno," Ran said. "You know that your mom doesn't like for you to have anyone over when she's not home. I mean, she is tough. She runs the place like an army prison."

"Yeah," Biscuit added, "we should call her Sarge."

"Hmm," Ran thought out loud. "Sarge is not a bad nickname … I mean, if you don't care if we call her that. Do you, Scott?"

"Nope, don't care at all, but I'm not sure what she'll think, though. You'll all be on your own with that one. Maybe you better not call her Sarge to her face."

"Well, Marie will rat on you if we come in, you know," Biscuit added.

"On most days, yes, but not today," I said. "She has her goofy girlfriend, Jessica, over, and if she rats on me, I'll rat on her. That's checkermate."

"What does that mean?" Ran asked.

"It means that when you play Chinese Checkers and the guy that you're playing can't make any more moves, you say 'Checkermate,' and it means that you won," I explained.

When we got to my house, Marie, Jessica, and Sam were watching some dumb program on the television. It looked like another dumb pony cartoon, just the kind of dumb cartoon that dumb girls love. Mom had made a pitcher of root beer Kool-Aid for us. I yelled in to Marie that it was time for lunch and that I was going to make a bologna sandwich and get a cookie for dessert. She was not interested in the bologna sandwich, but she didn't want me to get into the cookies because she was afraid that I would take an extra one.

All three of them came walking into the kitchen—goofy Marie, goofy Jessica, and goofy Sam, the three goofs. Marie said that she would get a cookie out for everyone except for Ran and Biscuit. I told her that if they couldn't have a cookie, then Jessica couldn't have a cookie. About that time, Ran, Biscuit, and Jessica said that they were not hungry anyway. I said fine, and I went into the pantry to pour three glasses of root beer Kool-Aid. The glasses were little dark plastic glasses, so when I slipped the fake mosquito ice cube into Marie's glass, no one noticed. I sat at one end of the table with Marie at the other end. Sam was stuck in the middle. I finished my sandwich pretty quickly and downed my root beer. Jessica had taken a seat on a stool next to the table between Marie and Sam. Ran and Biscuit just stood over by the back door watching everything that was going on. Marie and Jessica were so yappy that I didn't think she would ever drink enough of her Kool-Aid to see the fake mosquito ice cube. Sam was just keeping kind of quiet and munching on his bologna sandwich. He never had much of a clue what was going on most of the time anyway.

I watched as Marie finally lifted her glass back to finish off her Kool-Aid. As I watched, her eyes got real big, and she immediately spit out the Kool-Aid, spraying it all over Jessica and Sam. Immediately after spitting out the Kool-Aid, Marie screamed. When Marie spit out the Kool-Aid, Jessica fell back off of her stool and landed on Sam, knocking both of them to the ground. Sam had been holding his sandwich in one hand and his Kool-Aid in the other. When Jessica landed on him, the impact caused him to toss his glass of Kool-Aid and the sandwich toward Marie. She got hit directly in the face with the flying bologna and was doused across her face and shirt by the Kool-Aid.

Ran, Biscuit, and I all started laughing at the same time. Of course, Marie immediately thought that I had a hand in the whole mess. I immediately put the most innocent look that I could muster up on my face. "What do you mean, Marie?" I said.

"There is a bug in my ice cube, and you put it there," she said.

"No way," I replied. "Let me see."

By that time, the fake mosquito ice cube was on the floor. I quickly grabbed it and replied, "Yup, that is one nasty-looking, slimy mosquito in that ice cube. I bet that it's been melting in your Kool-Aid and you've been drinking dead mosquito juice. Dead mosquito juice will make you act real buggy and itchy."

After I said that, both Marie and Jessica acted like they were going to gag. Marie also started to scratch her head and arms. Ran and Biscuit were laughing so hard that they had to leave the kitchen and go out into the back yard.

"You know that if you drink dead mosquito juice, your eyes will get big and buggy and you nose will grow out to about a foot long," I added with a laugh.

"You did this!" Marie blurted out.

"Nope, you made the ice cubes, Marie," I replied. "You really need to wash out the ice tray before you make ice cubes, in order to make sure that bugs don't get frozen in the ice cubes."

GARY S. EDELEN

Marie and Jessica started to gag again. "Give me that ice cube so I can show Mom," Marie said.

"Can't do that," I said. "Seems like the ice cube has melted and the mosquito must have flown back outside." Marie had not seen me hand the fake mosquito ice cube back to Biscuit. "I think that you had better clean up this mess before Mom gets home."

"You need to clean it up," Marie said.

"Nope, you made the mess, so you get to clean it up."

"Well, I'm going to tell Mom that you put a mosquito in my ice cube and caused this mess," she said.

"That's fine with me, and you can explain to her why Jessica was in here and you doused her with Kool-Aid."

Marie just gave me a dirty look and finally said, "Jessica, will you help me clean this up?"

Finally, Sam, who had gotten up off of the floor, asked if he could have another cookie, since his cookie had been soaked with Marie's dead mosquito juice. Marie smacked Sam on the back of the head and told him to help her and Jessica clean up the kitchen. I just walked out and joined Ran and Biscuit. It was time to head out for a while. Mission accomplished!

It was not long before we ended up at our perch outside of the ballpark where we liked to watch the softball games. It was just on the other side of the left-field fence. It was a shady place, and since it was kind of wooded, no one ever bothered us there. It was a great place to watch the softball games too, because we felt kind of special, since we could see the games but the people in the stands couldn't see us.

Today had started out pretty good, and it had given us much to talk about. Of course, someone had to dampen our outlook. Moose had met up with us and said that his parents were going out shopping for back-to-school stuff. That phrase is one of the most hated things that you never ever want to hear when you're

158

out of school for summer vacation. The thought of back to school made me shiver. Then I got to thinking about Lori Ann Lake. She was so pretty. I guess that she was about the only thing that made it worth my time to go to school. Well, maybe not. Nothing made the idea of going to school sound attractive to me, not even Lori Ann. I knew that Principal Pennyberry would be just waiting for me to walk in the front doors. I was going to be guilty before I even did anything. I was always found guilty even before I did anything, as far as Miss Pennyberry was concerned. I didn't think that it would be fair to hold anything over me for my little innocent pranks from the last day of school last year, anyway. Heck, maybe she had not even noticed that I had glued her yardstick to the top of her bookcase last May.

I should have been proclaimed a hero for putting an end to that feared yardstick. It had tanned many a hide around that school, and I could speak with a bunch of authority on that very subject. Maybe she had figured out that I was the one who poked a leak in her cartridge pen last year. It was a slow leak, but I remember how it had leaked out on top of all of the papers on her desk when she laid it down and left her office for a while. It leaked out all over a bunch of report cards and created a big mess. My only regret was that my report card was not in the pile and didn't get messed up. I should have thought that one out a little better. A couple of my grades could have used some messing up before my mom got to see them.

Maybe Miss Pennyberry had discovered the reason that her office had come to smell so bad. Right before the school year ended, I thought that the left-over tuna fish salad would be a good fertilizer for her resurrection lily that she kept in her office. I mean, about a pound of tuna fish salad buried into her plant was supposed to work as a good fertilizer, wasn't it? Well, that is my story and I am sticking with it. I was just trying to help make God's green little Earth a little greener. But then, maybe she had not been able to pin anything on me. I doubt that. I think that she blamed me for any unsolved things, just on general principle.

Well, anyway, Lori Ann would be in my class again, and maybe this year I would get to sit next to her. She sure was cute with her long brown hair and her pretty brown eyes.

"Not too much longer until *The Tall Texan Wild West Show* comes to town," Ran announced.

That popped me right out of my thoughts about returning to school in the fall and also my thoughts about Lori Ann. "Yup, he'll be here soon," I agreed.

"Yup, he is one tall cowboy, and all of the bad guys are afraid of him," Mortie said.

"Well, if you just think how tall he is, you would be afraid of him too if you were a bad guy," I told Mortie. "His feet almost touch the ground as he rides his brave horse, Firestorm. Heck, he almost never even has to get off of old Firestorm when he catches up with the bad guys. He just takes out his trusty lasso and six shooter and then they always give up."

"He's probably about eight feet tall and tough as steel," Mortie added. "I wouldn't want to mess with him, EVER!"

"Well, we'll just have to wait until the State Fair," I said. "The bad thing is that he doesn't appear until the last night of the State Fair, and we have to go to school the very next day. That is just about as unfair and it can be. The pope should make a pope rule that Catholic schools do not have to go to school the day after the last day of the State Fair.

"I would vote for that," Biscuit said.

"You don't get to vote on pope rules," I said. "Only the pope gets to vote on pope rules, and he always wins all pope rules with his pope votes. Everyone knows that. Every time that they pick a new pope, he gets to make a new pope rule about something. That's why they burn white smoke out of the chimney in the Vatican when they elect a new pope. The head pope picker, the guy who picks out the pope, only puts white paper in the fireplace so that it will only let out white smoke to tell everyone that he is done picking and he has picked out a new pope and the new pope will be coming out soon. The white smoke also tells everyone that the new pope will be wearing white, so everyone knows who to be looking for. If he was going to be wearing black pope clothes, the pope picker would be burning old newspapers in the fireplace, because the black ink makes black smoke, and the people would be looking for a pope wearing black."

"I saw a picture of the pope, but he was dressed in red," Mortie said.

"Nope, that wasn't the pope," I said. "That was a cardinal. There are a bunch of cardinals, and they all have to wear red so you can pick them out in a crowd. Cardinals are pope trainees. When they have to get a new pope, all of the cardinals have to take the train to Rome, where the pope picker picks the new pope from one of the cardinals at a pope convention."

"What color outfit does the pope picker wear?" Ran asked.

"He's gotta wear both black and white, like a referee uniform, cuz he's kinda like a referee, and all of the pope trainees need to know that he's the guy in charge," I said.

"Maybe if the pope comes to our church, we can tell him that he needs to make a new pope rule about no school the day after the State Fair," Ran said.

"He won't be coming here," I said.

"How do you know that?" Ran asked.

"Simple," I said. "The pope is always an Italian guy, and Italian guys only like to eat Italian food, except for fish on Fridays. They like to eat fish sandwiches on Fridays, and they like hush puppies with their fish sandwiches. Well, we also don't have enough Italian restaurants around here. Sometimes the pope wants his fish sand-wich cooked at an Italian restaurant to remind him of home when he travels away from Italy. On top of that, there aren't very many fish places around here in the first place, so it would be hard for the pope to get his fish sandwich and hush puppies. They might have to send the bishop down to the Ohio River to catch a catfish for the pope's fish sandwich if the fish restaurant was closed. We have a cheeseburger restaurant across the street, but all they serve are cheeseburgers and fried chicken. Popes don't eat cheeseburg-ers or fried chicken, so he wouldn't be coming here."

"What about the nuns?" Biscuit asked. "He could eat nun cooking. I bet they learn how to cook pope food when they're in nun training. They might even be able to cook the catfish for the pope's fish sandwich."

"Are you kidding?" I asked. "Have you ever seen a nun cook anything, ever? I don't think that they're even allowed in the cafeteria at lunchtime during school. They have to eat bread and drink holy water all of the time. They don't even do their own cooking over at their convent. They have some lady that comes in and cooks their bread and probably their fish on Fridays for them."

"Nope, I think that they get their fish from the fish fry," Ran said.

"Yeah, I forgot about the fish fry on Friday nights. That's prob-ably why we have the fish fry, so the nuns have something to eat on Fridays," I said. "I don't even think they get any type of training about cooking when they're in nun school."

"Guess that the pope won't be stopping by then," Ran said.

"Well, whachawanna do later on after supper?" Mortie asked.

"Well, there should be a softball game tonight, but I'm not scheduled to work any of them. Stubby got to do all of the games tonight," I said.

"Maybe we can mess with Stubby some more," Mortie said.

"Maybe, but we'll see," I said. "Maybe we'll get lucky and they'll have some of the women's softball games tonight. Maybe the Peachtree Baptist Church will be playing tonight, and that real beautiful pitcher, Marlene Modelle, will be pitching. She is s-o-o-o-o pretty. Maybe!"

Chapter 19
MARLENE MODELLE

Well, the day had gone pretty good, and I guess that it carried on over to the night. We really didn't have anything real important to do that night, so after meeting at our special spot, just outside the ballpark by left field, we decided to watch the games. Actually, the choice was easy to make, because right after we got there, the teams started to arrive for the first game. It was the women's softball league night, and with a little bit more good luck, the Peachtree Baptist Church softball team with their beautiful pitcher, Marlene Modelle, would be playing. However, they definitely were not going to be playing in the first game.

It's always fun to watch the women play softball. They really are pretty good softball players. Now they might not be able to hit the ball over the outfield fence, but they could knock it all the way out to the fence, and they were a lot better to look at than the men when they were running the bases … well, at least most of them were.

The first game was between two teams that I didn't remember seeing before. The women were okay looking, but they were definitely not in the same "good looks" league as the Peachtree Baptist team. Their shortstop, however, was the best-looking gal on the team, and she was pretty, pretty, pretty. She reminded me of an older version of Lori Ann Lake. Now Lori Ann is very pretty, so when I say that this shortstop was pretty, she was really pretty. I mean really p-r-e-t-t-y. I even thought about talking to her after the game. I normally don't flirt with older women, and I guessed that the pretty shortstop was around eighteen years old, which definitely made her an older woman. The more I thought about it, the more I wanted to get to know her a little better. Heck, she could have a younger, pretty sister. I was pretty sure that getting to know her better was exactly what I was going to do.

Then, right before the game started, my plans came to a screeching halt. As the players were going to the dugout to start the game, I saw the little pretty shortstop pause at the gate by the dugout that exited to the stands. Some guy that was about three times bigger than me leaned through the gate and gave her a kiss on the cheek. I heard him say that it was for good luck. Well, it wasn't lucky for me. I mean, he was a monster! When I say that he was about three times bigger than me, I don't mean that he was fat. I mean that he was a football lineman-type big! His arms were bigger than my legs. She looked like a tiny ballerina on her toes next to him. What was worse, he had a flattop haircut. Only dunces and dumb athletes wear flattops anymore. I bet that if I could have stood him on his head, he wouldn't have fallen over, because his flattop was so flat. His hair had to have about a quart of grease in it to make it stand up that way. If he ever ran low on oil in his car, he could just pull over and squeeze some of that oily slop out of his hair and drip it straight into the engine.

He was not even good looking, not that I'm an authority on good looking guys, but having the body of a bus and the face of a Mack truck is not good looking. His girlfriend was supposed to look like Tankette, not the pretty little shortstop. Oh, Tankette is a girl who lives around here. She is big and tough! I heard that she eats buckshot for breakfast. Even most of the guys around here are afraid to mess with Tankette, because she could whip the snot out of just about all of them. Hmm, she might even be able to whup Mr. Flathead Flatop, the big goon. Well, this guy should be dating Tankette and leaving the pretty little shortstop for me. I just knew that she would be much better off getting a good luck kiss from me than the barfy, flathead, flattop goon. If he had a car, I bet that it was called the Goonmobile.

Oh well, the pretty little shortstop would just never know what she was missing out on, or at least that was what I told myself. I would just have to sit and admire her … um … athletic abilities from our perch.

I decided to drown my sorrows in a frosty malt cup and watch the game. Actually, the game was pretty good. The left fielder was running to scoop up a low line drive right in front of us, and when she stretched to reach for the ball, her shorts ripped right up the back! She was also pretty cute, and when that happened, all of us just about fell off of the log we were sitting on. It was like a little bit of heaven had been revealed to us right then and there. None of us wanted to spoil the moment by yelling out, lest she realize that we were back there admiring the view, and oh what a view it was! I think that my pulse had gone into overdrive! As soon as the play was over, time was called, and as she ran to the dugout, she made sure that her glove was covering up the rip in the back of her softball shorts. She was replaced by a very big left fielder. I don't mean that she was fat or anything, she was just pretty daggone big and mean-looking to top it off. We all agreed that under no circumstances did we want her softball shorts to rip up the back. I knew that if that happened, we would be blinded for life. We all agreed that the rip up the back of the first left fielder's softball shorts was going to be the highlight of the game. Heck, it would probably be the highlight of the night. It dawned on me that this was definitely an offense that I would have to confess to Father Taurman when I went back to school and was marched back to the confessional once again. That should keep the old buzzard from dozing off in the confessional, for awhile.

As it turned out, the pretty little shortstop's team lost by one run. I watched the goon put his gorilla arm around her and try to console her. He looked like King Kong holding that pretty blonde-headed lady in the movies. I know that she had to be putting on an act to look like she was enjoying it. Only a blind female gorilla in heat could find the goon attractive. It almost made me puke! I wished that there had been a foul ball that popped up and over the fence by the street during the game. It would have been nice for it to hit the roof of the Goonmobile and leave a dent. But that didn't happen. As I watched them walk toward what had to be the Goonmobile, I thought that maybe she had vision problems to be hooked up with a goon like him. She would have had to. But then, if she had vision problems, how did she get a couple of hits? I chalked it up to blind luck. Blind luck … not bad!

About this time, Moose and Mortie came running through the woods behind left field to join us. "Where have you guys been?" I asked.

"We snuck under the fence behind the scoreboard," Mortie said. "Just watch Stubby when he gets back to his seat on the scoreboard for the next game."

"What did you guys do?" I asked.

"Well, you know how Stubby always goes over to the concession stand between games to load up on candy and stuff?" Mortie asked. "Well, we wanted to sweeten the pot for him."

"You mean sweeten his pot," Moose said with a laugh.

"Yeah, sweeten his pot," Mortie agreed. "Well, we took a bottle of the dark Karo syrup and spread it all over the box that he sits on during the games. The box is dark, so you really can't see the dark syrup that we spread all over the box lid."

"There will be a whole new meaning when his mom calls him her sweetie," Mortie and Moose said between laughs.

"Not bad, I wish I would have thought of it," I said. As I looked out toward the scoreboard, I saw something that was going to make my day! I hadn't seen it during the first game, but the Peachtree Baptist women's softball team had been warming up on the other side of the field. As I looked across the field, I spied her. Yup, there she was—the beautiful Marlene Modelle warming up. She looked as beautiful as ever.

"I, I, I, I need to visit the concession stand," I said as I jumped up, ran over to the concrete block wall by left field, and scurried up, over, and down it. I was going to see if I could arrange to "accidentally" bump into Marlene. I calmed myself down and tried to put on my most cool guy look and appearance as I approached Marlene. Yup, she was bound to notice me. Her team had just finished warming up, and they were getting ready to take the field. No turning back now and no stopping me. I was a man on a mission! Marlene was the woman of my dreams! Nothing was going to stop me—that is, until I ran into a major roadblock.

The roadblock had a name, and the name was Stubby. Stubby had come running around the bleachers from the other side and ran flat into me at full speed. Now, Stubby was not THAT big, but he was compact and he did outweigh me by quite a bit. When I say that he ran into me… well, that is not the whole story. When he ran into me, he was running so fast that he ran over me, knocking both of us over and under the bleachers. It was like getting hit by a two-ton wrecking ball and then having it land on you. "What in the heck are you doing, Stubby?" I yelled.

"Gotta get to the concession stand before they run outta popcorn," he said.

"They never run out of popcorn," I yelled back.

"No, the fresh-popped popcorn! I wanna get it before they run out, or I'll have to wait until after the next game to get any," he said.

When I finally got that blabbering, walking, gobbling blob off of me, I looked around, only to see Marlene walking through the gate toward the dugout. My plans had gone up in a cloud of smoke! Nope, they had gotten flattened in a cloud of dust made by a starving, charging rhino. Oh well, I might as well go back and watch the game with the guys over in the woods by left field.

"What did you do and where did you go?" Ran asked.

"I was going to introduce myself to that pretty blonde pitcher for Peachtree Baptist team," I said.

"Well, what did she say?" Ran asked.

"Didn't get to talk to her. I ran into Stubby, or should I say that he ran into me at full steam, and that ended the meeting right there."

"You got Stubby-ized!" said Mortie.

"He must have been going to get something to eat," Ran said.

"Yeah, I think that he was in 'food heat' and the drive overpowered any good sense that he had," I said.

"Stubby only has two senses—eat and poop, and you don't ever want to get in the way of either one," Mortie chimed in.

"Never did like him much and now I really don't like him at all," I said.

"Well, that's too bad, but stick around, because look over there where Stubby's crossing the outfield heading for the scoreboard,"

Ran said as he pointed the way. "I think that Stubby is gonna be caught up in a real sticky situation real soon."

While the guys were waiting for Stubby to make it over to the scoreboard, I looked over to our side of the field to see who the Peachtree Baptist team was playing. I immediately got a little bit nervous. The Sixth Street Baptist Church women's softball team was warming up. The Sixth Street Baptist had a team that was very good. Everyone on their team was B-I-G. Their arms were bigger than my legs, and they were very hairy arms at that. They had builds that would have made Mr. Thunklebuster, our football team's coach, very envious. Any one of them could have played offensive guard or tackle. As a matter of fact, I think that I had heard somewhere that a couple of them may have been wrestlers from the professional women's wrestling circuit. They were downright scary. They didn't just beat the teams that they played— they murdered them! I think that they could have beaten a whole bunch of the men's softball teams that played here. If they couldn't have beaten them on the diamond, it was an even bet that they could whup a lot of the men's teams in the boxing ring or on the wrestling mat, or just out back in the alley. They were just plain super scary. They had those ugly dark uniforms that just looked mean. I bet that they never washed them. They even had hairy legs, the ones who wore shorts. I didn't like them much. Nope, I didn't like them at all. However, the Peachtree Baptist's players all looked like beauty queens and wore bright, good-looking uniforms. Both teams were undefeated.

After Peachtree Baptist took the field to start the game, I noticed Stubby starting to take a seat on the box on the scoreboard. I quickly got everyone's attention and pointed at Stubby. Just like Mortie and Moose had planned, Stubby had climbed up to his perch on the scoreboard, and since his hands were full of popcorn and candy, he didn't even notice the Karo syrup on the box as he sat down. At first when he sat down, he didn't do anything, kinda just like everything was okay, and he started eating his popcorn. A few seconds later, he started to frown and wiggle a little bit. Then he put his popcorn and candy down. He stood up to scratch his botchacooka and when he did, he brought up his hand in front of his face. He frowned and then sniffed his hand. He had rubbed it in the Karo syrup that was on the back of his pants from when he sat in the sticky stuff. Next, he then wiped the back of his pants with his other hand. Now both hands were sticky. After sniffing both hands this time, he started to lick his hands. I guess that he liked the Karo syrup. We couldn't hear him from where we were sitting and could only imagine what he was saying or thinking. Next, we watched as he climbed back down off of his scoreboard perch and went behind the scoreboard. He then sat down in the grass and started to scoot around on his botchacooka in an apparent effort to wipe the Karo syrup off of the back of his pants.

"He had better be careful about sliding his rear end across the ground back there," Ran said. "There are a ton of fire ant nests back there."

When Stubby got up, the back of his pants looked like a mass of grass that had been uprooted and glued to his botchacooka. We were rolling on the ground and laughing at him.

Stubby finally gave up and climbed back onto the scoreboard, but this time he sat down next to the box that the Karo syrup had been spread upon. He dabbed his finger in the Karo syrup on the box lid and then licked his finger. He did this a couple of times. It didn't take long before he started wiping his popcorn kernels across the box top in the Karo syrup and then eating each and every sticky kernel. It ended up being one of the best pranks that we had ever pulled on dear old Stubby.

About that time, we heard the umpire call "Batter up!" It was going to be a good game and a close one too. Marlene pitched a great game, only giving up a couple of walks, but one of them had led to a score when the umpire had called three more walks in a roll. She had gotten the first two batters thrown out at first base before the four walk calls in a roll. With the score now 1-0 in favor of Sixth Street Baptist, Marlene finally got out of the inning by getting the final batter to hit a pop fly for the final out of the inning.

Even in a tight game like that, Marlene never showed any sign of fear. I watched as she just brushed back her hair and tucked her glove under her arm as she left the pitchers' mound. She looked like a Greek goddess. I have never seen a Greek goddess in person, but I have it on good authority that they are supposed to be real pretty, so if I met one, I bet that she would look just like Marlene. She seemed to know that she was going to win, and I knew it too.

The Sixth Street Baptist pitcher was really pretty lucky, because I think that the umpires were all Sixth Street Baptist Church parishioners. Someone had really stacked the deck for them. The pitcher looked like a tough cookie. I gave her the nickname "Gronk," because she looked like a gronk. Not sure what a gronk looks like, but she looked like one anyway. She was the meanest looking member of her team. I think that while she was on the pitcher's mound, she had chewing tobacco in her mouth, because I saw her spit a bunch of times.

Well, it came down to the bottom of the last inning. The score was 1-0 in favor of the Sixth Street team. Peachtree Baptist Church had the final "at bat." Gronk must have been getting tired, because she finally gave up a single to the third batter of the inning. She had gotten the first two batters to hit pop fly outs. The hit seemed to make her really mad, and I was glad that I was not the batter facing her. Just the look that she was now giving the next batter was enough to give me cold chills. She kind of reminded me of that really mean professional wrestler, Mangling Max. He even bit people. I bet that she bit people too.

Anyway, the next batter ended up hitting a bunch of foul balls into the stands. This didn't do anything to make Gronk get into a better mood. She seemed to be getting even madder. After a whole bunch of pitches and a lot of foul balls, the batter ended up getting on base because she got hit by the pitch. I think that the hit was intentional, but the umpire who had been giving Gronk good calls all night long didn't have a choice other than to send the batter to first base when she got hit. I guess that was a lucky break, but it looked like the pitch hurt the batter a little. She looked a little dazed when she trotted out to first base.

Now Marlene was up to bat. Beautiful Marlene was facing off against the ugly Gronk. I was sitting on the edge of the log in the woods next to the left-field fence. I couldn't see the look on Marlene's face as she stared at Gronk, but I know that it must have been a fearless look. Yup, fearless and beautiful. I just knew that she would never back down from Gronk. It was the Beauty and the Beast on the softball field.

Marlene fouled the first pitch out into the street past third base. Everyone could see Gronk laugh and taunt Marlene after the foul ball. Marlene just stepped back up to the plate, took her normal two practice swings, placed the bat up over her right shoulder, and cocked her arm for the next pitch. She looked so pretty and unafraid out there facing Gronk.

The second pitch had the same result, except this time when the ball landed, everyone heard a loud THUNK as it hit a car parked on the street. I hoped that it had been one of the Sixth Street Baptist fans' cars, maybe even Gronk's car. I know that is not a Christian thought, but this was a serious matter, and no time to be nice.

Marlene was down 0-2. Now Gronk really started her taunting and telling Marlene that she might as well save the embarrassment and just swing for the final strike and end the game. Again, I saw

Marlene bring her bat around in her two practice-swing warm up swings that I had seen so many times before. Marlene never said a word, but I could tell that she was determined to win this show-down with Gronk. Even from the side, I could tell that Marlene had no fear—only determination and confidence. She was not going to be beaten by this barbarian bozo bulldozer lookalike.

Then Gronk threw the pitch. I could see Marlene rear back while taking aim to hit the ball. She looked so beautiful when she reared back to hit the ball. Anyway, as the ball arrived at the plate, Marlene brought the bat around, and everyone in the park, probably in all of Louisville, heard the impact of her bat as it met the ball. It was a long, hard, fast line drive just out of range of the left-field player's outstretched glove. The base runners had imme-diately taken off as the bat made contact. They were going all out to get at least one base runner across home plate.

It was then that I noticed that the path of the ball was headed straight for us and not slowing down one bit! Now, I wasn't worried about getting hit by the ball, because the fence protected us. Just then, another one of my flashes of brilliance struck me. This was a time that demanded my quick thinking and quick actions! "Quick! Mortie and Biscuit! Grab the ball when it rolls up to the fence!"

Mortie and Biscuit jumped into action immediately. I glanced over to the infield and saw Marlene approaching first base as the other two base runners were rounding second and third bases. At the same time, I saw Biscuit pull up on the bottom of the fence, and Mortie reach under the fence. Mortie managed to grab the ball just as the Sixth Street Baptist left fielder grabbed the ball. There was a brief but serious tug of war. However, I figured that since the Peachtree Baptist Church team had to deal with the crooked umpires all night, especially my beautiful Marlene, who had gotten way too many bad pitch calls called against her, it was my duty to even out the odds on the playing field. With the left

fielder bending down to pick up the ball, the umpires and specta-
tors in the stands couldn't see Biscuit and Mortie, especially since
they were in the darkness that was cast down under one of the
advertising signs hanging on the fence above them.

"Hold on for just a second, Mortie," I called out. When I saw
the leading base runner heading for home, I yelled for Mortie to
let the ball go. The left fielder picked up the ball and turned toward
home, only to see the leading base runner crossing home plate and
being closely followed by the second base runner. Marlene was
not only a very good pitcher and hitter, but she could run like the
wind. Marlene was beautiful when she ran. She had just reached
second base at the moment that the left fielder threw the ball in to
the shortstop. It was an easy standup double!

Marlene had delivered when the chips were down, giving the
Peachtree Baptist team the win. Of course, my very minor role as
Marlene's softball guardian angel didn't hurt matters. Heck, the
two base runner probably would have made it across home plate
even if their special guardian angel had not been watching out for
them. Well, maybe. Nevertheless, it was always better to play it
safe, especially given the fact that I thought all of the umpires must
have come from the Sixth Street Baptist Church congregation.

The Peachtree Baptist Church team and all of their fans in the
stands were jumping and yelling with delight. We were pretty
happy ourselves too. Me, I was on cloud nine. I asked Mortie if the
left fielder had said anything to him. He said that she had called
him a name, and he thought that even though he had never heard
it before, he was pretty sure that it must have been a bad name
because of the way that she said it. Since that was the final game
of the night, we were able to march on into the ballpark to soak
up some of the celebration. Everyone patted Marlene on the back
and called her a hero. She was a hero, my beautiful Greek Goddess

hero. I wanted to tell her that I had helped her out but thought better of it.

About that time, I saw the Sixth Street Baptist team's left fielder and her coach arguing with the umpire and pointing to the left field grass. Someone near me also saw that and asked what they were arguing about. I told him that I thought it had something to do with the grass needing to be cut or the sun getting in her eyes. I almost messed up on that explanation, because it had been a night game.

It was finally time for me to introduce myself to Marlene. This was it! Once again, I decided to walk right up to Marlene and tell her just how much I liked her game, among other things. There she was, standing right over in front of the concession stand, soft drink in hand. This was my moment! Nothing would stop me this time. I straightened out my hair with my hand, dusted off my shirt and shorts, put on my cool guy look and started to walk straight for her.

Then all of a sudden, out of nowhere, WHAM! I found myself flat on my back again, seeing stars instead of Marlene. Stubby had come flying across the field straight from the scoreboard. We had both reached the gate from the infield to the stands at the same time. However, Stubby was running like a guy whose hair was on fire. Actually, as I later found out, his botchacooka was on fire. It appears that when he was dragging his botchacooka across the ground, he dragged it over a nest of fire ants. They must have gotten stuck in the Karo syrup. No matter anyway, because enough of them had crawled into his pants that they had begun biting him in very tender places. He was screaming, "Ants biting my butt!" as he charged through the crowd. He didn't even stop to collect his pay from Steve, and that never ever happened.

I regained my footing only to see Marlene walking out onto the street, surrounded by her teammates. The love of my life was driving off into the sunset! Once again, Stubby had wrecked my plans. There was nothing more that I could do. I just sighed. After a round of frozen malt cups for the four of us, we decided to call it a night.

Chapter 20
BIRD WATCHING

"Scott, my bicycle just won't keep air in the tires. The tires are in real good shape, and I have taken the bicycle tubes out and checked them twice, but they still won't hold air," Sam said. "I don't know what I'm supposed to do now."

It was still kinda early in the day, and I really didn't feel like fooling around with my little brother, but since I kinda was somewhat responsible for his problem, I felt that maybe I should talk to him. "When you took the tubes out, did you put the whole tube in a bucket of water, and did you make sure that it had some air in it when you stuck in under water?" I asked.

"Yeah, and there weren't any bubbles coming up in the water," he answered.

"Did you have the valve stem under the water too?"

"Yeah, I had the tube and the valve stem completely under water. I had filled up the big metal tub that we give Troubles a bath in to test the tubes."

"Well, what did you do after putting the tube back into the tire and then pumping it up with air?"

"I rode the bike up to the Texaco station and let all of the bad air out like you taught me to do, then I got the Texaco man to fill the tires up with Texaco air."

"Well, there's your problem. What kind of bike do you have?"

"It's a Western Auto Western Flyer."

"Sam, everyone knows that all Western Auto Western Flyer bicycles won't hold Texaco air. Texaco air only works for Schwinn bicycles. You have to use Phillips 66 air for a Western Auto Western Flyer bicycle! Gee whizz, Sam, do I have to tell you everything?"

"Oh, I didn't know that. I'll pump up the tires right now and then ride over to the Phillips 66 station, let the bad air out, and then get the Phillips 66 guy to put new Phillips 66 air in my tires for me. Thanks, Scott," he said as he started to run out to the garage out back to pump up his tires.

"Hold on, Sam," I called. "My advice didn't come for free."

"Whacha mean?"

"Well, my advice comes with a price."

"I don't have any money. Marie has all of the money around here, but she won't give me any money unless I play her stupid girl games with her and her friends," he moaned.

"Well, I think that we can work out a deal," I said. "This is my week to clean the kitchen every night. I think that if you take over my week cleaning up the kitchen chores for the rest of the week, that will be suitable payment."

"A suitable payment," he said. "Does that mean that I have to wear a suit when I clean the kitchen?"

"No, that's a saying like, 'that would be a fair payment.'"

"Good, because I don't have a suit, and I don't like dressing up. But I don't think that it's fair cleaning up the kitchen for the rest of the week, and next week is MY week to clean up the kitchen. That means that I would be cleaning up the kitchen every night for almost two weeks in a row. I don't think that's fair."

"Well, just think about all of the times that you've come running to me to fix your problems, and I always fix them for you now, don't I?"

"Yeah, but for a price."

"Well, yes, my time, knowledge, and experience do come at a cost, and it's always far less than what you would have to pay to someone else to get your problems fixed. Now do you want to run the risk of having the next time that you have a problem or an emergency and you need my help, and you come to me for help, but I decide that I'm not gonna help you because you don't think that it's fair to have to pay me to help you?"

"Well, okay, I guess that you're right," Sam mumbled.

"Then it's a deal," I said.

"It's a deal," Sam replied.

As Sam went off to get ready to take his bicycle to Phillips 66 for some good air, I turned away and smiled to myself. I thought that I really should not have charged him for my advice. I guess that I felt that way because I had been letting most of the air out of his bicycle tires most every night for a couple of weeks now. Then I came back to my senses. Nope, little brothers are born so that big brothers can take advantage of them. It kinda makes up for some of the torment that they cause their big brothers. That was Sam's purpose in life. I decided that it was time to run over to Ran's house in order to plan out our day.

"Hey Ran, whachawanna do today?" I asked.

"I dunno. Whachawanna do, Scott?"

"I dunno, but I wanna do something worthwhile."

About that time, Biscuit and Moose were walking up the street, and as they got close, they yelled out to us. "Hey, ya'll, whacha doin today?"

"I dunno. Whacha ya'll doin?"

"We're goin' over to Miss Bloatwig's house," Biscuit answered as he fooled around with one of the two pairs of binoculars he was carrying. "She is one mean old lady, and she hates everyone."

"She even hates cheeseburgers," Ran said.

"How do you know that?" I asked.

"Well, she is mean, and she does seem to hate everything that's good, so that means that she probably just has to hate cheeseburgers, because they are super good," Ran explained.

"Yeah, guess so. It does make sense," I said. "Still, why in the world do you all want to go see her?"

"Who said anything about going to see her?" Moose said. "We're going to her house … or really, going behind her house. You know that she lives next door to the Quarry Swim Club, up on the ridge, right behind the main building, and there is a little bushy area behind her garage that looks right down over everything. Well, Mortie and I found a way to get there by sneaking behind a bunch of garages and back yards, in order to be able to get to that spot behind her garage. We were over there the other day, but today we brought binoculars so we could get a better view of the sights."

"Now that sounds interesting," Ran said. "My dad has a really good pair of binoculars, and I'm sure he wouldn't mind me borrowing them for a little bit."

Watching pretty girls in bathing suits sounded interesting to me. I finally said that I thought we all needed to explore this new observation point that looked over the Quarry Swim Club, so that we could make sure that no one was drowning.

About this time, Mortie came out with his dad's binoculars, along with a second pair of binoculars. "Are we gonna go bird watching today?" he asked.

Biscuit replied, "Yeah, we're gonna be watching a bunch of chicks!"

Well, it didn't take long to get to this new observation point, although it did take a little bit of climbing and sneaking behind all of those peoples' houses to get there. It was perfect and even better than I had expected. If you were down in the Quarry Swim Club, there was no way that you could have looked up and been able to see us. We sat under a bunch of big honeysuckle bushes. The bushes just bent out and were full of leaves and honeysuckles. Underneath, we had a lot of room to sit down and peek out to see the views below. The pool was already really crowded.

"Hey, look at all of the girls in bikinis," Biscuit said.

"Those aren't bikinis," I said. "They're two pieces."

"No, they are bikinis," Biscuit responded.

"Biscuit, they only have bikinis in Florida and California, where all of the really cute, suntanned girls live. They don't have bikinis in Kentucky, because we are located above the bikini zone on the weather map that you see on TV," I said.

"Well, I don't care what you call them, but they sure look good to me," he replied.

"Hey, Scott, there's Lori Ann Lake," Moose said.

"Gimme those binoculars," I said as I yanked the binoculars away from Moose, almost strangling him with the binocular strap in the process.

Yes, there she was, sitting out on her beach towel in her beautiful orange two-piece bathing suit, with her beautiful, long brown hair hanging down over her beautiful shoulders, while hiding her beautiful brown eyes behind her beautiful sunglasses. She was just about the most beautiful girl that I had ever laid eyes on, I thought.

Well, Lori Ann and Marlene. But Marlene was not there and Lori Ann was. *Hmm, that would be a tough choice*, I thought.

"Hey, Scott, you're about to melt my binoculars," Moose said. "Can I have my binoculars back now?"

"Yeah, just one more minute," I said. Here I was, the guy of her dreams, and she didn't realize it. Well, she had not dreamed that dream yet, I guess. I finally gave the binoculars back to Moose.

"Hey, the lenses are all steamed up," Moose said.

"That ain't all that is steamed up," I said.

All of a sudden, I heard Mortie say, "Hubba hubba hubba!"

We all looked over at Mortie. He was sitting there, staring out through his binoculars with a huge smile on his face. He finally said with a big grin," I think that the moon is going to be out all afternoon today."

"Whacha talking about?" I asked.

We all looked to see what he was looking at, but he was not looking anywhere close to any of the swimming pools. "Whacha looking at, Mortie?" Ran asked.

"Heaven, I think that I can see heaven," Mortie answered.

By that time, we were all really confused. "I think that he must have banged his head on a tree limb or ledge while climbing up here," Ran said.

"He's acting really weird," Biscuit chimed in.

"I think that he's been in the sun too long," Moose said.

I looked at Moose and said, "We have been sitting under this honeysuckle bush in the shade with a really good breeze. The sun is not even hitting him."

"Maybe it's something that he ate," Ran said.

"He looks like he's in a trance," I said.

"Yes, I am in a trance, a beautiful trance that I never want to end," Mortie replied.

Finally, Ran said, "Mortie what's the matter with you? Tell me or I'll tell Dad that you borrowed his binoculars without asking."

"Okay," Mortie finally said with a sigh. "You guys see that third window on the second floor over the concession stand down there?"

"Yeah, those are the … WOMEN'S DRESSING ROOM windows," I blurted out.

"Yeah, you got it now," Mortie answered.

Then we all began to fight over the three pairs of binoculars, with Ran, Biscuit, and I ending up with the three pairs.

"Wow, you can see right in there, sorta" Biscuit exclaimed.

This was too good to be true, but it was real and happening right now. We could see legs and feet that appeared to be walking in and out of what we guessed was a shower area. "Come closer to the window, little ladies," we all begged together. We implored them to walk right over to the window, but they always seemed to just stop short.

"They know that we're watching them, and they're teasing us," Mortie said.

"No, they're not. They can't even see us up here," I said.

Someone was bound to walk right next to the window, we all thought. It was a dream come true for all of us. Darn it, now I had another thing that I would have to tell Father Taurman about in the confessional when I returned to school. Maybe I could water the story down so he wouldn't understand it. I mean, he is a priest, and priests only look at nuns, anyway, and looking at nuns will just … I would rather look at a cold waffle or something.

Well, we sat there for what seemed like hours, begging the girls in the dressing room to walk by the window on their way to get dressed. We all almost fell off of the ledge together when one girl stood in front of the window with her back to us. She was the cheerleading captain of the junior high school cheerleading team. Was she going to change into her bathing suit and go swimming? Maybe this would be it! It was at that point where we all just about lost our footing on our perch as we stretched out to get a better view. However, we all ended up disappointed, because someone threw her a towel and she headed out of sight. We had all come close to having a heart attack—all at the same time! But our dreamed-of vision was not to be.

Right about that time, we heard a growling close behind us. "Does Mrs. Bloatwig have a dog?" I asked.

"Yeah, she has a German shepherd, and he's pretty mean," Moose answered.

"Well, I think that we need to be getting out of here pretty quickly," I said.

"Why?" Biscuit asked, still trying to get a better look into the women's dressing room.

"Because Mrs. Bloatwig's dog is trying to crawl into the honeysuckle bush right behind us and he doesn't look like he's in a very good mood," I said.

"Yikes," Biscuit said, and he was gone and halfway back to the street in about two seconds' time.

Moose and Mortie were the next to leave, and they also left in a pretty big hurry. We couldn't all leave at the same time, because we had to go in single file and climb and squeeze down the path behind the houses and garages. As Ran and I eagerly waited for the other guys to get going, I noticed that the dog was still growling at us, but he wasn't getting any closer. He still looked pretty mean, but I couldn't figure out why he hadn't gotten to us yet.

As I was watching, I finally noticed that there was a wire fence that ran through the honeysuckle bush that kept him on one side and me and Ran on the other side. I tapped Ran on his shoulder and pointed to the fence. I told him to hold up a minute. We sat there and waited for about five minutes before starting to make our way down the path and out to the street.

While we were waiting, I teased the dog, making him bark and growl even more. Then I fished out a couple of my cookies that I had been keeping in my pocket and slid them through the fence to the German shepherd. That changed everything. By the time the German shepherd had eaten all four of my cookies, we were the best of friends. He even let me reach through the fence and pet him behind his ears.

After making friends with the dog, we decided that it was time to head back and join the rest of the guys. When we finally made it to the street and joined the rest of the guys, they asked what had taken us so long. I looked at Ran and then said that the dog had gotten through the honeysuckle bush, and Ran and I were forced to wrestle the dog down. I told them that it was tough wrestling the dog and not getting bitten, but the two of us were too much for the dog. Ran jumped in and said that by the time we got finished with the dog, he had turned tail and run back to the house.

Then Ran and I just strolled right in front of the guys as if we were the toughest guys around—kinda like the Tall Texan.

Speaking of the Tall Texan, I told the guys that for an extra five dollars each, after the Tall Texan Show was over, we could go backstage and actually meet the Tall Texan, Wang Chow KaPow, Chief Thunder Belly, and Princess Running Summer Snowflake.

"Wow, we could actually get to meet them and talk to them!" Biscuit exclaimed.

"Yup, that's right, for as long as we want, or at least until they have to pack up their stuff in their stagecoach and head out to the next State Fair," I said.

"What other State Fairs are you talking about?" Moose asked. "We only have one State Fair a year."

"All of the states have to have a State Fair every year," I explained. "When the Declaration of Independence was signed and the states were set up, each state was required to have a State Fair, so that the people could get together and talk about important stuff once a year. They invented cotton candy at one of the southern State Fairs because they had a bunch of extra cotton sitting around, and they needed something to snack on. They just put some pink colored sugar on the cotton and stuck it on a stick and started selling cotton candy. That's why you always see cotton candy at all of the State Fairs."

"Oh, I always wondered about that," Moose replied. "And I bet that's why they have pony rides at the State Fair too.

"Yup," I said. "In the old days, when our parents were kids, people used to have to ride their ponies to the fair and park them in the pony parking lot. When their kids got grumpy, the parents would take their kids over to the pony parking lot and let the kids ride around on the ponies to shut them up. Now it's just an old custom to let the pony ride company bring their ponies to the State Fairs so that the parents will still have a place to take their kid, where they could shut them up from all of their whining and crying. It still works pretty good. It always shuts up the kids, except for the little babies, because since they are so little, they can't hold on and they keep falling off of the ponies and then yell even more. When that happens, the moms and the dads haveta take turns going out to the parking lot or into the bathrooms and try talking the babies into shutting up. I think that the only way they really can get the babies to shut up is by sticking a bottle in their mouths."

"Hey, back to the Tall Texan," Ran said. "An extra five dollars each is kinda expensive, and I don't know if we can get that much money together by then."

"We already have a pretty good start with our fundraising," I said. I think that if we keep on doing what we have been doing, mostly at the ballpark, we should be able to save enough to be able to buy the backstage tickets. I'll stay on top of it and keep you guys informed."

Later that evening, we all gathered at my house. There were no games down at the ballfield, so we had to come up with something else to do. As we sat there, we watched as a city bus drove by. We all liked the new buses that had been put into service. They were a lot bigger, and they were air conditioned. "Those buses are neat," Mortie said.

"Yeah, I'd like to take a ride on one," Biscuit added.

"Well, all that they do is go downtown, turn around, and then go up to the Loop and turn around, and then go back downtown," I said.

"I'd like to just ride around the neighborhood," said Moose.

"Well, that would be dumb," Ran said. "You would just pay the fare to ride up to the Loop and back. Sounds like a waste of money to me."

Hmm, I thought. *Maybe Moose had a good idea.* I needed to think about it a little bit. The more that I thought about the picture of the new buses, the more an idea seemed to come together in my mind. My street was on the bus route, and the buses came by on a pretty regular schedule until about midnight. Now, I knew that the bus driver wouldn't stop and let us get on and ride through our neighborhood for free. However, if he didn't know that we were even riding, then maybe we could get our free ride. "Hey, Ran, you know that the old buses looked kind of mashed on their back end, right?" I asked.

"Yeah, kind of looks like the bus driver must have backed the bus into a wall or something."

"Well, the new buses don't look like that in the back anymore," I said. "Do you remember that the old buses' back fenders or bumpers were almost flush with the back end of the bus, and the new buses' bumpers stick out about six to eight inches from the back of the bus?"

"Yup, I have noticed that too."

"Now the best that I can remember, the advertising sign on the back of the old buses was in a sign holder that was almost flush against the back of the bus right under the windows across the back, and the new buses have signs and sign holders that stick out at least four to six inches."

"Yup, I think that you're right on that too," Ran said.

"Well, we might be able to hitch a ride around the neighborhood anyway, and ride for free," I told everyone.

"Whatcha mean?" Biscuit asked.

"I think that we could just hop on the back bumper on the new buses and hold onto the sign holder and just ride around the neighborhood as part of the regular bus route."

"Oh yeah," Biscuit replied. "We just stop the bus at the bus stop and tell the bus driver that we want to hop onto the back bumper and take a ride. I don't think that is gonna work."

"Well, it's kinda like that," I responded. "Maybe we don't ask the bus driver, but I think that we could still board the bus at the bus stop. The bus comes down this street right in front of where we are sitting right now. Am I correct so far?"

"Yup," came the unanimous reply.

"Well, when the bus gets down to the end of the street, he has to stop at the stop sign before making his right-hand turn down the next street. Well, old lady Cratcher always leaves her car parked on the street right by that bus stop. I think that when the bus comes down the street and stops at the stop sign, we have enough time to hop onto the back bumper. All that we have to do is watch for the bus to turn down our street and head for the stop sign. We know the bus schedule, so we know when to get ready to hop onto the bus."

"Won't the bus driver see us waiting to hop onto the bus?" Moose asked.

"Nope, he'll never see us. We'll just hide on the sidewalk side of old lady Cratcher's parked car, and when the bus stops, we just run out and hop on. It's that easy, really," I said.

"Okay, let's try it," Ran said.

Well, we waited around, but we really didn't have to wait around that long. Sure enough, Moose and Mortie came running down the street from the other corner." The bus is coming! It just turned onto Norris Place and is heading this way, and it's about six blocks away!" Mortie yelled.

"Okay you all, let's get down to old lady Cratcher's car."

Biscuit and Moose said that they were going to watch us on this one to see if it worked before they tried it. Mortie and Ran were ready to join me on the inaugural first free bus ride through the neighborhood.

We saw the bus pull up to the other end of the street and wait for the traffic to pass before turning down Richmond Drive, our street. The three of us crouched low behind old lady Cratcher's car. Just then, it dawned on me that about right now wouldn't be a good time for her to come out and decide that she needed to go somewhere. Luck was on our side, though. The bus made the turn, motored down the street, and stopped right in front of us, just as I had planned. Actually, it was better than I had planned, because the back end of the bus lined up right even with the end of old lady Cratcher's car, which made it easy to slip away from her car and onto the bus back bumper. Heck, we ended up having a few seconds to spare.

We held on tight as the bus started its slow turn around the corner. We had made it! As we rode down several blocks, we saw some of the neighborhood kids that we knew. We just waved to them as we passed. I guess that we were pretty lucky that none of the parents or neighbors that we knew saw us as we motored by.

As the bus slowed down to turn onto a busy street, we decided that we would hop off and wait for it to return. Since the turn-around at the Loop was nearby, we knew that we wouldn't have to wait long. We could hop back on once the bus left the busy street and stopped at the first stop sign. Sure enough, in about fifteen minutes or so, the bus returned, and we re-boarded it at the designated stop sign. Fortunately for us, there were a bunch of bushes right next to this stop sign that made it really easy for us to hide from the driver and then hop back on.

When we got to my street, we hopped back off of the bus when it came to the stop sign. Moose and Biscuit were sitting on my front porch and asked how the ride had gone. I shushed them up right away. They were sitting on my front porch where my mom or Marie or Sam could overhear them. That would mean big trouble for me!

We all walked down the street together, and then Ran and Mortie started telling the other guys how easy it was to get on the bus and ride around. It had been a bunch of fun, and we couldn't hardly wait for the next bus to come by. There was more than enough room on the back bumper for all of us to hop on.

The days were getting a little bit shorter, making it a little bit darker a little bit earlier now. This worked out great for us. It would be even easier to hide from the bus driver before hopping onto the back bumper and taking a ride. For the next several hours, we repeated our first ride, only by now, Biscuit and Moose had decided to join us. We agreed that we were pretty lucky, because no neighbors or parents ever saw us one single time. Ching-Ching, the paperboy, saw us ride by him and yelled out for us to wait for him, but the bus was already moving down the street. I yelled back to him that we could take him with us another time.

Well, it was getting kinda late, so we decided to call it a night and then get back together tomorrow.

Chapter 21
ENTER KATHY

"Moose, who's the girl with you?" I asked. "You know, we're a guys-only kinda club."

"Hey, Scott, she's my cousin Kathy, and she's staying with us for a while this summer," Moose answered. "I'm supposed to entertain her, so she's gotta hang out with me."

"I dunno know about that," I said.

"Yeah, we don't need a goofy girl hanging out with us," Ran said.

"Who's a goofy girl, brillo head?" Kathy replied to Ran.

"You guys might not want to be messing around with Kathy," Moose said. "She's not an ordinary kinda girl."

"Whacha mean by that?" I asked.

"Well, she plays on all of her school sports teams—the girls' ones, I mean," Moose said. "She can pitch as good as the guys on the baseball team, and she's just kinda got a knack to being good at about anything that she tries."

"Yeah, but I bet she's not so hot when it comes to guy stuff like slingshots and stuff," Ran said.

"Okay, brillo head, find a target and I'll see just how good you're with a slingshot," Kathy called out to Ran.

"I'm not a brillo head! My hair is naturally curly, and some even say that it is wavy."

"Brillo head," snorted Kathy.

Well, Ran was the best slingshot guy around, and nobody ever beat him. We set up a target about thirty feet away. It was an empty paint can, and it would be easy to tell if they could hit it. Ran went first and, as usual, he hit it with all five of his shots. "Let's see you beat that, Miss Goofy Girl," Ran said as he handed his slingshot to Kathy.

Kathy just smirked and took the slingshot. We watched as she took her time gathering up some pebbles from out in the alley. "I think that she's scared," I said to Mortie.

"You may be surprised," Moose commented.

Well, we were surprised when Kathy's first four shots hit the paint can square on. She then looked at Ran and said that it was too easy. We watched as she looked around the alley for a special pebble. Finding a larger pebble, Kathy took aim again. BAM! She not only hit the empty paint can dead on, but she shot it clear off of the stand that we had set it on. "Wow," we all said at once. We could not believe what we had seen.

Moose smiled and said, "I told you so."

"Any more contests, brillo head?" she asked Ran.

"Nope, that was pretty good shooting, if I do say so myself," Ran said.

"Okay, you're in, Kathy," I said. If she was that good at sling-shotting, I just figured that she must be pretty good all around, and she was kinda cute, in an okay for a girl kinda way.

"Where did you learn to shoot like that?" Ran asked.

"It's a long story. I'll tell you sometime," Kathy answered.

I could see that Ran was also impressed by Kathy.

About that time, we heard, "You boys are really goofy looking!"

Here we were not bothering anybody, when up walks a bunch of the goofy girls, and then they start sounding off at us! "What's your problem, you ugly bunch of clucking hens?" I asked.

"We don't have any problems except for you bunch of gross looking boys," replied Margie Zaster, the head clucker.

"Well, Miss Margie Zaster the Disaster, you need to look in a mirror before you say any more. It appears that you must have run your face into a couple of trees on the way over here," I replied.

"We know that we are all quite beautiful young ladies, and we know that deep down inside, you all have a deep desire to be our boyfriends," she said.

"Wrong again, Miss Zaster the plaster face. The only thing that we feel deep inside when we see you all is gas, and I am starting to feel that right about now. Since you're all downwind, you might want to leave right away. The bunch of you are definitely not beauties, and the only way that you could get in a beauty contest was if you all were on leashes in a dog show, and even then you would come in last," I said.

"Well, Mister Goofball, if there was a beauty contest in our neighborhood, we would win it without any questions," she replied.

"What, would you all be the only contestants?" I asked while laughing. "I'll enter my dog, Troubles, and mess you all up when Troubles comes in first."

At that, Ran, Mortie, and Biscuit all burst out laughing. "Woof, woof, woof," we began to call.

"Scott, you may want to hold a beauty contest," Kathy whispered to me. "Go on and set it up. I've got an idea, and I'll tell you about it once you get it set up."

"I'll tell you what, Miss Margie Mirror Breaker, we'll hold a beauty contest, and you can get whoever you want to enter, and I'll bet that you won't win," I said.

"Well, maybe not, if you're judging," she said.

"I'll make you a deal," I said. "I'll get an impartial judge to judge the contest. We can hold it in your back yard during the day. We need to do it while your parents are at work so that they won't try to influence the judge. The winner will get a date to the ice cream parlor with our Mystery Mister Hunky."

"Who is your Mystery Mister Hunky?" she asked.

"Can't tell you, because it's a secret. All I can tell you is that he has become a legend around here this summer. Many stories have been told about Mister Mystery Hunky. What do you say?"

"Is he really a handsome, hunky guy?" she asked.

"Oh, he is as hunky as they come," I said.

"Okay, it's a deal, but I get a day to gather the girls to be in the beauty contest. Since it will be held in my back yard and I have a little built-in swimming pool, I want it to be a swimsuit beauty contest," she said.

"It's not a swimming pool, it's a fish pond," I said.

"I say that it's a swimming pool, and it will be a swimsuit beauty contest."

The thought of seeing these girls in swimming suits made me sick to my stomach, but I finally agreed.

"Will Mister Mystery Hunky be watching the contest?" she asked.

"No, I'll have him there so he can be hooked up with the winner, but he can't see you all before or during the contest, and you all can't see him before or during the contest."

"When is the contest?" she asked.

"Tomorrow at noon," I answered.

"Okay, it's a deal," she said. The bunch of goofy girls giggled and then headed off like a bunch of ugly cackling geese.

"And they wonder why we call them the Goofy Girls' Yippity Yappity Club," I said.

Kathy leaned over to me and whispered that she already knew who to ask to be a contestant in the contest. "I promise you that when she shows up, you will want to make her the winner. Trust me on this one, Scott."

"Who are you gonna get to be Mister Mystery Hunky?" Ran asked.

"None of us," Mortie said.

"I'm leaving town if I have to be Mister Mystery Hunky," Biscuit said. "I would rather have to go and spend an afternoon in Miss Pennyberry's office when she is in a really bad mood than go to the ice cream parlor with any of those pukey girls."

"Hey, I would never do that to any of you guys. However, I do have someone in mind who I would do this to," I said.

"You must really not like that guy, whoever it is," Ran said.

At about the same time, me and Ran smiled at each other and together said, "Stubby!"

"Oh that is too good," said Mortie, "but how are you gonna get him to be Mister Mystery Hunky?"

"Easy," I said. "He's so desperate for a girlfriend that he would be happy to win an ice cream date with an eighty-year-old nun. I'll tell him that we have set him up as the grand prize for a beauty queen swimsuit contest winner. He'll bite on that as soon as the words get out of our mouths."

"He might be better off with an eighty-year-old nun than with one of those goofy girls," Biscuit added.

"Hey, since it's a swimming suit contest, why don't we have Stubby show up in his swimming trunks?" Mortie asked.

"Yeah, we can tell him that he has to wear Speedo trunks, and we can have him wear a mask like the Lone Ranger," Ran said.

"That's perfect," I said.

It didn't take long for me and the guys to find Stubby. He was organizing his candy stash that he kept in his garage. "Hey, Stubby, do I have a deal for you," I said.

When Stubby turned around and saw me, he said, "I don't know about that. Your deals don't seem to work out too good for me, Scott."

"Oh now Stubby, that's not true," I said. "I always have your best interests at heart. I treat you special! Let me tell you about it. We need one of the best looking, most handsome, most well-built guys in the neighborhood … you know, a regular hunk."

Once I said that, Stubby tried to pull in his stomach, flex his flab, and assume a Hollywood look. "That does sound a whole lot like me," he said.

Boy, he must really think pretty highly of himself, I thought. He looked more like Clarabelle from the *Howdy Doody Show*, except with black hair.

"I am pretty hunky, if I do say so myself," he said.

"Yeah, exactly," I said while managing to hold back a laugh.

"What do I get out of it?" he asked.

"Well, none of us qualify, because none of us have your looks," I said with a sigh.

"Yup, that's true," he said.

I heard Ran murmur, "Thank goodness."

"You will get an expense-paid date with the winner of a swim-suit bathing-beauty contest."

"The winner?" he exclaimed.

"Yup, the winner, just you and her," I said. "It will be an all-expenses paid trip to the ice cream parlor of our choice, on any day that you want that we pick out, from a menu selection that will be made public at a time of our choosing."

"It's a deal!" he said.

"Now hold on," I said. "Since it is a swimsuit beauty contest, you have to show up in Speedo swimming trunks, and you will also have to be wearing a mask like the Lone Ranger."

"A mask," he said.

"Yup, because you will be introduced as Mister Mystery Hunky," I said.

"Mister Mystery Hunky," he repeated. "I like it, and I am pretty hunky, if I do say so myself," he said for the second time.

"More like chunky Fred Flintstone," Mortie whispered.

"Yeah, the mask makes it a mystery, and all of the girls like a mysterious hunky man like me," Stubby went on.

I almost blew it right there, but I managed to hold back my big laugh.

"Okay, I'll do it!" he said.

"Fine, we'll come by tomorrow at around eleven thirty in the morning to get you and take you to the contest, but you can't tell anyone about it."

"Okay, and no problem," he said. "Mister Mystery Hunky has spoken! Yeah, hunky me for the girls to see."

The next day, the contest was ready to get started on time. Since the goofy girls hadn't noticed that Moose ran around with us, they agreed that he could be the impartial judge. I had to bribe Moose to agree to do this, because he didn't much like any of the goofy girls one bit.

They had done their best to stack the deck in their favor. They brought in the ugly girls, the skinny girls, the chubby girls, and the girls with braces. I had told Moose that he had to act like every one of the girls was pretty. He said that he didn't know if his acting skills were that good. He said that if he could pull this off, he wanted to receive an Oscar for his acting performance. I told him that I would signal to him by a scratch to my right ear for the contestant who I wanted to win.

All of the girls were prancing out by the fish pond when the final contestant appeared. As soon as I saw her, I knew that we had our winner. Her name was Bertha Blunk. Bertha was not a very friendly person, and I couldn't figure out how Margie Zaster had talked her into entering a swimming suit bathing-beauty contest. She was really trying to stack the deck in her favor by inviting Bertha

Bertha was big, about an inch under six feet tall. She must have weighed about 225 pounds. She threw the shotput on her school track and field team. She had facial hair, and it was rumored that she used chewing tobacco. I don't think that she ever had a boyfriend, because all of the guys were afraid of her. When Moose saw her, he looked real scared. Bertha had a nickname. We called her Tankette—but never to her face, for fear of getting our brains beat out.

As soon as Moose looked at me, I scratched my right ear. He then looked back at Tankette and tried to smile and act like he thought that she was beautiful. I think that he might really deserve an Oscar for this performance. I found out that Kathy had talked Bertha into entering the contest. I was starting to become real impressed by Kathy. We kinda thought alike.

Finally, he had all of the contestants line up. There was only going to be one first-place winner and no second or third place winners. At the same time, on the other side of the garage, we swung the garage door halfway open, just enough so that the contestants couldn't see Mister Mystery Hunky. However, we could see both Stubby and all of the goofy girl contestants, as they were separated by the garage door. Stubby had been ushered out wearing his Speedo swimming trunks and mask. It was not a very nice sight. He was grinning from ear to ear.

There was a hush over the contest as Moose got ready to announce the winner. "I have to announce that this was an easy contest to pick the winner," he said. "Our winner has a degree of beauty that I struggle to define. The words just do not do her justice."

That is an understatement, I thought.

All of the girls were acting giddy about now, even Tankette … I mean, Bertha. "The winner of this year's swimming suit bathing beauty contest is BERTHA!" Moose announced.

The other girls' mouths all dropped almost to the ground, all at the same time.

"Bertha, come over here and claim your date with Mister Mystery Hunky," Moose said.

Stubby was still grinning ear to ear. Then, as Bertha approached the garage door, we swung it open so everyone could see Stubby. We had cued Stubby that when we made that announcement, he was to close his eyes and pucker up. He was more than eager to do so, because in his mind, he was about to have a kiss planted on his face like he had never received before in his life. And that is exactly what happened! Tankette ran over to him, wrapped her arms around him, and planted a kiss that can only be described as … well, it was so yucky that I can't even describe it.

When Stubby opened his eyes, he was filled with terror.

"Come on, Ducky Poo!" Tankette said to Stubby. "We are going to hop into that little pool, and I'm going to let Mister Mystery Hunky tickle my fancy." Tankette had Stubby in her very firm grasp, and she lifted him up and carried him straight to the fish pond. Then she jumped in on top of him.

"Should we throw him a rope or a life preserver?" Ran asked.

"Nope, just leave him to his pleasure … I mean, her pleasure," I said.

The girls didn't know quite what to say, but I bet that was one time they were glad that they were not the winners of a swimsuit bathing-beauty contest.

"Okay, guys, it's time to move on," I said. And move on we did at a pretty fast clip, laughing all the way.

Chapter 22
THE BUS RIDE

A little later, we ended up over at my house. Mom had already made it home from work, so I knew that I had better be on my best behavior. Mom was a pretty good mom, at least that's what I always thought. I mean, since her and my dad had gotten a divorce when I was three years old and he left town, Mom was the only parent around. I kind of compared her to other parents, and she usually measured up pretty good. However, she was pretty strict, at least with me—and my friends too, when they were over at my house.

Of course, since Marie was the only girl and Sam was the baby of the family, they got special treatment. I would hear "Mommy's little girl" or "Mommy's baby boy." Anytime that I heard either one of those phrases, or anything even closely resembling them, I wanted to go puke my guts out. It usually meant that there was going to be trouble ahead for me. And they would just look up at Mom with their little sickening smiles.

Ugh! Mom thought that they were sweet and innocent, but I knew just how mean and evil they really were. Their smiles reminded me of the Venus flytrap plants that I saw in the *Konga* movie the previous year. Those Venus flytraps were pretty until they chomped you and swallowed you. My sinister little sister and her "lead by his nose" little brother were always lurking around, just waiting for any opportunity to rat me out on some tiny little almost-invisible error in my behavior or judgment. The more that I think about it, the more I believe that I didn't have any errors in my behavior or judgment. At least not around them. I bet that they framed me, and the evidence was circumstances evidence, at best!

Anyway, I would have been a lot happier if they had been sold to pirates, especially if I made the sale and got to keep the money. With my luck, the pirates would have returned them for a refund, probably about a half hour later, and then probably sued me for damages. My friends all liked my mom, even though she was pretty strict. As I have said before, they thought that Mom ran our house like a prison camp or a military base. They even started calling her "Sarge," but not to her face. So how did she find out about this nickname? we used to wonder. Marie probably ratted them out, hoping to get them barred from ever coming over to my house.

Well, I was surprised to learn that Mom kinda liked the nickname. She even was able to get her hands on some army sergeant stripes and have them sewn on her white sweatshirt sleeves.

Well, this particular afternoon, we were standing by our back gate in the alley. We had an old wire fence attached to an old wooden gate that always looked like it was about to fall down. Mom was always telling us not to lean on the fence, for fear that it would fall down. Well, as we were all standing back by the gate talking, Mom came out on the back porch and saw us. Biscuit was kind of leaning on the fence. All of a sudden, we heard a loud "GET OFF OF THAT FENCE!"

Biscuit jumped straight up into the air and came to land in the middle of the alley, all in one jump! It was my mom telling Biscuit to quit leaning on the fence. She said that she was just giving him some gentle guidance. When Biscuit landed in the alley, he said, "Yes, Sarge, or sir, or yes, ma'am!"

At the same time, all the rest of us quickly stepped away from the fence and into the alley. Ran and Mortie even saluted Mom, and I think that she even liked it. "You boys better get to finding out what you want to do, because it's going to be raining in a few minutes," she said.

"It's okay, Mom. We're just getting ready to run over to Ran's house to help his little brothers and sister with their chores," I answered. Helping out little brothers and sisters always worked to put parents in a good mood, and this time was no exception. That didn't mean that we had to do it. It meant that we could tell our parents that was what we were going to do, so they would leave us alone. Besides, none of the parents ever checked with the other parents to see if that is what we actually did. We could always say that we had every intention of doing what we said, but we became distracted. We would be automatically forgiven for our failure to do what we had said that we were going to do. Parents have a kind of built-in forgiveness button. If you had a real good excuse and offered it up with a sincere, innocent look, you were actually punching that button and getting off scot-free. It was another one of my good techniques.

As we turned to walk off, Ran said, "We're not gonna help those little brats do anything."

"I know," I said. "It was just an excuse to leave and not have Mom ask a thousand questions about where we were going and when would I be home."

"Yeah, I guess that was a pretty good line to use," Ran said.

It did start to rain, but it was not a hard rain, so we decided to just sit under one of the big oak trees until the rain had left the neighborhood. As we sat there, one of the old buses drove by. "Wish that it was a new bus instead of that old bus," Mortie said.

"Why's that?" I asked.

"Well, we could hop on the bumper and ride around the neighborhood on the back bumper if it was a new bus," he said.

"We can still do that even on an old bus," I replied. "Ran and I hopped on one earlier this afternoon and rode it for about three blocks."

"How did you stay on?" Mortie asked.

"Pretty much the same way as on the new buses ... only, it is a little bit tricky and a little bit harder," I answered. "You see, when you jump up on the bumper, you have to grab the back sign-holder right away, because you don't have a good enough perch on the back bumper, since it just barely sticks out from the back of the bus. The top of the sign-holder only has enough room for you to get your fingertips on it. But if you time it right and do both things at the same time, between your feet and your fingertips, you can hold on. That old bus will be coming back this way soon. Why don't we head down to the end of the street and hop on at a spot where we can ride for about three blocks?"

They all agreed and off we went to the bus stop that was located three blocks away. This was a good bus stop to hop on the bus back bumper, because our hiding place was hidden behind the bushes next to the stop. As we were sitting there, our friend Ching-Ching, the paperboy, came by.

"Whacha ya'll doin?" he asked. His real name was Buddy, but we called him Ching-Ching because he was almost always wearing his coin changer that he used when he was collecting money for his newspaper route. The coin changer made a CHING-CHING sound when he made change, hence the name.

"We're waiting on a bus. We're gonna take another bus ride," I answered.

"Like the one that I saw you and Ran take on the back bumper of the bus?" he asked.

"Yup, but this one will be on one of the old buses and not one of the new ones. It works the same way. You just have to get a good fingertip hold on the sign frame, and you put your feet on the bumper of the bus," I added.

"Can I do it with you guys too?" he asked.

"Sure you can, but you've just got to be quick," I answered.

"Great, this will be a lot of fun," Ching-Ching said with a whole bunch of excitement in his voice. Ching-Ching always had a whole bunch of excitement in his voice, and he was always kind of high strung. It never bothered us, because we all liked him. We just figured he was like that because he used to drink double servings of A&W root beer, and it was always served straight up. Ching-Ching never used ice. He said that he liked his root beer straight up, just like the cowboys do.

About that time, the old bus turned around the corner and approached our stop. As soon as it stopped, we all ran out and hopped on the bus back bumper while grabbing for a fingerhold on the sign-holder. Now, I should point out that Ching-Ching had been out collecting money for his paper route. He wore his coin changer on the front of his belt when he was collecting.

It had been raining and the bus was still wet, making it a little bit harder to get a good footing on the back bumper. As the bus started rolling down the street, Ching-Ching lost his footing and was hanging on to the sign holder by his fingertips. As he tried to pull his feet up to the bumper to get his footing, he kept swinging back against the back of the bus. Every time he bumped into the back of the bus, his coin changer would also hit the back of the bus, and a whole bunch of coins would fall out onto the street. When I saw what was happening, I hopped off the bus and started gathering up the coins off the street. When I looked back at the bus, I could see Ching-Ching still hanging on and banging against the bus, followed by a CHING-CHING-CHING-CHING-CHING while he was yelling for help. It was like pennies falling from heaven, I thought.

Ran had also hopped off the bus and was gathering up coins from the street. The sight of Ching-Ching banging against the back of the bus and hearing his loud "H-E-L-P" was one of the funniest things we had ever seen or heard. We laughed until we couldn't laugh anymore. Ching-Ching was finally able to hop off the bus when it stopped three blocks down the street. Normally we would have kept the money, since we did find it lying around in the middle of the street. Kind of like "finders-keepers." However, we liked Ching-Ching, and we felt that after this experience, he deserved to get his money back.

"I'm never gonna ride a bus again, at least not ride it on the outside," Ching-Ching said as he walked up to us. He looked like he had been whupped, and whupped pretty bad.

"Maybe bus hopping is not for you, Ching-Ching," I said as we handed his money back to him, all the time laughing at his performance.

"We'll see you, Ching-Ching. We should have kept the money that we found in the street," Ran said. "We could have used it for the extra backstage tickets for *The Tall Texan Wild West Show* at the State Fair."

"Nope, that was really Ching-Ching's money, and we all like him, even if he is a little goofy sometimes," I said. "I have been keeping track of the money that we've earned, and I think that we are about there as far as being able to afford to buy the tickets, anyway. I think that we'll call it a night."

As I headed home, I wondered what kind of shenanigans tomorrow would bring.

Chapter 23
ANOTHER DAY

"Well, the summer is almost over with," I said.

"Yeah, where did it go?" Ran asked.

"Seems like we have only been out of school for about a month," Mortie added.

"I think that the summer vacation should last at least through September," Biscuit said.

"I kinda like school!" Moose said.

We all turned around and gave Moose a dumb-looking stare. "Are you nuts, Moose?" Ran exclaimed.

"You gotta be crazy to like school," Mortie chimed in.

"Hold on, guys," Moose said. "I mean, I don't like school, but I kinda like school."

"You're not making one bit of sense," I told Moose. Now Moose was Mortie's age, about one year younger than us, but he went to a different school.

"Your school must not teach math or give homework, if you like it," Ran said.

"They definitely don't have nuns then," I said.

"Yeah, they do; as a matter of fact, they teach all of the same classes as everywhere else," Moose replied.

"Then why do you 'kinda' like school?" Mortie asked.

Kathy had come over with Moose and said, "You all had better let him explain."

"Well, I don't really like school, but I kinda like someone that goes to my school."

"O-h-h-h-h, I think that I am beginning to understand this now," I said. "Is that someone in your class?"

"Yup," came the answer.

"And might that someone be a she or a her?"

"Kinda," came the next answer.

"Kinda!" I exclaimed. "There isn't any kinda! There is only a yes or a no answer for that question."

"Well, yes," came the answer.

"Well then, I take it that you're sweet on some girl in your class, Moose."

"Well, kinda."

"And what is her name?" I continued.

"She's really pretty," Moose sighed with a twinkle in his eye.

Maybe it was not really a twinkle. Maybe it was his brain over-heating. "Her name?" I repeated.

"Heather Downey."

"Heather Downey?" I questioned. "That little red-headed girl who always wears saddle oxfords to school?"

"Yup."

"Heather Downey, the girl who rats out all of the boys in her church group every time they play hooky from Bible study?"

"Yup."

"Heather Downey, the girl who is the smartest brainiac in the class and lets everyone know it?"

"Yup, she is so pretty."

"What's gotten into you, Moose?"

"She told me that I was cute, and no one has ever told me that I was cute ever before in my whole life, except for my grandmother, and I think that my mom put her up to it."

"I don't know what to say, other than you really deserve to go back to class if you like Heather Downey," I sighed.

"Yeah, but she sure is pretty," he sighed again.

"Yup, she's pretty all right, but we are gonna have to keep an eye on you. You may be going wacko or something," I said.

"Back off, Scott," Kathy said. "I know Heather, and she's not as bad as you think. I'll vouch for her."

"Hmm, okay, Kathy. If you say that she's okay, that's good enough for us."

By that time, Kathy had pretty well been able to fit into our group. Even though she was a girl, she was still pretty cool. Maybe there is hope for the rest of the girls out there. Then again, I don't think that there was any hope for the Goofy Girls and their Yippity-Yap Club.

"Well, at least we have one thing to look forward to before we go back to school," I said.

"What's that?" Ran asked.

"The Tall Texan will be at the State Fair tomorrow, and we'll all get to see him in real life."

"And don't forget about Wang Chow KaPow," Mortie said.

"Yeah, yeah and don't forget about Chief Thunder Belly and Princess Running Summer Snowflake," Biscuit added. "I bet that they'll be there too."

"Yup, I bet that the Tall Texan just rides into the arena sitting tall in the saddle of his trusty horse, Firestorm," I said.

"I bet that he also gets his faithful rifle, the Texas Sureshot, out for some fancy shooting. I heard that he can shoot the bird sitting on a jet plane's wing flying way up in the sky and only clip its tail feather, because he does not like to harm animals," Moose said.

"Yeah, probably if it is a sunny day," Mortie said.

"Well, I want to see Wang Chow KaPow do his judo hops to the bad guys. He is really tough," Ran added.

"I bet that Chief Thunder Belly will have a headdress with about a hundred gazillion eagle feathers on it, and Princess Running Summer Snowflake will be the prettiest girl in the show," I said.

Well, one more day and they would all be right there at our own State Fair!

We sat for a while talking about the Tall Texan and then decided that we needed to do something productive, as my mom liked to say. " Whachawanna do, Ran?" I asked.

"I dunno. Whachawanna do, Scott?"

"I dunno," I answered.

We had been sitting in the basement of Ran's house because it was always cool down there during the summer. "What's in those big boxes over there?" I asked.

"I dunno," Ran replied.

"I know," Mortie chimed in. "It's toilet paper, a whole bunch of toilet paper."

"What are you doing with a whole bunch of toilet paper?" I asked.

"I was helping some of the Boy Scouts unload their trailer after their last camping trip. One of the Boy Scout bosses came up to me and said to stick the box of toilet paper somewhere where it would be out of the way and dry. It was kind of dark, and it looked a little damp in their storage room, so I brought it here."

"How long has it been here?" I asked.

"Oh, about a year or so," Mortie replied.

"Did they ever ask for it back?" I asked.

"Nope, I think that they forgot about it," he said.

"You know that the Boy Scouts camp out in the wilderness all of the time and try to be real rugged like," I said. "I heard that when they're camping in the wilderness like the pioneers, they use corn cobs and leaves, just like in the old days. The pioneers didn't have toilet paper back then, you know."

"Well, I know that my dad would like to get rid of that big box," Ran said.

"I got an idea," I said. "Let's grab the box and head for my alley."

We all lifted up the corners of the box and then carried it over to the end of the alley behind my garage. "What are we gonna do now?" Moose asked.

"Let's play roadblock," I said. "Each of you grab a couple of rolls of toilet paper and follow me. Okay, Ran, you hold this end and tack it to the telephone pole, and I'll unroll it by going over to the telephone pole across the street and then continue back to where you are. I've got some duct tape that will hold it. I'll just keep running back and forth until the roll is empty, and then we'll unwind your roll too, Ran. Moose, you, Kathy, and Mortie do the same thing between those two signs on both sides of the street over there."

Off we went until we had built two walls of toilet paper stretching across the street. It was a thing of beauty to behold, and the most amazing thing about its construction was that not a single car or bus came down the street while we were hard at work. We then gathered up all of our stuff and climbed up in a yard that overlooked the street. We didn't have to wait too long before a car and then a second car pulled up to the barricade. We were all just sitting there chuckling and wondering what the drivers were going to do.

Finally, a couple of cars drove down the street. One of the drivers got out of the car and walked up to the barricade. She kind of poked her finger at the toilet paper and then just stood there. I wished that I would have had something that made a loud flushing sound. That would have set her off. She then walked over to one of the telephone poles and peeked around. From there she could see the other barricade that was wrapped between the two signs.

The driver in the car behind her was hanging her head out of the window and watching what was going on. The first lady then turned around and called to the lady hanging her head out of the car window that there must be some sewer issue going on. They then both backed up their cars to a point where they could turn around. This was fun.

Next, a couple of little girls on their bikes rode up to the barricade. They stopped, looked at the barricade, and then I heard one of the little girls say, "This just reminded me that I have to go to the bathroom real bad." They then just turned around and peddled back from wherever they had come from, and they peddled in a big hurry!

Finally, one of the new buses came around the corner. We thought that this would be a lot of fun watching the big bus having to back up and detour around. To our amazement, the bus never even slowed down. He just plowed through both barricades, just like they were made of toilet paper. Well, they were made of toilet paper.

Well, we figured that this had been enough fun for now, and it was time to move on to something else. "Maybe we had better clean up all of this toilet paper," I said. "We need to destroy the evidence so no one will be able to blame any of this on us."

"Yeah, especially my dad," added Ran.

It only took a few minutes to clean up all of the toilet paper, since most of it was still in long strands and had not blown away. We deposited the toilet paper in old lady Cratcher's garbage can and then strode off in search of our next adventure.

Chapter 24
STUBBY'S BIG PAYOFF

When we got to my house, Marie came out and told me that the stupid Stubby had been looking for me. "He said that you made a deal with him earlier this summer, and it is time to pay up. What did you promise him, a carton of candy bars so he would sneak you into the ballpark this summer?" she asked.

"No, I promised him a big smooshy kiss on his lips from you," I said.

"Oh gross! Well, that is never going to happen, so you had better come up with something else, you stupid boys," she said.

"Yeah, I think that you're right," I replied. "You're way too ugly for Stubby to ever want to kiss, even if you were the last girl in the universe."

As we began to walk back down the alley, I began to realize that I had to come up with something and come up with it really quick. After all, school started in two days.

"I bet that old Stubby is back waiting for you to make good on the deal that you made so that we could shag balls at the ballpark this summer," Ran said.

"Yup, that's what I figured too," I said.

"Well, you promised him an ice cream date with that little blonde-headed girl, and you know that there is absolutely no way in the world she would ever get near him," Mortie added.

"Yup, I know, but there just has to be a way to work out this deal."

"You said that you were gonna tell him that she changed her mind," Biscuit said. "But if he ever finds out that you never even asked her to have an ice cream with him, he will never let us shag balls or anything else at the ballpark."

"Yup, that is one detail that I didn't really think about, because I was just really interested in us earning enough money to be able to go to the State Fair and see *The Tall Texan Wild West Show*. We do have enough money, and we even ended up with a lot more than I expected," I said.

"Well then, what are we gonna do?" asked Moose.

"I dunno," I sighed. "I'm just gonna havta try to figure out a way out of this problem."

We all kicked around a bunch of ideas as we headed for our favorite resting spot in the woods by the left-field fence outside of the ballpark. I had really enjoyed a bunch of games from that very spot all summer long. It had been our special place. I thought back about all of the pranks we had pulled on Stubby, the smoke bombs that floated into the infield and stands, and, of course, my beautiful, blonde Marlene Modelle. I was really going to miss her. She was one of the prettiest girls I had ever seen in my entire life. I could visualize her there on the pitcher's mound in her blue shirt, her white shorts, and her blonde hair.

Her blond hair! That gave me an idea. "I think that I have the answer," I said. "Do you guys remember Marlene Modelle, the pretty blonde pitcher that we helped to beat the ugly Six Street Baptist Church's team?" I asked.

"Yup, I remember her, but what does she have to do with this problem?" Ran asked.

"Well, I promised Stubby that I would get him a date with that cute little blonde, but I didn't say which cute little blonde," I answered.

"Okay, I guess, but you will never get Marlene Modelle to go have ice cream with Stubby. You don't even know her, know where she lives, or even have her telephone number. No girl in her right mind would want to go have an ice cream or anything else with Stubby," Ran said.

"No, I'm not gonna ask Marlene. It's just that her blonde hair gave me an idea," I answered. "I didn't say EXACTLY just which little blonde girl I would get to go and have an ice cream with him."

"Yup, but Stubby assumed that you were meaning 'his' cute little blonde-headed girl," Mortie said.

"Goes to show you that you never assume. The devil is in the details, and Stubby should have read the fine print," I said.

"Well, okay, but then what little blonde-headed girl in her right mind are you gonna get to go have an ice cream with Stubby?" Ran asked.

"Who said anything about her being in her right mind? I have the right cute little blonde girl in mind," I said.

"What? Who?" they all asked at once.

"Hey, Kathy, I think that I am gonna need your help on this one. Tankette!" I proudly announced.

"She's not cute and she's not little," Biscuit said.

"She's definitely not in her right mind," Ran added.

"That's a plus. Well, she is a blonde, and I can prove that she is little and that she is cute," I said.

"Well, you can't shrink her, and all of the beauty parlors in the world couldn't make her cute," Mortie added.

"Well, first, she is cute, because we all know that every grandmother thinks that her grandkids are cute, and Tankette had a grandmother, and she must have thought that she was cute," I said.

"Maybe, but only if her grandmother was named Sherman, like in Sherman Tank," Biscuit said, and we all shared a bit of a laugh.

"Remember, she did win a bathing-beauty swimming-suit contest this summer," I said.

"That is a stretch, but she's not little," Ran said.

"Okay, and she is definitely little. If you compare her with any professional offensive lineman, she will look little," I said.

"That is stretching it a little again," Ran said.

"That is stretching the truth to Cleveland and back, and then balling it all up in a knot and throwing it into the river," Mortie added.

"But it is a truthful statement," I replied.

"Okay, then how are you gonna get Tankette to go along with the deal?" Ran asked.

"This is where Kathy comes in. How many boyfriends has Tankette had?" I asked.

"Zero; all of the guys are afraid of her," Kathy answered.

"Well, do any of you remember when she saw that she had won Mister Mystery Hunky, better known as Stubby?" I asked. "It seemed to me that she kinda liked him, even though she could plainly see him."

"Yup, and she did go on and give him a big mushy kiss when she grabbed a hold of him," Mortie said.

"I couldn't look, because I was about to puke my guts out when I saw her in that two-piece bathing suit," Moose said.

"Well, I think that Tankette kinda liked Stubby, and that she probably would like to get together with him again," I said.

"Howya gonna talk her into it?" Ran asked.

"Just leave that up to me and Kathy," I said. "Kathy, do you think the two of us can talk Tankette into this?"

"This will be easy as pie," she replied.

We soon found ourselves knocking at Tankette's front door. The door was flung open, and in front of us stood almost six feet of pure terror. "Hi, Tan ... I mean, Bertha! You look especially pretty today. Could we talk to you for a little while?" I asked. "We've got something that you may be interested in."

As Kathy and I walked into the house, I noticed that Ran, Mortie, Biscuit, and Moose were standing lined up in a row directly behind us. They all knew that they were facing the Grim Reaper's younger sister, and they were going to beat a quick getaway if needed. Sacrifice Scott for self-preservation was their motto that day.

"Why would I want to talk to you ugly little brats?" she asked. "Well, Kathy, you aren't an ugly little brat, but you're hanging out with a bunch of them."

"Oh Bertha," I interjected, "you wound me to the very marrow of my bone when you say something like that to me, especially since I have come in peace and bearing gifts." That was a line that I had heard somewhere on TV, and it worked there, so I thought that I would give it a try here.

"What gift?" she demanded.

"Well, why don't we all have a seat on your front porch and we can talk about it?" I replied. That seemed to do the trick, as I noticed the foaming near the corner of her mouth had slowed down. "I have to admit that you sure did look pretty, much prettier than all of those goofy girls, when you won the bathing beauty swimming suit contest," I said. I had really screwed up my face, trying to put on my most sincere look for that one. *God will punish you for telling all of your lies*, Sister Mary Wackenhammer had always told me. *Please God, this is for a good cause, so please overlook this minor stretching of the truth*, I prayed.

"Oh yes, I did look pretty good that day," Tankette said as she patted her hair in the manner that all girls do when you compliment their looks. This was getting tough.

Kathy said, "Well, you seemed to enjoy your time with Mister Mystery Hunky."

"You mean that cute little Stubby?" she asked. "He is kind of cute and cuddly."

"Yup, he's the one," Kathy replied.

"Oh, he was a little beast, he was," Tankette giggled. "I don't think that he ever wanted to let go of me. I almost had to fight him off, that cute little monster." She let out a sigh as she thought back about that day.

"I know," continued Kathy, "and I think that he likes you, Bertha. I think that he likes you a whole lot. I can't describe just how much he wants to see you. The words just won't come to me."

Boy, Kathy was GOOD at this!

"Well, how would you like to be able to get together for an ice cream with him?" I asked.

"Oh, I bet that he has already forgotten about me," she said.

"Oh no, Bertha, he said that he could never forget you or the special sight of you in your two-piece bathing suit," I continued.

"Sorry, Scott, I gotta leave," Moose suddenly said. "I'm having a relapse of something, and I don't feel too good." Moose took off running down the street.

"He said that about me?" she asked.

"Oh yes, and more," Kathy replied. "He said that you're the girl of his dreams."

The girl of his dreams in his nightmares, I thought.

"Well, yes, I think that I would like to have an ice cream with Stubby," she beamed.

"Well, how about if we have Stubby show up over here tonight at about seven?" I asked. "I'll bring the ice cream and stuff over before he gets here."

"Well, my parents are going out with my aunt and uncle tonight. I have to babysit for their little baby, but she'll probably be asleep by then," she said.

"Okay, that should work. I'll send Mister Mystery Hunky over here at seven."

She thought about it and then said, "Why don't you all just show him in and then leave real quick? Then I'll come into the living room and surprise him. I'll leave the door open!"

"I think that's a great idea, and I know that it will be a super surprise for him," I said. "See ya later, Bertha."

Well, it was pretty easy to find Stubby. If he wasn't outside, he was in his garage organizing his candy stash. When we walked up, he turned around and said, "I've been wanting to see you."

"Now before you say a single word, we have to attend to some business," I said. "I promised earlier this summer that I would arrange an ice cream get-together for you and a cute blonde-headed girl."

"Yes, you did," he eagerly replied.

"Well, tonight is your lucky night," I said. "That's right, you heard it right! Tonight is your lucky night!" I could tell that old Stubby was getting all geared up now. "Tonight is the night that you get to have that ice cream get-together. However, since I am your friend through thick and thin, I am making the deal even better. I have arranged for the two of you to have a nice romantic ice cream get-together at her house. Her parents won't be home, and she'll be there all alone, except for her aunt's little baby, who will already be fast asleep."

"Oh golly gee!" Stubby exclaimed. "An evening alone with the girl of my dreams."

Oh yes, the girl of your nightmare dreams, I thought again. "You will need to be there by seven," I said.

"But I don't know exactly where she lives," he said. "I kinda know where she lives, cuz I rode my bike in front of her house, but I wasn't sure just exactly which one was hers, and when we went over there that night, we came up from the alley in back. It was dark when we went there that night that I fell out of the tree, and I wasn't sure just where we were."

"Don't worry, because I know exactly where she lives," I said. "Her family moved two streets over to Rutherford Avenue about a month ago, and I know exactly which house they are living in now."

"Scott, you're just a great friend!" he exclaimed. "No one has ever treated me the way that you do! I'll never forget tonight."

"I'm sure that you won't," I said.

We all met Stubby a little bit before seven. Rutherford Avenue wasn't very far away, so it didn't take long to get over to her house.

"Okay now, Stubby, there is only one thing that the little blonde-headed girl told me to have you do. By the way, she knows who you are, and I think that she is sweet on you."

"Yes, yes, what does she want for me to do?" he asked.

"We'll walk you up to the door. The front screen door is open. She wants you to stand in her living room, but you have to promise to keep your eyes closed."

"Eyes closed, eyes closed," he repeated.

"I think that you may also want to be wearing a big pucker on your lips."

"Big pucker, big pucker," he said.

"I'm pretty sure that she wants to surprise you with a super big mushy kiss!"

"Mushy kiss! Mushy kiss!" he exclaimed.

"Okay, here we go. Close your eyes and keep them closed."

"Eyes closed, eyes closed," he said.

Kathy and I led him up onto the front porch and then opened the front screen door and walked him to the center of the room. It was dim but not dark in there. "Okay, this is where we leave you now. Remember, eyes closed."

"Eyes closed, eyes closed," he said with a huge grin. Then he puckered up his lips about as far that they would pucker.

We stepped out onto the front porch and waited. About two seconds later, we heard, "DUCKY POO!'" followed by a loud smooching sound. The next thing that we heard was a loud, blood-curling scream coming from Stubby.

"Oh, that is so sweet! You're so excited just to see little ole me," we heard Tankette say.

Kathy was peeking through the screen door. "She's got him pinned to the floor! It was a body slam! She's got Stubby down for a three count! There's no way Stubby is gonna get loose!"

"Come on, Kathy, we need to leave those two little lovebirds alone," I said. "Time to head out."

I was darn proud of myself for figuring out just how to get out of that situation. Of course, I had to admit that Kathy was a lot of help. Heck, she wasn't bad for a girl. Heck, she wasn't bad at all!

Chapter 25
THE TALL TEXAN

The big day had finally arrived. Here we all were at the State Fair! Paul, Ran's big brother, had driven us to the State Fair and dropped us off. Ran, Mortie, Biscuit, Moose, and I— we were all ready to finally see our hero, The Tall Texan, in person. We had saved up enough money from shagging balls at the ballpark, and, of course, by other means, to pay for both our admissions to the fair and also to *The Tall Texan Wild West Show,* plus the backstage tickets. We didn't even have to sneak in.

We had arrived early so that we could get the really good seats. All of the seats were general admission, so we knew that we had to get there early in order to get the very best seats up front. Oh, the show was being held in the baseball stadium part of the fairgrounds. They had done a pretty good job of not making it look like a baseball field and making it sorta look like a prairie field from the Wild West. They even had some tumble bushes that were blowing around the field … I mean, prairie.

Getting there so early did present some problems, though. We needed to super guard our great seats, so when someone had to go to the bathroom or make a run to the water fountain, we made sure that at least two of us were sitting at the outside edge of our group of seats so that the empty ones would be in the middle. Also, only one person was allowed to go per bathroom break. We limited visits to the water fountain in order to keep the call of nature from calling before we were ready to be called. However, any way you looked at it, we had a long wait before showtime.

"I bet that ole Stubby would have liked to be here with us," Moose said.

"Yup, but he would have had to be in the show," I said.

"Whacha mean, Scott?"

"Well, I think he means Stubby would have had to appear as an extra in the show, you know, playing the part of the buffalo. They don't make buffaloes that grow to be that big," Ran said.

It was starting to get dark. At long last, the stadium finally filled up. Then from somewhere, we were not sure from exactly where, a cowboy voice asked if everyone was ready for a rootin', tootin', good time. Of course, everyone yelled, "YES!"

The stadium lights were dimmed way down low. Then you could hear it, and we all got chills. "Tall Texan, No Way to Disguise … Tall Texan, Terror to Bad Guys!" It was the Tall Texan theme song being played right here in Louisville, Kentucky! It played again, and everybody in the stadium started to whoop and yell. It was just about the most exciting thing that I have ever seen or heard!

All of sudden, a whole bunch of little cowboys came bursting out from one end of the stadium. It was really strange, because they were all little guys and they were riding little bitty horses. They were all dressed in black, every single one of them, and they all wore black bad-guy masks. I guess it was because we were at one end of the stadium and they were at the other end of the stadium that made them look little.

"Who are those little guys?" Ran asked.

"I dunno; maybe the bad guy's kids, and they must be learning how to be bad guys," I said.

"Yeah, that makes sense… bad guy trainees. I always wondered how they learned to be bad guys in the Old West," Ran replied.

"I read somewhere that there used to be a bad-guy school out in Arizona or somewhere like that where the adult bad guys could send their kids to learn how to be bad guys when they grew up," I said. "You know, they had to learn how to dress all in black and grow black mustaches, and how to wear bank robbing masks and to rob trains and stagecoaches, and just be mean little hombres. They teach them how to spit there too."

"Yeah, I think that you're right," Ran said. "I think that it was called the Bad Lands, and good guys were not allowed in there."

"That makes sense to me," Mortie said. "They had to learn somewhere."

"I wonder if they got diplomas when they graduated from bad-guy school?" Moose said.

"Nope, instead of diplomas, I think that the schools gave all of the graduating little bad guys their very own first box of dynamite for blowing up banks and stuff," I said.

"I bet that their bad-guy parents were real proud of them when they graduated from bad-guy school back then," Biscuit said.

Well, the little bad-guy cowboy trainees, or whatever you wanted to call them, were making a whole bunch of noise and riding around in circles while yelling and shooting their six shooters into the air.

"Do they ever run out of bullets?" Mortie asked.

"Only on the television," I said. "In real life, they all have a six shooter in both holsters, a six shooter stuck in their pants, a derringer pistol stuck in each front pocket, and a spare six shooter hidden under their cowboy hat. They also carry a couple of hunting rifles and about three or four throwing knives and a Swiss Army knife," I said.

"Why do they have a Swiss Army knife?" Biscuit asked.

"One of the teachers in the bad-guy school originally came from Switzerland. He had used a Swiss Army knife in Switzerland when he used to climb up on the Alps. He knew that the Swiss Army knife would be a useful weapon and tool for all of the bad guys. They could use the knife part for stabbing and stuff, and the spoon part for eating grub on the trail, and the corkscrew part for corkscrewing," I finished.

"What is corkscrewing?" Biscuit asked.

"Gee, Biscuit, don't you know anything?" I asked. "Corkscrewing is what you do when you have finished taking a drink from your canteen in the Old West. You have to put the cork back into the canteen real tight so that the prairie bugs can't get into your fresh canteen water. There's nothing worse than prairie bugs in your fresh canteen water. You just stick the corkscrew into the cork and screw the cork into the mouth of the canteen real tight," I said.

Well, while they were riding around at one end of the stadium, we didn't notice that a couple of teepees had popped up at the other end of the stadium. Now that was at about the farthest point away from our seats that you could get. It was way, way across the stadium ... I mean, prairie. Then we all saw her come out from the teepee. It was Princess Running Summer Snowflake! She looked kinda short from my seat, but I guessed it was because she was so far away from us, and that must have made her look kinda little. She was just walking around and picking up daisies or flowers or something off the ground. She didn't seem to notice the short little cowboy bad guys riding around.

Then we watched as the short little cowboy bad guys got off of their little bitty cowboy horses and started to sneak up on Princess Running Summer Snowflake. We all yelled to Princess Running Summer Snowflake to watch out behind her, but she didn't seem to hear us yelling. "I bet that Princess Running Summer Snowflake will just turn around and beat the snot out of those little cowboy bad guy turds," Mortie said. "They're so little, she could probably whup all of them at the same time."

However, as they got closer to her, she seemed to look like she was about the same size as them.

"I don't understand. It's like Princess Running Summer Snowflake is shrinking," Biscuit said with a confused sound in his voice.

Then the little bad guys jumped her, and all of them grabbed her at the same time. We could hear her screams from our seats. Then out of the other teepee appeared the great Chief Thunder Belly!

"He'll get those little cowboy squirts now," Moose yelled.

Chief Thunder Belly was big and strong. He was almost as big as the Tall Texan. About that time, we watched half of the little cowboy bad guys turn and run toward Chief Thunder Belly. Then it started to happen again. The closer they got to Chief Thunder Belly, the shorter Chief Thunder Belly appeared to be getting. It must have been the angle from where we were sitting. The little cowboy bad guys all got out their lassos and lassoed Chief Thunder Belly, all at the same time. They pulled him to the ground and tied him to a totem pole.

Bad guys like to tie good guys to totem poles or telephone poles and stuff like that. If they were really mean, they would tie you to a tall cactus! Once they got Chief Thunder Belly tied to the totem pole, they got out a book of matches. They were going burn him at the stake. We heard a big WHOOSH, and then some funny wiggly stuff started fluttering around Chief Thunder Belly.

"What is that?" Ran asked.

"That is colored cellar flame," I said. "It's some kind of colored wax paper-like stuff that when you wiggle it, it kinda looks like fire flames."

"Does it burn?" Mortie asked.

"Only if you catch it on fire," I said. "Maybe they're just trying to scare Chief Thunder Belly first before lighting him on fire." Then the little bad guy cowboys went back and started to pull Princess Running Summer Snowflake toward another totem pole. I saw one of them grab her by her long black hair, and then I was horrified. He lifted up her black hair in his hand. He had scalped her right in front of everybody! I could see her bloody head. It was terrible, and I knew that her princess buckskin dress would soon be all bloody.

But wait a minute … that wasn't blood. It was red hair! Princess Running Summer Snowflake had been wearing a wig! No wonder she didn't cry when she got scalped. When you really get scalped, you cry a bunch! She then grabbed her black hair and put it back on her head so she could be unscalped. Then she started screaming again. I guess that the wig must have had some pins in it that were sticking her in the head by now. It seemed like there must have be a hundred little cowboy bad guys running around, yelling and shooting their guns into the air.

Then we all heard it. First it was kind of soft: "Tall Texan, No Way to Disguise … Tall Texan, Terror to Bad Guys!" Then it was repeated louder. "Tall Texan, No Way to Disguise … Tall Texan, Terror to Bad Guys!"

"He's coming, he's coming, he's coming!" Biscuit exclaimed.

The Tall Texan theme song blasted through the stadium! Then out from a thick cloud of smoke at the other end of the stadium came … a short little guy on a real short little bitty black pony!

"What?" I asked in amazement.

The "Tall Texan, No Way to Disguise … Tall Texan, Terror to Bad Guys!" was now blaring from the PA. This guy looked like the Tall Texan, but he was, he was … little! He looked like a miniature Tall Texan. Did the Tall Texan have a Tall Texan kid? We were confused. We kept looking behind him for the Tall Texan to appear, but only the little guy was to be seen. The little guy sat on a little bitty black pony that was an exact copy of mighty Firestorm, but only in miniature. It had to be the Tall Texan's kid, but then the Tall Texan had never gotten married, not even to Princess Running Summer Snowflake.

The little guy's legs did hang down to almost the ground, just like the Tall Texan's did, but this guy was in miniature. *They're munchkins; all of them are munchkins,* I thought. Maybe this was a trick.

Just then we saw another little guy on another little pony come galloping out through the cloud of smoke. It looked just like Wang Chow KaPow, but he was in miniature too. This was getting really strange. Then we heard a voice that sounded like the Tall Texan say, "Steady, Firestorm, I need to take aim with my faithful rife, the Texas Sureshot."

At that point, I saw the miniature little Tall Texan aim a rifle toward the little cowboy bad guys. There was a loud POW, and Princess Running Summer Snowflakes' ropes fell away, like they had been cut by a speeding bullet. You know that the Tall Texan has never missed his target in his entire life. Then Wang Chow KaPow hopped off his little pony right in front of a whole bunch of little bad cowboys.

"He's gonna do his judo hops now!" Ran exclaimed with delight. "He'll pop them good now!"

We watched as the miniature Wang Chow KaPow ran up to the first group of little bad guys and then started jumping up in the air and kicking out his feet. He could even do kicking flips. The little bad guy cowboys watched him for a little while, and then they all took off running.

"Hey! He didn't even touch those little bad guy cowboys with his judo hops," Ran said.

We watched as the miniature Tall Texan rode over to where Chief Thunder Belly was being roasted alive. Then the Tall Texan grabbed his canteen, shot off its lid, and emptied it onto the fire until it was out. Next, the Tall Texan rode up to Princess Running Summer Snowflake and said, "Princess, you untie your father, brave Chief Thunder Belly, while me and Wang Chow KaPow round up every one of these dastardly villains."

We watched as the miniature Tall Texan rode the miniature pony Firestorm around in circles, herding all of the little bad cowboys into a group. I couldn't call the miniature pony a horse because it was smaller than a horse that you ride on a merry-go-round. Then the miniature Wang Chow KaPow stopped his judo hopping and tossed a rope to the miniature Tall Texan. As the miniature Tall Texan began to circle the band of little bad cowboys, he drew them into a tight circle. Finally, the circle had grown so tight that none of the miniature little bad guy cowboys could move or get away. Then the miniature Tall Texan and the miniature Wang Chow KaPow rode up to the miniature brave Chief Thunder Belly and the miniature Princess Running Summer Snowflake, and the miniature Tall Texan said, "Chief, they won't be bothering you anymore. I'll hand these evil bad guys over to your brave braves now, so they can watch them until the sheriff gets here. We sent the sheriff a smoke signal on the way over here to tell him that we were going to rescue you and Princess Running Snowflake and that he would need to lock up all of the bad guys after we captured them."

"You're our hero, Tall Texan!" Princess Running Summer Snowflake said.

"I only do what's right and nothing more," said the miniature Tall Texan. "The sheriff is on the way to get these hombres. Now I have to go and save some more honest, good people who live in the Wild West."

"Let me give you a kiss before you leave, Tall Texan," Princess Running Snowflake called out.

"Blow me a kiss if you wish, but the Tall Texan is too much of a gentleman to steal a kiss from a beautiful princess!"

Then the miniature Tall Texan and the miniature Wang Chow KaPow turned their little bitty ponies around and headed out of the stadium. You could see Princess Running Summer Snowflake holding her hand over her heart as she waved goodbye. Finally, we heard the familiar theme, "Tall Texan, No Way to Disguise ... Tall Texan, Terror to Bad Guys!" Then came the announcement: "We hope that you have enjoyed today's Tall Texan Wild West Show, and autographs are now available behind the stadium. A backstage ticket is required for admittance."

We all looked at each other in a state of confusion. "Well, let's go get some autographs," I said. "We need to figure this out."

When we got to the autograph table, it got worse. They were all there: The Tall Texan, Wang Chow KaPow, Chief Thunder Belly, and Princess Running Summer Snowflake. The problem is that they were all really short. I mean really short. Ran was a little taller than me, and he was a whole lot taller than any of them!

"They look so big on TV," I said.

"It's the camera," the guy next to me said. "You know, it's Hollywood!"

"They're all so little though," I said to him.

"I know. You've seen them before," he said.

"Whacha mean?" I asked.

"You know, *The Wizard of Oz.* They were the kids who played the Munchkin babies in Munchkin Land," he said.

"What? The Tall Texan and all of the rest are really Munchkins?" I said while I scratched my head.

"Yeah," the guy said. "They were about eight years old back then, and after the *Wizard* movie, they didn't have any more movie offers. A few years later at one of their Wizard Munchkin reunions, they got together and came up with the idea for the Tall Texan. They use trick camera shots to make them look big. Now they're making a ton of money from their cereal commercials and Tall Texan toys and stuff. It helped that the Tall Texan's father owns the studio where they film the shows. You know, in Hollywood the cameramen can do all kinds of trick shots that make things look big. Don't you know that Godzilla is really a little model that's about twelve inches tall? They had a guy dress up in a Godzilla suit in the middle of tiny buildings for the action scenes. The little guys ended up really making some good money, and their show is super popular too, don't you think so?

"I'm never gonna eat another bowl of that Texas Tumbleweed Munchie Crunchies again," I said.

We all stood there watching all of our favorite actors and actress. Most of the time when you see your hero in person, they look even bigger. This time it looked like someone had left the entire cast out in the rain and they all had shrunk. They didn't even sign their names. They used rubber stamps. Wang Chow Kapow had pulled off his headband, and when he spoke, he just sounded like a guy from England and not China or Japan! He was actually holding a cup a tea! Then I noticed that his tomahawk was make out of rubber. A rubber tomahawk! No self-respecting hero sidekick would ever be caught with a rubber tomahawk. Even worse was the fact that Princess Running Summer Snowflake had pulled off her black wig and now sat there giving out her autographs in her red hair.

I called to her across the table, "Hey, Princess Running Summer Snowflake, an Indian Princess is not supposed to have red hair."

She looked up at me and said, "When they come from Ireland they do, laddie!"

I was starting to get dizzy. Then I heard the Tall Texan speak, and it was not even his real voice. Well, maybe it was his real voice, and Hollywood had someone talk his lines for the television program. The little guy who was standing right in front of me had a little squeaky voice, kinda like Mickey Mouse. When one of the helpers asked him if he wanted something cold to drink, the Tall Texan asked for a glass of milk! No real cowboy ever drinks milk, EVER! They don't even look at a cow unless they want a hamburger or cheeseburger.

Finally, we watched as the Tall Texan took off his cowboy hat and his wig and then wiped his bald head with a handkerchief. The Tall Texan was bald! No real Western good guy was bald! It was in the Western good guy handbook. You had to have long, wavy, perfect hair!

This was more than any of us could take. We had seen our greatest hero shrunk down to a pint-sized toy cowboy who rode around on a little bitty pony that had escaped from Munchkin Land. It was time to go home.

"I gotta get outta here right away!" I said. "Ran, call your brother and tell him to come and pick us up. I want to go home and burn all of my Tall Texan comic books and put Princess Running Summer Snowflake's picture on the floor of Troubles' doghouse."

"I'm with you there," Ran replied.

What a way to end my special summer.

Chapter 26
RETURN TO PRISON

The next morning I heard a sound that I had not heard in a few months. It was the clanging of that stupid alarm clock. There is no worse sound than a clanging alarm clock on a school-day morning. It's even worse when you hear it the morning of the first day of school. Is it any wonder that a whole bunch of people are in bad moods in the morning after listening to an alarm clock clang into their ear? Only school teachers and drill sergeants like clanging alarm clocks. I think that soft music would work much better. Maybe the voice of a pretty girl like Marlene Modelle gently calling for you to wake up. What am I talking about? If I didn't have that stupid alarm clock, I probably wouldn't wake up until noon, or at least 9:00 a.m.

Waking up to go to school is the worst feeling of all. I would rather sit through one of Marie's dance recitals than have to go to school. Well, maybe not. Marie's dance recitals are pretty yucky. I didn't think that it was possible, but she even looks goofier in her dance recital dress and her dance recital hairdo. She looks like a stressed-out ostrich in tights and slippers on those days. Yeah, I guess that having to go to school is slightly better than having to go to Marie's dance recital. I just knew that I was not going to like this day.

To make matters worse, Marie and Sam were happy to be going back to school. That was all the proof I needed to conclude that they are just plain goofy ... bad goofy! They ought to have their heads examined. I bet that on a windy day you can hear a whistle sound come from their heads as the wind blows between their ears.

At least I didn't have to walk to school with them. Their happy moods would have been enough to make me want to puke. Well, another nine months of torture and drudgery was ahead for me.

To make matters even worse, I'd heard my class was getting a new nun that they just brought in from the nun marine boot camp. Her name was Sister Mary Brutus. Jeez, that name just does not inspire me to strive for "academic excellence." It motivated me to stay out of swatting distance and duck a lot when she takes a swing at me. I had it on good authority that she was a former prize fighter in the heavyweight division. I bet she's missing several teeth and has a big nose that probably had been broken in the ring several times. The word was that she had a skull and crossbones tattoo under her nun outfit. I wouldn't have been surprised if she had a flat top haircut under her nun bonnet, but unless she was out in a really strong wind, we would never know. Those nun bonnets never come off, even in a bad windy storm. They have so much starch in them, they are bulletproof. I heard that the army was looking into using them as something that they could replace their metal helmets with. I was pretty sure that those bonnets got glued or duct taped on. Maybe they were stapled on.

I didn't like Sister Mary Brutus already, and I was pretty sure that she wouldn't like me. I bet that Miss Penneyberry had already given her the full update on me. Of course, any update would be from her point of view, where she completely disregards my gift for original thinking when it comes to school matters. She didn't appreciate my genius! I bet that Sir Fig Newton was given a hard time by his teacher and school principal when that apple fell on his head and he discovered applesauce.

Well, I knew that this year was not going to be fun, at least for me. I could see it already. "Mister Stiles, you can stay after school and dust out every chalkboard eraser in the entire building." I wouldn't be surprised if they even brought in more dirty chalkboard erasers from other schools for me to clean, just to prolong the torture. "Mister Stiles, move your desk up to the front corner of the room so I can keep my eye on you. Mister Stiles, you have been assigned to my room because I am the designated angel of despair, torment, and hopelessness for all problem students, more commonly known as The Angel of Death."

Well, at least I knew that I was personally responsible for the early retirement of a couple of those black-clad merchants of torture and misery. They better not forget that little fact. I was pretty sure that they had to send the last nun who had locked horns with me to the funny farm. They called it early retirement, but I am not quite sure about that. She ended up running out of my classroom, screaming. She went straight over the top of the Carmelite monastery walls next to school, where she is locked behind those really tall brick walls even to this day. What was her name? Oh, it was Sister Mary Tolerance. *Maybe I should send her a Christmas card this year,* I thought. *Yup, a Christmas card that has a picture of me in it. That would blow the beads right off her rosary.*

I got my school satchel and headed out the door for school. Mom called out to me, "Have a good day, Scott!"

Good day. I would almost rather stay home with a case of diarrhea. As I walked the long road to school, I began to really wonder what was in store for me. Would this be the year that they would finally break me? I really didn't think so, but they were a mean bunch, those nuns. Those nuns were really trying hard to beat an education into me, one yardstick at a time. It seemed to me that getting an education was a very painful experience. I had always heard that the eighth grade was the toughest of all the grades to get through. It was the last chance for the nuns to give you a hard way to go, especially if you didn't want to become a priest. If you told them that you wanted to become a priest when you grew up, they would completely change the way they treated you. They would even smile at you and be nice to you.

Only one guy in our class had decided to head in that direction. I looked at that vocation, but it seemed like it compared to life in a prison or something. If you're a priest, all that you get to drink is water and wine, and all that you get to eat are fish sandwiches and vegetable soup. You can't even look at a cheeseburger! Anyway, the nuns would never have believed me if I told them that I wanted to become a priest. They would be wondering just what my angle was, and I guess that they would have been right. One little screw up and the jig would be up.

Nope, no priesthood would be in my future. Heck, priests can't even have girlfriends. As a matter of fact, I didn't even think that they were allowed to look at girls unless it was in church, school, at the bingo, at the fish fry, or at the church picnic. Even then, you had to carry your rosary and a bottle of holy water in case a pretty girl was to come up and talk to you. A rosary and holy water will ward off the devil every time. At least that's what I heard.

Sister Mary Wackenhammer said that I should take a bath in holy water every night and then wear a rosary under my shirt every day. The only girls that the priests are really allowed to look at are girl nuns, and nobody really wants to look at a girl nun. They make your eyeballs hurt! That was not for me.

Nope, I guessed that I would have to face one more year of letting them try to beat me into submission. I was just about at the end of my walk. When I looked up at the last street crossing, there was good ole Saint Penitentiary Grade School ahead of me. It seemed to be like a giant mouth that was waiting to swallow me up as I approached. *Maybe we'll have a new warden this year. Maybe Miss Pennyberry got drafted into the Marines and shipped overseas. I bet that she would make an awesome master sergeant.* She could eat buckshot and poop bullets, I was sure of that. Yup, I bet that when she did that, she could hit the target bullseye at fifty yards. Bend over and fire! Put it on automatic! Yuck, I don't even like to imagine that.

Well, I started to feel a little better as I looked ahead to the front doors. There stood that pretty Miss Bunch. She was so pretty, but way too old for me. I heard that she was about twenty-three years old, practically an old maid. At least I would enjoy seeing her around, even if she was an old maid.

"Well hi, Scott, I am especially glad to see you again," she said.

She was glad to see me! Wow, she remembered me! Out of all of the students at Saint Penitentiary Grade School, Miss Bunch remembered me! Well, maybe this might end up being a good year after all.

Then I heard it. It was that voice that seemed to rise up from Dracula's grave. It was a voice that would scare John Wayne, and nothing much scares him. "Hello, Mister Stiles," came that voice that sounded like the evil twin of the Wicked Witch of the West.

"Hello, Miss Pennyberry, it is so good to see you again," I lied.

"I have been waiting all summer long to see YOU again, Mister Stiles. Come with me," she commanded in that voice that told you to follow or never see the light of day again.

I followed her straight through to the gates of hell and into her office. She turned around and looked straight and me and smiled. It was the kind of smile that a shark gives you right before he chomps you.

"Why, Miss Pennyberry, you look so much younger this year. Have you lost weight?" I asked.

I could see right away that my attempt to talk my way out of whatever she had in store for me was not going to work. My "sincere" compliment had been swatted away, just like a fast pitch getting smacked out of Yankee Field by Mickey Mantle. I bet that she figured out that I was the one who put a pack of fizzies into the holy water font last May. Maybe it was the ad for a new school principal that I posted on the church bulletin board. Oh boy, busted again!

She gave me that evil Wicked Witch of the West look and smiled down at me.

Here it comes, I thought.

"I intend to take the necessary steps to make sure that you measure up this year, young man," she said with a mean, nasty-looking grin.

Rats, I thought. *I bet that she's got a new yardstick.*

Author Bio

Gary Edelen is happily retired after a long career in the finance industry. Gary and his wife, Faryl, reside in Middletown, Kentucky, where he enjoys composing and distributing humorous stories of his travels hither and yon to his friends and relatives.

CPSIA information can be obtained
at www.ICGtesting.com
Printed in the USA
BVHW072049240720
584504BV00002B/13

9 781525 569357